[illegible]



# ON THE ROAD TO DAMASCUS

Anthony Viney

Anthony Viney

Happy Reading!

Published by Zenobia Books
ISBN: 978-1-3999-4648-3



Cover design by Rebecca Connell

*For my father*

# Timeline

| | |
|---|---|
| 2500 BC | Coastal towns in Syria settled by Phoenicians |
| 1550 BC | Egyptians take control of much of Syria |
| 856 BC | Assyrian empire takes over northern Syria |
| 333 BC | Alexander the Great expels Persian forces |
| AD 272 | Roman Emperor, Aurelian, captures Queen Zenobia of Palmyra |
| 395 | Syria comes under control of the Byzantines |
| 636 | Arab conquest of Syria |
| 1097 | Crusaders come to Syria |
| 1271 | Krak des Chevaliers captured by Mamluks |
| 1401 | Mongol invasion begins |
| 1516 | The Ottoman Turks occupy Syria |
| 1918 | Damascus liberated by Allies and Arab Nationalists |
| 1946 | French forces leave Damascus and French Mandate ends |
| 1973 | Syria loses Golan Heights to Israel |
| 1982 | Hama is bombed following an uprising by the Muslim Brotherhood |
| 2000 | Bashar al-Assad becomes President of Syria |
| 2011 | Start of Syrian civil war |

*Every man at some term or turn of his life has*
*longed for the supernatural powers and*
*a glimpse of Wonderland.*

Richard F. Burton, *Tales from*
*A Thousand and One Nights*

# Chapter One

*Anti-Lebanon Mountains, Syria 2011*

Rising to a thousand feet, a peregrine falcon engaged in a display of loops, spirals and pirouettes. The mature female dropped steeply towards the plateau, then spotted three corpses lying at the foot of the rockface. She had never tasted human flesh. But denied her customary fare of hamsters and small reptiles, now lying low in the scrub, her menu was about to change. She sensed that the body count was going to rise. All she had to do was wait.

Chandler seized the revolver from his rucksack and raised the weapon a few inches above the rock. Keeping his head firmly down, he let off four rounds in quick succession in the direction of the ridge. Chandler heard the men laughing above him. He curled into a ball as a burst of machine gun fire peppered his sanctuary. The muscles in his chest tightened and his breathing became more rapid. Chandler loosened his grip on the Webley. With one hand holding the barrel, he lifted the pistol above his head and tossed it clear of the boulder.

From his kneeling position at the top of the gorge, Jabril flung down his rifle. A scattering of spent cartridges lay at his feet. He was unsure whether the Martini-Henry had given up the ghost through overheating, or whether the firing mechanism had decided to jam. Either way, he knew the game was up.

Standing shoulder to shoulder, Chandler and Jabril looked up towards the ridge. They watched a figure take centre-stage, then draw a large hunting knife from a sheath hanging from his fatigues.

'You should have hung onto the revolver,' Jabril said.

'I'm sorry, I was unsure – I've let you down.'

'Try to remain still – it will be over soon.'

'Jabril ... please.'

'Kismet, Mr Chandler, kismet.'

# Chapter Two

*Crowns in my purse I have and goods at home.*
*And so am come abroad to see the world.*
Shakespeare

*Beirut. One week earlier.*

Draining his third beer in a bar in central Beirut, Robert Chandler thought about all the reasons why he should *not* visit Syria. He had watched Al Jazeera footage of tanks on the streets. Listened to Foreign Office advice telling Britons to leave. Considered his travel agent's warning that his medical insurance would be cancelled if he ignored government strictures. Most worryingly, he continued to ruminate on his solicitor's insistence to draw up a will – just in case.

Chandler looked across the crowded bar to the open doorway. A heavy flow of traffic ground its way through Hamra Street. Taxi drivers issued a cacophony of shouts and honks, while passers-by did their best to ignore them.

He was unable to work out how so many taxis attracted so few customers. A triumph of hope over experience, he concluded.

Ordering another beer – a Lebanese brew to satisfy his thirst for variety – Chandler checked his notes. They contained a spiderwork of words and half-formed sentences, brought together in a series of loops and arrows. Some phrases given prominence with heavy underlining in red marker pen. Others hung around with nowhere to go. He had long promised himself a laptop, assuring members of his writers group in London that he fully intended to make the great leap forward into the digital age. A computer, they insisted, would take away the drudgery of longhand. Allow him to make instant corrections at the click of a button. He knew their arguments made sense. But today wasn't the day for this old dog to learn new tricks.

Whether propping up the bar, or writing prose, Chandler was never content with half measures. He demanded the *full* story. In doing so, score a few points over old Sharkey in the writers group. As unelected chief critic, Sharkey had never missed an opportunity to hammer Chandler over his lack of narrative tension. '*Rather tepid, Robert ... you need to grab the reader from the off.*' And ready to maximise the humiliation by ensuring that the other wordsmiths were always present.

Earlier that morning, Chandler had nearly succeeded in his mission to net one of the journalists. The Middle East correspondent from CNN was about to offer him a cigarette in the hotel lobby when, to Chandler's dismay, news of the shootings in the south broke out, whereupon the entire rat pack scurried for the exit. Bearing witness to another border crossing by Palestinian refuseniks, they had calculated, in advance, that Israeli snipers would be ready for them. A newsworthy outcome assured. Twelve dead, a hundred wounded – including an eighteen year old from the university. Later, under flashing cameras, his friends holding an ill tempered vigil in the hospital. On one matter, press and public were agreed – the boy would never last the night.

Chandler could already see tomorrow's breaking news:

*Carnage on Israeli Border*
*Hezbollah Threatens Retaliation*
*UN Calls for Restraint*

Then, a more intimate headline intruded:

*Unpublished Author Once Again Sidelined*

✧

Chandler made his way along Hamra. He took in the sights and smells of the city centre. Beirut was buzzing. He was struck by the city's normality. With its brash collection of shopping malls and banks, it rivalled anything he was accustomed to in London. Office workers rushed past him, desperate to find elusive tables in the shade. Small coffee shops lining the route looked fit to burst. Stallholders furiously dished out paper plates, piled high with falafel and grilled kebab. But for the smart business executives, looking for respite before the afternoon shift, nothing could compete with the croissants and chocolate cupcakes on offer at the all conquering Costas and Starbucks.

At a steady pace, it took Chandler an hour to reach the old quarter. Disappointingly, the shell shocked hotels and apartment blocks were nowhere to be seen. Overtaken by smarter outlets catering to a younger set. He turned into a narrow side street, then spotted a boarded-up restaurant, built in the colonial style. Its pockmarked exterior testified to a war that had once consumed the city. Perfect, he thought. Chandler reached into his bag, only to discover he had left his camera in the hotel.

It was late afternoon when the taxi dropped Chandler back to Hamra. Weaving through the crowds, he observed a child, standing in the forecourt of Byblos Bank. No more than seven or eight, his hair cut close to his scalp. He wore a pair of oversize shorts, heavily frayed and spattered with mud. The boy stood awkwardly. His left leg appeared shorter than his right. With his dishevelled figure silhouetted against the gleaming white marble, fringing the entrance of the bank, he held a single plastic carnation. Probably from the camps, Chandler mused.

Like all the other beggars he'd encountered in Beirut, Chandler sensed a moral rebuke. He tried to avoid eye contact. Too late. He searched for loose change. None. Wide-eyed, the boy held out the carnation. Chandler hesitated, shook his head apologetically, and moved swiftly on.

✧

Chandler's room in the Mayflower was clean, with adequate furnishings. Grand enough in its day, he reckoned. Once it had boasted itself as a watering hole for Kim Philby and Graham Green. Today, the little hotel in Yafet Street was outflanked by the newly built Crowne Plaza around the corner. What really drew Chandler to the Mayflower, however, was that it remained a haunt for journalists – the old school types who still hankered for a stiff drink or two, before filing their evening dispatches.

He removed his jacket, then filled the sink. He searched for soap. Chandler began to massage his scalp, taking comfort from the full head of hair he had inherited from his father. As a young man, genetics had gifted Chandler with a muscular build. Long gone. Getting dressed, he watched his shirt buttons lose their tug of war with his heavy paunch. His expansive jowls gave him the look of a bull dog well past its prime.

Lifting a wallet from his back pocket, Chandler took out a thick wad of notes. He separated the Lebanese pounds, intended as a tip for the cleaners. Next, from a larger pile, he began to count the U.S. dollars, telling himself that Uncle Sam's greenbacks remained the currency of choice among the barstaff.

He rehoused the cash, then removed a passport size photograph of his nephew, Kevin. The youngster's sullen expression reminded him of his futile attempts to inspire the lad with tales of their ancestors' heroics. Even Chandler's stirring account of his great-uncle Albert's doomed bayonet charge at Suvla Bay had fallen on deaf ears. Biting his lip, he thought back to his visit to his sister, a week after Kevin was born. Her first words; '*Robert, all these presents, it's too much.*' Then, the bodyblow. '*I've asked Jack to be Godfather.*'

Chandler's status as outsider had been a constant feature of his working life. Back then, each day spent behind his desk in the Council Tax Department had seemed an eternity. Every minute stretched by his colleagues' idle office chatter.

Every day marred by their endless recitations on the joys of married life – Friday nights at the cinema, romantic city breaks, even their weekly runs to Tesco. It was all too much. His world had become dominated by *couples.*

Mercifully, Chandler had found some solace in the photocopying room during lunchbreaks. Time to polish the drafts of short stories he hoped to present to the writers group. Made up of retired malcontents, the assembly rarely gave his historical fiction a platform. Forced to listen to Felicity Hamilton's latest attempts to bag a literary agent, and Pamela Bostock's pleas for a pensioner discount for membership fees, his enthusiasm had wavered. Working alone at night, Chandler concentrated on character and plot. In the stillness of his apartment, he half-believed that the lost souls of the Dardanelles were somehow watching over him.

Over time, Chandler's disconnection from office life had earned him a nickname: *the invisible man*. He didn't mind. He even relished the title. When the prospect of voluntary redundancy arose, he seized it without a moment's thought. A chance to travel, maybe catch history in the making. Like his great-uncle, grab an opportunity to rise above mediocrity – to leave his mark. Whatever the cost.

Chandler checked his mobile. He noted two unread messages, both from Sharkey. Promptly deleted. Scrolling down, he located the Artemis travel agency.

'Any luck with the driver?' he begged.

'Mr Chandler, we have some problems, the situation in Syria is difficult, all our Lebanese drivers are refusing ... they have families you understand.'

'I appreciate that, but you promised me a driver for tomorrow. I have to get to Krak des Chevaliers ... it's the main reason I'm here.'

'In normal times the castle is open to tourists,' the agent replied, 'but tomorrow is Friday. Everything goes crazy on Fridays, you know, after prayers.'

Raucous laughter rose from the journalists downstairs. Chandler pushed the phone closer.

'You have visa?' the agent continued.

'Yes, I told you, a tourist visa from the Syrian Embassy in London.'

A long pause.

'Mr Chandler, I think *one* of our drivers may be willing to go in. He is Syrian ... from Latakia. It will be quite a drive for him to get to Beirut, but he has agreed to leave early. Now, his French is good and his English is perfect. You must pay for his accommodation of course, his meals too. You have MasterCard?'

Chandler dictated his credit card details. A minute's silence.

'Good, the card is accepted,' the agent announced warmly, leaving Chandler's account two thousand dollars lighter.

'One more thing,' Chandler said hesitantly, 'if we're turned back at the border, will I get my money back?' '*Mr Chandler*,' the agent fired back, 'you cannot expect our driver to risk his life and look for a refund too!'

Chandler set down the phone and reached into the mini bar. For a moment, he told himself that he should cut down on the booze, then reminded himself that some of his best stories had been twinned with a heavy binge. All the more reason, he concluded, to bring a few unfinished drafts with him. Chandler reckoned that there would be ample opportunity to locate sufficient quantities of local brews to energise his final edits.

Opening the steel box, he spotted two quarter bottles – a French Colombard and an unspecified grape from the Bekaa Valley. He twisted the cap from the Lebanese Vin Rouge, then set his alarm for seven. For a few minutes, he lay on the bed, studying the photographs that populated his guidebook. He held up a picture of Krak des Chevaliers. Amidst all the upheavals of the previous months, the towering crusader castle stood defiant, demonstrating to Chandler, and Syria's dwindling band of visitors, that the fortress was in for the long haul.

As the effect of the wine took hold, Chandler wondered how he might be received. Naturally people would be suspicious. In the empty hotels of Aleppo and tourist-free souqs of Damascus, they would be unlikely to take his credentials at face value. Chandler could already hear them.

*The Englishman isn't telling us the full story.*
*He must have something to hide.*
*This man has other fish to fry.*

And, in a way, they were right.

# Chapter Three

*I shall go out with the chariots to counsel and command, for that is the privilege of the old; the young must fight in the ranks.*

Homer

'Sami, it's time to get up, your father has to leave.'

'Mother, it's too early. Please, five more minutes.'

'No Sami, get dressed now, I told you, he has a big journey, you won't see him till next week.'

The boy rubbed his eyes and swung his feet from under the duvet. He stood up and stretched his arms. With eyes fixed firmly on the floor, he picked his way carefully between the rows of toy soldiers and tanks arranged on the tiles. Perfect miniatures. At the doorway, he glanced back at his little army. A sturdy column of T-62s, their armour delicately painted sand-yellow and grey, shielded a platoon of infantry. The stage set. October 7th 1973, and the little boy ready for battle with the occupiers of the Golan Heights. Of course,

Sami already knew the outcome. His grandfather, Qasim, had told him all about it. A heroic lightning charge across the valley, a treacherous counterattack by the Israeli usurpers, followed by a steady rout along the road to Damascus. Today, however, Sami was determined that catastrophe would not be on the cards. When he returned from school, he would take personal charge of the offensive, ignore his commander-in-chief's order for a general retreat, and re-write history.

✧

The wall clock chimed seven as Nadia lay out the breakfast table. A full spread of flatbread, humous and cream cheese, sprinkled liberally with coriander and parsley. Completing the feast, she placed three hard boiled eggs in a bowl on the centre of the table. Qasim's favourite. Nadia poured out black coffee for the men and pure orange for the boy. She reserved a quarter melon for herself, determined to stick to her unforgiving diet.

Their house in coastal Latakia lacked a sea view. Situated in downmarket Sharia 14, it presented a lifeless structure. Built of breeze block, to accommodate their immediate family, it included a small annexe for her father-in-law, Qasim. The annexe had been designed by her husband, and was hastily erected by his cousins. But, the Mansour dwelling proved a bitter disappointment for both Nadia and her parents. She envied the well manicured gardens and ornamental fountains enjoyed by their wealthier friends, living in the American Quarter. She also missed the Ottoman splendour of their first marital home behind the city walls in Damascus.

Of late, Nadia had become increasingly reflective. Her thoughts constantly rewound to happier times, when Jabril finally clinched the position of chief librarian at the university. Back then, Nadia convinced herself that she could not be luckier. As their daughter, Zafirah, embarked on a degree in fine art, Nadia felt blessed. The birth of their son, Sami, the final bonus. Friends and relatives marvelled at Jabril's good fortune, telling him, 'first you find the most beautiful wife in Syria, now you have the most handsome son in all of Damascus – perhaps another tank commander for the Republican Guard?'

'Insha' Allah, Insha' Allah,' came Jabril's glowing reply.

Lifting a small chunk of melon, Nadia watched her father-in-law. Confined to a wheelchair, Qasim was unable to get his knees beneath the kitchen table. The old soldier reached over to engage in hand-to-hand combat with the flatbread and cheese, but struggled to bridge the gap. Nadia sighed as she watched the old man endure a downpour of breadcrumbs and olive oil.

'I'll just stick to coffee,' Jabril grunted. 'I need to be in Beirut for nine. You know what the traffic is like.'

Nadia scanned his uneaten breakfast, then lifted the coffee pot. She glanced at Qasim. He commandeered a small piece of flatbread and stubbed it into the humous. His hand shaking, Qasim brought the morsel slowly to his mouth. Nadia snatched a napkin and wiped his beard before the humous had time to migrate to his shirt.

'Hurry up Sami, your father has to go.'

She heard her son slam the bathroom door, but suspected he had returned to inspect his soldiers in the bedroom. The

First Armoured Division seemed to hold a greater allure than the prospect of brushing his teeth.

'Jabril, Youssef rang early this morning. He asked me to remind you about the itinerary. You're to take the Englishman through the Masnaa crossing.'

'Why didn't you wake me?'

'You told me it was just another run. What's going on?'

Jabril drained the last of his coffee. 'It's a bit more than that,' he muttered.

Nadia turned towards her father-in-law. She observed a widening stain on Qasim's crotch – unsure whether the culprit was another spillage of olive oil or Qasim's incontinence.

'Really? And how long do I have to put up with it?'

'With what?'

'With all the *secrecy*.'

Jabril stood up and reached for his jacket. For a moment he strained to listen for signs of movement upstairs. 'I see, so now driving a taxi isn't good enough,' he said.

'But it's not a taxi service is it? Lifting Turks and Russians. Never having the slightest clue where you are. You know the neighbours are talking.'

'Let them talk. It's Youssef's money that puts food on the table.'

'Have you any idea how much Sami misses you?' Nadia shot back.

'I know.'

'Did he tell you his friends have stopped coming to the house?'

'No,' Jabil replied with surprise.

'They're saying that you're the President's little poodle.'

'I hope you're not blaming *me* for all this. You know who the real cause of the trouble is?'

'Oh, not again,' Nadia snapped. 'Every time we argue, you bring *this* up.'

'Why not? We were doing fine until she—'

'Jabril, your daughter has a name – *Zafirah, Zafirah, Zafirah*, or have you forgotten?'

'How could I? The apple of her mother's eye, isn't that what your family say? Just *perfect*. Then the dirty little whore runs off with that Armenian and we're *all* finished. Oh, and where is she now? *Haifa*. What a catch for her fancy Jewish friends.'

Nadia lifted three paper napkins. She arranged them neatly over Qasim's lap. 'Jabril, please, you can't blame all our troubles on Zafirah. You should take some responsibility yourself.'

'No, Nadia, my actions don't come into it. You heard what Youssef said – *I'm so sorry, with your daughter in Israel you're too much of a security risk to run the library. The Director can't take any chances.*'

Nadia began to clear the breakfast table. *Noisily*. She glanced at Qasim. He smiled back at her. In his large fist, he squeezed a hard boiled egg to pulp. She did her best to hold back the tears, and still no sign of Sami.

# Chapter Four

*The meeting of two personalities is like the contact of two chemical substances. If there is any reaction, both are transformed.*
Carl Jung

With a nod from the pretty receptionist, Chandler set down his rucksack in the lobby. He hesitated at the entrance of the lounge and observed its only occupant. Like an impatient job seeker, the man was perched bolt upright on the edge of a leather armchair. He wore a slim-fitting cream blazer and navy chinos. His straight nose offset by generous lips. Chandler struggled to determine his age. Dropping his gaze, Chandler was struck by the size of the man's feet. They appeared tiny, delicate – almost inconsequential. Moving into the lounge, Chandler caught a strong whiff of cologne. Everything about the man hinted effeminacy. If this *was* the driver assigned to him, he thought, the prospect of sharing a car and accommodation with a pretty boy, in a foreign country fast becoming a warzone, had little appeal. Then again, the man sitting before him had, the agency insisted, been the only driver willing to cross the border. Perhaps he'd been too quick to rush to judgement. Either way, Chandler didn't have much choice.

'Good morning, I'm Jabril, from the agency,' the man said. 'Did they ring you?'

'I spoke with them yesterday. I hear you're the only volunteer.'

Jabril let out a short chuckle. 'Yes, you could say that. The local drivers ... Lebanese – they read too many scare stories in the press.'

About to reply, Chandler spotted the CNN journalist stroll briskly towards the reception desk. He recalled their brief encounter the day before and his near offer of a cigarette, before the flight for the exit. Today, the journalist ignored him.

'I think I'm holding you back from your breakfast,' Jabril said.

'Don't worry, I'm only fit for coffee and cigarettes this early.'

'A man after my own heart.'

'I'm impressed with your command of English,' Chandler said. 'I always thought that *French* was the language of choice in Syria, after Arabic of course.'

'It's more the language of *culture*,' Jabril replied. 'And our colonial heritage.'

For a moment, Chandler continued to size up the driver, then ordered coffee.

'So, tell me, how does a driver acquire such good English?'

Chandler watched Jabril's eyebrows rise.

'Sorry, I didn't mean to ... '

'No need to apologise. I spent three years studying English in Moscow University. Nineteenth century literature, my speciality.'

For a few seconds, Chandler felt threatened. He feared his own literary credentials were about to crumble. 'So, I suppose *English* is now in your blood,' he remarked acidly.

'I think I fell a little in love with Austen,' Jabril continued, ignoring the barb, 'after a difficult relationship with the Brontës.'

'What about Chaucer?' asked Chandler, defiantly.

Jabril grimaced. 'Canterbury Tales? A fine collection of stories, but a little too bawdy.'

'Is that a problem for you?'

'Not at all. I spent a year working in England. I'm a great follower of Benny Hill,' Jabril fired back, grinning.

Chandler let out a deep breath. He sensed that he may have met his match but thought it unwise to go head to head.

'What about you?' said Jabril. 'Are you familiar with Arab literature?'

'No, to be honest, my knowledge of the Middle East is pretty limited – my Arabic non-existent.'

'None at all?'

'Not a word ... but maybe you'll have me fluent by the time we return.'

'Insha' Allah,' Jabril sighed.

Chandler remained unsure what to make of the driver. Barring his ambivalent sexual leanings, Jabril had all the makings of an ideal travelling companion. Clearly well educated and erudite, if lacking in deference. Chandler wondered whether he might make a constructive critic for his short stories. At the same time, he struggled to reconcile Jabril's literary pedigree with his job as driver and bag carrier.

'This morning I rang a friend in the north,' the driver went on, his cheerful demeanour overtaken by an air of solemnity.

Chandler detected a change of plan.

'We have to alter the itinerary – take the southern crossing and head east for Palmyra. There's less trouble there.'

'This isn't what was agreed.'

'I'm sorry ... please understand, there are too many problems in the north. There is trouble in Homs and the main highway to Aleppo is cut off. I think we should start with Palmyra. The ruins are stunning. After that, we can, how you say, *play it by ear*.'

Jabril noted Chandler's dejection. An unpromising start. 'Don't worry, we will get you to your castle, just not today. You must be patient. Now, if you want to finish your coffee, I'll carry your bag to the car.'

✧

Standing next to a metallic blue BMW saloon, Jabril checked his watch. Well past ten. He feared the traffic in central Beirut was approaching its customary gridlock. They should leave soon. But first, he needed to ring his handler.

'Youssef, I told you not to speak to Nadia. All this talk about a change of itinerary – it only makes her suspicious.'

'Jabril, I think you need to exercise a little more control over that wife of yours, it's not good for your rehabilitation.'

'I'm sorry, I didn't mean to—'

'Just be careful, Jabril. Now, any word from Zafirah?'

'She isn't speaking to me. I don't know if she's been in touch with Nadia, she tells me nothing.'

'No contact at all?'

'I told you, nothing since she left for Israel. Maybe the odd text to Nadia.'

'Now you're getting me worried. First your daughter elopes with the Armenian dog and sets up camp in Haifa. Then, messages to your wife. It doesn't look good, does it?'

'Youssef ... you're reading too much into it. You know I want nothing more to do with her ... she can go to hell as far as I'm concerned.'

'Oh she *will*, she *will*. Listen, have you checked the Englishman's luggage?'

'Yes, while he was finishing his breakfast.'

'Well?'

'A bit of an odd collection. An old copy of *A Thousand and One Nights* and a guide to Syria. The usual clothes. Oh, and a cheap camera,'

'Is that it?'

'There *is* something else, I'm not sure what to make of it. I found a stack of papers stuffed into plastic envelopes. Stories, I think, all handwritten.'

'Is he a journalist?'

'No, I don't think so, certainly not with *that* camera.'

'Did you check for recording equipment?'

'Of course, but there's nothing, unless he has it hidden on him. I'll search his jacket when I get a chance.'

'He doesn't sound much like a tourist.'

'Hard to tell. He's keen enough to see the sights – Aleppo and Krak des Chevaliers. He seemed pretty upset at the change of route. I told him about the trouble in Homs.'

'Oh there's trouble there alright. Tearing down statues, burning cars too. Naturally when *our* boys arrived they ran off like frightened rabbits. Mind you, we managed to catch one of them ... a young lad from Tartus.'

'Who's he working for, Youssef? Is he with the Muslim Brotherhood?'

'Don't be so melodramatic. He's just a little runt looking for excitement. From a good family, I hear. His father is a policeman.'

'Are you going to let him go?'

'Certainly not. We need to set an example. We'll soften him up with a little electricity. By tonight he'll be crying like a baby.'

'Then you'll release him?'

Jabril heard Youssef stifle a giggle.

'All in good time, my little cousin. But first we'll cut out his tongue.'

# Chapter Five

*Art is not a pastime but a priesthood.*
Jean Cocteau

As senior curator at the Ben Gurion gallery, located in the prestigious museum quarter of Haifa, Baruch Abelman had no time for indulging young upstarts – even those with a sound command of the English language. Especially when they had the impertinence to *drop by* without an appointment.

He sat with his head bowed and leafed through the pages of Zafirah's portfolio – photographs of abstract paintings firmly secured. Every few moments, Abelman looked up and smiled, before shaking his head with an air of disappointment. He was determined to give nothing away. He drew satisfaction from any sign of the artist's discomfort.

'If you want to see something more *representational*, I can—'

'Well, Miss Mansour, you certainly push the boundaries. I see hints of Mondrian ... no, maybe Kandinsky.'

Zafirah watched Abelman run a bony finger along the photographs. He licked his lips.

'The exhibition for emerging artists next month,' Zafirah said hopefully, 'what do you think?'

Abelman cocked his head. 'There's no question that your work meets our high standards – we're always on the lookout for innovative talent.'

Zafirah's heart began to race. She leaned forward ...

'It's just ... ' whispered Abelman.

'Just?'

Abelman closed the portfolio. 'You have references?'

'Of course,' said Zafirah, beaming. 'I've brought them with me – from the University of Damascus.'

Abelman drew breath. '*Damascus*, yes ... quite.'

'First class honours,' Zafirah shot back forcefully.

'Miss Mansour,' continued Abelman, 'in *normal* times we would be delighted to showcase work by our nearest neighbours. Only last year our No Borders exhibition proved a great success'

Zafirah clasped her hands over her stomach.

For a few seconds, Abelman's composure began to slip. His face reddened. He pushed the portfolio towards Zafirah. 'But since the rocket attacks our patrons have become a little jumpy. They're calling for a more *traditional* emphasis – something to reflect our national aspirations.'

As if in protest at the curator's obduracy, Zafirah's unborn started to kick.

Abelman raised his palms. 'Miss Mansour, I have a meeting with the Director at twelve. I'm happy to share your interest with him – but you'll appreciate the pressure we're under.'

Zafirah pulled herself up from the chair. She reached for the portfolio.

'When is the baby due?' asked Abelman, glumly.

'*Soon.*'

'Well, good luck with that.'

✧

Eyes glued to the screen, Theo gripped the mouse and scrolled down to the next website. *Thinking of a Career in Construction? Opportunities in Tel Aviv!* Theo sighed. Why the hell is there nothing more local? he thought. He failed to spot Zafirah bearing down on him.

'*Bastards*', she grunted.

Theo spun in his chair, for a moment lost for words.

'They probably think I'm a bloody security risk,' Zafirah spat out. 'Funny, isn't it? That's just what they told my father at the library. It obviously runs in the family.'

Theo shook his head. 'I told you it would be a waste of time – Syrians are hardly flavour of the month these days.'

Zafirah's eyes flashed. 'Maybe you should stick to job hunting.'

Theo stretched out his legs. 'Listen, I've just had a thought – there's a new Armenian restaurant opening up near the old Templar buildings. They're bound to be looking for wall displays – I can put in a word if—'

'Leave it Theo ... just leave it.'

# Chapter Six

*Omens are the individual language in which God talks to you.*

Paulo Coelho

Chandler's bemusement with the slow moving traffic leaving Beirut gave way to impatience, then nervousness. By the mid-morning the road leading to the Masnaa crossing had all but emptied. The usual flow of cars, packed with children and grandparents, overladen trucks and brightly painted buses, had dwindled to a trickle. He checked the temperature gauge. Thirty degrees. Inside the car, things began to cool down once the air conditioning kicked in. After his verbal brinkmanship at the hotel, Jabril had become disconcertingly quiet. He reached for one of Chandler's cigarettes, prompting Chandler to wonder if there was an Arabic code that, in the case of tobacco, ensured an unspoken sharing of resources. It would never happen in London, he reckoned.

They crossed the Lebanese frontier without incident, before reaching a customs house bedecked with Syrian flags.

'Remain in the car,' Jabril ordered. 'There'll be thirty dollars to pay for entry.'

'Any excuse to raise revenue, I suppose.'

'You could say that,' Jabril replied. 'So, do the English have a problem paying their taxes?'

'Not usually,' Chandler replied dryly. 'Provided they're lawful, of course.'

Jabril raised an eyebrow. 'Perhaps we should leave the politics for later.'

Thirty minutes later, and back on the road. Chandler noticed a change in décor. Brightly coloured bunting, bearing the Lebanese cedar, had given way to a forest of flags. They lined each side of the road, bearing the emblem of the Arab Syrian Republic. Large posters, sporting photographs of the Syrian President, assailed them every few hundred metres. Replete with the uniform of the Republican Guard, and wearing fashionable shades, the President smiled down on them. With his elongated neck and stationary wave, the leader appeared to invite them to join him on his peacock throne.

'We should stop here,' Jabril said, pulling over to a rundown block of shops at the side of the road. Chandler hadn't bargained on a rest stop so soon after crossing the frontier.

'We can grab some coffee. If you wish, you can buy Syrian currency. We've three hundred kilometres before we reach Palmyra.'

Chandler looked for signs of life. He took in the restaurant's dilapidated frontage and dirty windows. He detected the whiff of raw sewage. Inside, he watched Jabril take measured bites from a large falafel, then decline the offer of coffee from a sullen waiter.

'Well Jabril, no awkward questions at the customs house then. Looks like we're home and dry.'

'Don't count your chickens, we've a long way to go. And remember it's *Friday*.'

'Oh, I forgot,' Chandler said, 'everyone goes a little crazy on Fridays.'

'Today, everyone is nervous. I think there'll be more trouble in Homs, maybe Aleppo too.'

Chandler was about to respond when he spotted an elderly man shuffle into the café. He was dressed in an old army overcoat and wore a pair of unlaced shoes. In one hand, he carried a string of beads. In the other, a discoloured tobacco tin. He bore down on his target.

'Here, I have Greek and Roman coins, some Persian also. All genuine.'

'He knows English?' Chandler said.

'Probably French and Russian too,' Jabril replied, smiling.

Chandler lifted the coins one by one. Some bore a sickly metallic green, others burnished brown. *The weight of history*.

'On this, you have Alexander the Great and this one ... Darius, King of Persia.'

Chandler focused on a solitary silver coin, still lodged in the tin. The old man noticed his interest.

'This one, *Roman*,' he said enthusiastically.

Chandler fingered the coin. Emperor Augustus stared back at him.

'You give me fifty dollars ... good price.'

Chandler looked across the table to Jabril, hoping for a signal. Jabril raised his hands in a show of non-committal.

'Ten dollars, take it or leave it,' Chandler declared.

The man raised his eyebrows and clung onto Augustus. Chandler took a ten dollar bill from his wallet and slapped it on the table. Jabril nodded approvingly. The coin seller picked up the note and placed it in the tin. He looked intently at Chandler and held onto the silver coin.

'You make tough deal,' he said.

Chandler scooped up the green and brown coins and dropped them back into the tobacco tin. He stood up to leave. Pressing the silver coin into Chandler's hand, the old man pushed his mouth towards his ear.

'Please ... if you see him, it is a gift for the boy.'

# Chapter Seven

*The collection of stories known as A Thousand and One Nights is in itself a symbol of infinity ... a character in a story invokes a character who tells a story about a character who has a story to tell. Everything proliferates.*

A.S. Byatt

'*Arabian Nights*, you know, where Scheherazade tells the king stories to postpone her execution – have you read it?'

I think you mean *A Thousand and One Nights*, there's a big distinction.'

'I stand corrected. Anyway, have you read it? Aladdin, Ali Baba, Sinbad?'

'These stories may not be part of the original collection,' Jabril said disdainfully. 'Probably modern additions, invented by Europeans.'

Chandler wondered whether to pursue the debate. Once again, he began to feel outflanked.

'What's brought on this sudden interest, Mr Chandler? You've been quiet as a mouse since we left the café.'

Chandler stared out of the car window. Since his encounter with the coin vendor he had allowed himself to become immersed in the barren terrain surrounding the speeding vehicle. The landscape almost lunar, with no sign of life – animal or human. The closest he had come to a genuine desert.

'Sorry Jabril, it's something the old man said before we left the café. I'm still trying to work it out. He has me a bit spooked to be honest.'

'Spooked?'

'Yes ... unnerved.'

'What did he say?'

For a few seconds, Chandler remained silent. 'The silver coin, he said something about *a gift for the boy*.'

'What boy?'

'I haven't a clue.'

'*A gift for the boy*. Sounds like a new story for your *Arabian Nights*. Perhaps you should write it.'

'What makes you think I can write?'

'Have you tried?'

'A little, but nothing published.'

Jabril pulled a face. 'You know, storytelling is in our blood – it appeals to our emotions.'

'Storytelling doesn't feature much in the cultural life of Enfield,' Chandler muttered.

'So you must try to imagine the scene in an Ottoman café in Damascus,' Jabril went on. 'There, in the crowd, the storyteller, the hakawati, holds court. He keeps his audience transfixed with tales of epic battles and great leaders. He provides the perfect distraction for men at times of stress.'

'Stress?'

'Of course. Stress isn't a *Western* invention. Think of the expectant father waiting in the café for word of his wife and baby, his head full of worries, the news often bad. He needs diversion. The hakawati knows this and fills the space.'

'Then, like Scheherazade, he inflicts the poor sod with a cliffhanger to ensure he comes back the next day.'

Jabril chuckled. 'It's always good for business.'

'I think we're getting a bit off track, Jabril. Can we get back to Arabian ... sorry, *A Thousand and One Nights*? What story would you recommend?'

'Forget the individual stories,' Jabril shot back. 'On their own I find them rather childish and a little vulgar. But what *is* interesting is how the tales are held together. I believe the English call it a narrative frame.'

'Sounds confusing.'

'Okay, try to understand it in a different light. One day, you step into a fast flowing river. You think you're familiar with its ebb and flow. Then, the next day, there's a heavy rainfall. The river's character has changed, so you have to understand it differently. Get below the surface.'

'That's funny ... that's just what old Sharkey is always telling me.'

'Who?'

'Another writer ... call him a literary adversary.'

'There, you see, I *knew* you were more than just a tourist,' announced Jabril.

'Just as I suspect *you* are more than just a driver,' Chandler fired back.

Jabril's fingers tightened around the steering wheel. 'Mr Chandler, I think that it is now *you* who is talking in riddles.'

# Chapter Eight

*We know no spectacle so ridiculous as the British public in one of its periodical fits of morality.*
Thomas Macaulay

'Okay, Mr Chandler, *control* – you'll need your passport.'

Jabril brought the car to a halt a few metres in front of a 4x4, which sat squarely on the road ahead of them. A heavy machine gun was mounted on its roof, sitting at an angle. The gunner, wearing sandy fatigues, adjusted its sights. He ignored Jabril and Chandler, preferring to concentrate on the sullen row of civilians, mostly old men and boys, standing on the dirt track, running parallel to the highway.

Chandler watched the security personnel go about their labours. More a militia than an army. Some dressed in khaki. Others wearing baggy trousers or jeans. No insignia to identify whether they were paid up regulars or just enthusiastic amateurs. They stood about idly, occasionally laughing at the prisoners. Sweating, unshaven and obese, the guards appeared to have let themselves go. AK-47s, slung casually over their shoulders, were the only tools to distinguish them from a gang of roadside labourers.

'Paramilitaries?' asked Chandler.

'No, *mukhabarat* – secret police.'

'Is that meant to reassure me?'

A heavily set man, Chandler took to be an officer, approached the vehicle. He wore scuffed boots, camouflaged trousers and Arab headgear. He sported a pair of wide sunglasses and bore a broad confident smile. Jabril leaned over, then tapped his fingers on Chandler's passport. He flicked the camera off Chandler's lap.

'*As-salaamu 'alakum*,' the officer announced warmly.

'*Wa 'alaykum 'as-salaam*,' Jabril replied. He passed over his identity papers and driver's permit. The officer scrutinised the documents, then looked past Jabril towards Chandler, before glancing back at Jabril and muttering a few words.

'He wants to know where we're heading,' Jabril added. 'I'm not sure if he speaks English.'

'Speaks English? By the look of him, I don't think we have much to worry about,' said Chandler.

Jabril stepped out of the car and walked to the rear of the vehicle. Chandler strained to catch any fragments of their conversation. With each word, the officer's tone became more animated.

'*Amriikii?*'

Chandler tried to pick up Jabril's replies, before returning his gaze to the civilians on the dirt track. Squatting, their arms were tied behind their backs. Wrists bound tightly with plastic straps. A boy, no more than twelve, murmured a few words to the guard. His Arabic carried a pleading tone that Chandler had no difficulty understanding. The guard shouted towards the officer, then pushed the boy to his knees. He placed his boot firmly onto the boy's shoulder, toppling him backwards into the dirt. His father, kneeling next to him, began to remonstrate. Hearing the commotion, the officer turned on his heel and marched towards the prisoners. He reached the boy first, still lying prostrate in the sand. The officer bent down and whispered a few words to him, before moving towards his father.

Chandler had never witnessed a pistol whipping. So much blood. Split lips and broken teeth too. He heard the boy sobbing. The others in the line remained motionless, like shop window dummies. He thought about lifting his camera, but was interrupted by Jabril thrusting his head through the open window.

'Don't even think about it.'

'What's happening?'

'He's asking me if you're American.'

'I guessed that,' Chandler replied.

'And if you're a journalist.'

'Are you serious?'

'Keep your voice down,' Jabril snapped.

'C'mon, it's obvious he doesn't speak English.'

Jabril and Chandler watched the officer push his pistol under his belt and turn his back on the boy's father, who lay twitching by his feet, heavily bloodied. The officer walked towards a huddle of police, standing at the edge of the road. For a few moments, they stood grinning, as if sharing a private joke. The prisoners were manhandled to their feet. Flying kicks to encourage those too slow to respond. One by one, they were blindfolded, then pushed into the back of an open-topped truck. The young boy and his father left to last. Still whimpering, the boy was shoved into the front of the 4x4. His father had to be carried.

Wiping his hands on his fatigues, the officer lifted a mobile phone from his back pocket. He spoke for a few minutes. His eyes remained fixed on Chandler. Jabril leaned against the car bonnet, his attention focused on the civilians sitting in the truck. He didn't notice the officer move towards the passenger side of the car and reach for Chandler's passport. A full minute passed before it was returned.

Chandler spotted a globule of phlegm clinging steadfastly to the cover. Raising his right hand to his chest, the officer regained his smile. 'Mr Chandler, welcome to Syria.'

✧

For the next hour Jabril and Chandler said nothing. The saloon cruised steadily at ninety kilometres. By midday, cloudless skies and a blistering thirty-five degrees. The road skirted the Syrian desert. Chandler gazed eastwards – the featureless vista occasionally interrupted by herdsmen harrying cattle and sheep along ground as smooth and hard as marble.

Jabril glanced discreetly at his passenger. Chandler's notepad lay open and was balanced precariously on his knees. He had completed three pages of rough notes. Most were half finished sentences with their direction of travel unclear. Jabril was tempted to ask him about his scribblings, wanting to discover if they formed a discomforting commentary on the scenes they had witnessed at the checkpoint. But he held his curiosity in check. There would be ample opportunity to lift the lid on the doodlings when they reached Palmyra, he thought.

Chandler picked up his pen, paused, then tossed it onto the dashboard. 'You know, this isn't what I expected.'

Jabril remained silent.

'That business at the checkpoint,' Chandler continued, more forcibly.

'What did you expect?'

'I'm not sure, but not *that*. Did you see the state of the kid's father?'

Jabril pushed hard on the gas. The speedometer climbed to one hundred and twenty. 'Things are different here. We have enemies inside and outside of the country. Extremists who would—'

'*Extremists*? You mean those old men and boys on the road? I didn't see any of them carrying weapons, did you?'

'They don't need to,' Jabril shot back. 'A simple telephone message by mobile phone is enough. A short call to their cousins who *do* have the guns.'

'Jabril, are you seriously suggesting that the kid was passing high level intelligence to his political masters in Damascus?'

'He's old enough to become indoctrinated … to follow a few simple instructions.'

'He's only a child.'

'Then he'll grow up fast'.

'Really? So they'll help him reach maturity by kicking the shit out of his father. He won't get over that in a hurry.'

'That's exactly my point, Mr Chandler, he *won't*. The boy will bear a grudge. He will tell his relatives the whole story, grossly exaggerated, of course. His relatives will pass it on to their neighbours. Like stories from *A Thousand and One Nights*, the tale will travel endlessly.'

'They can't hold the boy forever,' murmured Chandler.

'Probably not. But long enough to buy us time. Give the police a chance to catch the ringleaders.'

'Oh right, catch the godfathers and the problem goes away.'

'It's called *counter insurgency*, Mr Chandler. Haven't the British always been past masters at it?'

Chandler began to lose steam. He suspected that he was about to be caught in another of Jabril's well practiced pincer movements. 'Look, I'm not trying to tell you how to run your country,' he muttered.

'So what *are* you trying to tell me?'

Jabril dropped the saloon into a leisurely cruise. 'You know, there's still time to turn back – visit the sites in Lebanon. Baalbek has—'

'No Jabril, let's press on.'

They spent the next hour enduring an uncomfortable silence. Jabril was the first to speak. 'Do you have children?'

Chandler picked up his change of tone. Less heat. 'No, none, no, that's not true ... once, nearly.'

Jabril swerved the car to avoid a hare bolting across the highway.

'My second wife,' Chandler continued 'we tried, but she always miscarried. The last time she reached eight months.'

'That's bad luck, Mr Chandler.'

'It doesn't matter. It's history now. Anyway, he was never going to make it ... respiratory problems, some other stuff too.'

Jabril shook his head.

'He'd be seven by now,' said Chandler, his voice trembling.

'How did your wife take it?'

'She never really got over it. The marriage ended soon after. We tried to keep in touch, but you know ... '

'Some things can never be fixed,' Jabril muttered.

Chandler struggled for an answer, then thought back to the boy on the road. 'You're right, and some things are too precious to be broken.'

# Chapter Nine

*Be just before you are generous.*
R.B. Sheridan

Chandler had an hour to wait before Jabril was due to return with the guide. Late afternoon, but still time to take in the panoramic views of Palmyra. He entered the ancient temple of Baal, then surveyed the Roman theatre and senate. Sidestepping the old market place, he strolled along the colonnaded avenues before seeking shade under a monumental arch. Chandler took a deep breath. The air tasted sweeter than the sterile emissions from the car's air conditioning. Around him, in the softening sun, Palmyra's great colonnades and arches began to take on a pink hue, while palm trees, fringing the ruins, reminded him that the Old City stood squarely in an oasis. He looked about him. Not another living being in sight. The full weight of history and Chandler its sole spectator.

He checked his watch, then sat down and lifted a thick file from his rucksack. It contained several bundles of papers, neatly divided into plastic polypockets. Chandler began to rearrange the packages. He wondered whether reading his stories to Jabril would yield a profit. Perhaps an opportunity to earn some authentic Arab praise. Challenge Jabril's political prejudices too. But he was keenly aware of the risk, afraid that his tales might be met with derision. What had old Sharkey said? 'I'm having difficulty with your narrative structure, old boy. Too much exposition. Remember, *show*, don't tell.'

Hearing the sound of a car engine, Chandler returned the bundles to his rucksack. Standing on top of the podium, he watched Jabril and the guide exit the saloon. The guide was short and stockily built. Wearing cheap spectacles, he carried, in one hand, a rough sketch of the site. In the other, a packet of Gauloises.

'Mr Chandler, it is difficult to speak of a *Palmyrene* empire as it was so short-lived. Her queen, Zenobia—' The guide's commentary was interrupted by a fit of coughing.

'Why didn't the empire survive?' Chandler asked.

'You must understand, Rome had too much at stake to permit Queen Zenobia to make a challenge. Opposition is contagious. The emperor couldn't let the threat grow.'

Chandler felt Jabril grasp his shoulder. 'It's simple,' Jabril declared, 'Rome had to make an example of Zenobia. Remember what I told you in the car about difficult lessons.'

'What happened to her?'

Jabril chuckled. 'Zenobia was paraded through the streets of Rome in golden chains.'

'But a peaceful retirement and a villa in Tivoli,' ventured the guide, more hopefully.

✧

The Oasis Hotel lacked authenticity. Agreeably, a step up from the Mayflower, but missing something. Chandler's room was spacious and en suite, boasting a full English breakfast and a well stocked mini bar. Framed photographs of London, New York and Paris hung on the walls. But its interior and furnishings struck him as bland. The hotel staff greeted him with a volley of pleasantries. He could have been anywhere.

Sitting in the lobby, Chandler observed the unassuming manner in which they went about their duties. The barman constantly checked an empty till. The porter appeared from the lift devoid of luggage. A sullen middle-aged cleaner pushed a mop along a marble floor that was already spotless. No other guests in sight. Probably frightened off by the first sparks of unrest in Deraa, Chandler reckoned. Business deals scuppered as the flames of rebellion spread along the coastal towns of Latakia and Banias, with the *suits* all too ready to jump ship. Still, with most of the journalists holed up in Beirut, Chandler felt privileged. Their absence, he told himself, was sure to leave *him* with a greater story to tell.

✧

Perched on the end of his bed, Chandler closed his guidebook as he heard a light tap on the door. Jabril let himself in, then sat crosslegged on the armchair opposite him.

'We need to make an early start if we are to reach Aleppo before sunset,' Jabril said.

'I was hoping we'd see Krak des Chevaliers tomorrow,' Chandler ventured.

'No, there are still demonstrations on the road to the castle – it's too dangerous, so it must be Aleppo.'

Chandler cast Jabril a rueful glance.

'Look, Aleppo will be a perfect venue for some rest and relaxation. If we've time, an evening visit to its famous hammam – I've already rung to tell them to expect us.'

Chandler pulled a face in an exaggerated display of impatience.

'Don't worry, we'll get you to your castle as soon as it's safe.'

Chandler nodded.

'Now, I trust you enjoyed the tour of Palmyra – you were privileged to have the ruins to yourself.'

'That's one way of looking at it,' Chandler said.

'And a most informative guide, don't you think?'

'With all the demonstrations, I don't suppose he has much of a future,' said Chandler.

'Probably not – an early retirement, if the tourists fail to return.'

'But no villa in Tivoli.'

Jabril grinned. 'Sadly not – such mercies are only reserved for royalty.'

Chandler lifted himself from the bed and paced towards the window. In the fading light he was barely able to detect the smudges of ruins lying beyond the palm trees.

'*Mercy* ... funny you should mention that ... after that stuff at the checkpoint.'

'It's still bothering you, isn't it?'

'Are you surprised? In England—'

'This isn't England, Mr Chandler.'

'No, I suppose not.'

'Listen Mr Chandler, a roadside beating ... Zenobia's exile to Italy, the difference is immaterial – it's the message that counts.'

'So, what you're saying is that we mustn't upset the apple cart.'

'What I'm saying is that we should keep our thoughts to ourselves. At the very least, confine your moral insecurities to fiction.'

Chandler cocked his head. 'Stick to my writing, you mean?'

Jabril smiled. 'Precisely. But remember, *telling* the story risks nothing. Wanting to *become* the story only invites trouble.'

# Chapter Ten

*I was stupefied with fear; my hair stood on end*
*and my voice stuck in my throat.*
Virgil

'Did you get my text?'

'Which one?'

'The joke I sent you, you know, the one about the whore in Damascus?'

'Oh, that one, sorry, yes – very amusing.'

Standing by the entrance of the Hotel Oasis, Jabril clutched his mobile and watched the sunrise. The streets were empty. The town slept.

'How are you getting on with the Englishman?'

'Fine.'

'Jabril, can you be more specific.'

'Well, he hasn't sprung any surprises yet.'

'What, *nothing*?'

'He was thrown a little by an incident at a checkpoint, but insisted we should go on.'

'I know all about that, Lieutenant Mahood briefed me this morning.'

'Did he tell you what happened to the kid and his father?'

'The ones taken into custody for questioning?'

'It was a bit more than that.'

'But *necessary*,' Youssef declared.

'I'm not trying to question his methods.'

'I hope not, Jabril. We need to stay strong. Deal with these bandits firmly.'

Jabril looked up towards Chandler's window on the third floor. The lights were off. 'Youssef, I think we may be wasting our time with this man.'

'How do you mean?'

'Well, I can't see any evidence of a hidden agenda. He seems more interested in visiting the sites. He was quite taken with Palmyra.'

'Is he asking any difficult questions, talking to people?'

'How could he? The place is deserted. He hasn't been annoying anyone, unless you mean the guide. He didn't leave him a tip.'

'This is no good. You need to give me something to work on or we'll both be in trouble.'

'I told you, I've searched his bag, I can't find anything unusual, just a few stories. I think he's hoping I'll offer some sort of critique.'

'A what?'

'An evaluation, perhaps a—'

'Jabril, don't get smart with me. We haven't all had the benefit of your education.'

'Sorry, I just assumed.'

'That's your trouble, you *assume* too much. Take things for granted. Never see what's under your own nose.'

'Youssef, please ...'

'Listen, if you paid a little more attention to your own affairs, you wouldn't have let that daughter of yours get screwed by the Armenian in Aleppo.'

'I think I've suffered enough for that.'

'Jabril, you're beginning to bore me. Let's get back to this man's stories – anything political in them?'

'No Youssef, perhaps a little idealistic. I didn't get time to—'

'Sounds dangerous.'

'No, I don't think so, maybe a bit naïve.'

'Jabril, this is more serious than I thought. If this man is spreading sedition, then we have a problem on our hands.'

'Calm down, he's a *writer*, not a revolutionary.'

'Words are powerful weapons, Jabril. I don't like the smell of this. Keep a close eye on him and report back immediately you find anything suspicious. Oh, and look out for anything he might be holding back – any weaknesses.'

'I don't understand.'

'Something we can use against him ... just use your imagination.'

✧

Chandler set his hand under the spray. Lukewarm. Never a fundamentalist in matters of hygiene, he applied the shower cream haphazardly. He let the water course over his scalp and allowed a heavy lather to bubble under his armpits, around his groin and between his buttocks. He watched the suds travel down his legs. In the rising froth of the shower basin, his feet took care of themselves.

Chandler stepped out of the shower, then wrapped a large towel around his waist. He wondered whether he should go down and wake Jabril, but thought better of it. There would be plenty of time to talk in the car later, so why prematurely interrupt his slumber? Better to keep occupied, he thought. He lifted his rucksack and sat on the bed. He spent the next few minutes arranging his stories in the order he had written them. Then wondered whether they should be classified according to theme, and arranged them all over again.

✧

'The trouble is concentrated in Homs, so we will have to be careful,' Jabril said.

Chandler stared blankly at Jabril across the breakfast table. 'Do we have to go through Homs to get to Aleppo?' he asked.

'No, there's a road that by-passes the city but there will be checkpoints, lots of them, after the riots yesterday.'

'Like the travel agent said – everyone goes crazy on Fridays.'

'Sadly, there is some truth in that,' Jabril replied. 'Some of our more ignorant countrymen get stirred up at the mosque. Afternoon prayers become an excuse for anti-government propaganda.'

Chandler tore off a piece of flatbread and reached for the

humous. 'Yesterday sounded pretty bad, didn't it? I caught the news on the radio. Thirty dead, I think they said.'

'You have a radio?' Jabril asked with surprise.

'No, just my mobile phone. I caught some snippets from the World Service. The reception here is surprisingly good.'

Jabril lifted his knife. With the precision of a microsurgeon he began to dissect a cucumber stretched out on his plate. 'You know, the city of Homs dates back to 2000 BC,' he continued solemnly. 'It's mentioned in the Bible. The site of the largest chariot battle ever fought.'

'Yesterday's battle tanks?'

'Homs has always been strategically important,' Jabril added. 'We won't give it up to terrorists lightly.'

'Terrorists?'

'Yes, *terrorists*,' Jabril snapped. 'Can you imagine your government passing control of Manchester to Al Quaida?'

'If you put it that way, probably not.'

'At last, I think we're beginning to get on the same wavelength,' Jabril replied triumphantly.

'I'm not sure about that. I'll stick to the BBC for the time being.'

✧

Seventy miles west of Palmyra, Chandler watched the moving landscape. Desert gave way to wide fields of wheat and barley. Approaching the city, he watched mechanical diggers sitting idly among small mountains of grey phosphate. A miniature railway lay ready to transport the deposits to a fertiliser plant in the east of the city. Jabril had been right to compare industrial Homs to Manchester.

Apart from old war movies, Chandler had never encountered a tank. He was about to make a more personal acquaintance. At the intersection between Homs and Highway Five, leading north to Aleppo, he spotted a dozen of the beasts. Painted sandy yellow and grey, they sat brooding on the edge of the road. In the searing heat, Chandler watched their crews sweat to clear debris from caterpillar tracks. Soldiers hovered nearby, laughing and smoking. Further on, an armoured personnel carrier snaked its way under a bridge.

Chandler glanced nervously at Jabril.

'Look, a Model T-62', Jabril exclaimed, with the air of a vintage car enthusiast. 'You don't see too many of these now ... most have been replaced by the T-72. Full body protection from RPGs ... infra red night sights ... a killing range of one thousand metres.'

'A classic then,' muttered Chandler.

Jabril leaned towards the dashboard, then turned up the air conditioning. They watched an elderly officer walk between groups of soldiers. He was wearing a dark green beret, a black eye patch and a bushy moustache. His jacket bedecked with stars and ribbons. He took salutes and handshakes from the soldiers. Nobody was missed. The soldiers took no notice of the blue BMW, its engine running, standing incongruously among the forest of armoured vehicles. Enough time for Jabril to launch another barrage. 'A crew of four, commander, gunner, loader and driver, 115mm smooth bore gun with 18 degree elevation, 580 horsepower diesel engine, a cruising speed of—'

'Jabril, did you hear that?'

'What?'

'Sounds like gunfire, over there, under the bridge.'

Jabril pushed his face against the window. He watched the personnel carrier menacing the entrance to the bridge. The rear doors were flung open and a well built man, wearing a balaclava, jumped out. He joined another man, also masked, standing below the parapet. Chandler scanned the right hand side of the road, fringed by ragged gorse. He spotted a solitary leather sandal. A few metres on, its owner lay face down in the sand, with his leg set at ninety degrees. For a moment Chandler wondered how the contortion was anatomically possible. Like a passing motorist at the scene of a traffic accident, he considered getting out to check on the welfare of the casualty. He resisted the impulse and decided to duck below the windscreen instead. Chandler's knees knocked and his hands trembled.

The balaclavas were followed dutifully by a squad of helmeted soldiers. They walked past a line of civilians, already well bloodied. Like enthusiastic gangmasters, choosing labourers for a day's heavy toil, the pair paused every few metres, before giving the thumbs up to the goons. The prisoners selected were pulled out of the line, then pushed roughly against the wall of the bridge. They resembled starfish clinging to life against a sea wall, their legs and arms splayed across the concrete. Then, without ceremony, dispatched with short bursts of automatic gunfire.

'Christ, Jabril, I don't believe this. It's fucking madness. Can't you do something?'

'Mr Chandler, keep quiet, it will be over soon. Leave your camera in your bag and don't move.'

Chandler felt his stomach muscles tighten. His bladder began to fill. 'Can't you stop them? Tell them I'm British – *anything*.'

'Don't be absurd. Now, stay in the car,' Jabril ordered. 'Keep your eyes off the soldiers. If anyone asks questions, say nothing. I'm going to talk to the officer in charge, I think I know him.'

Chandler remained frozen to his seat, battling the need to relieve himself. Keeping his eyes firmly lowered, he listened to the grind of tank tracks and revving of engines – the steady rumble interrupted by renewed bursts of gunfire. He watched Jabril emerge from the shadow of the bridge.

'Everything is in order, Mr Chandler. We're good to go.'

'*Good to go*?' You make it sound like a bloody hamburger joint. Don't they want to speak to me?'

'No need,' Jabril replied. 'I explained the purpose of our visit to General Abrash.'

'The one with the eye patch?'

'Yes, he's taken charge of Homs Governorate. He offers his apologies for the delay and wishes you a pleasant vacation.'

Jabril weaved the car through the jam of tanks and carriers. He grinned as they passed a gunner lifting himself from a turret. The soldier raised his arm and issued a victory salute. Reaching under his seat, Jabril flipped the latch on a small compartment. 'Here, take this. Arak, from the best distillery in Latakia.' Chandler grasped the small bottle and drained it in a succession of heavy gulps. He felt the pale liquid burn his tongue, before it coursed down his throat.

'I would love to join you, Mr Chandler, but, as you know, I am forbidden. Still, I believe it's good medicine for the nervous passenger.'

'Pure bloody nectar.'

✧

Cruising steadily along Highway Five, they spent the next few minutes in silence. Chandler leaned back in his seat and let the Arak do its work.

'This man, Abrash, the general, what did he say?'

'I told you, he said everything is in order.'

'C'mon Jabril, it can't be as simple as that. Didn't he want to know about me?'

'Mr Chandler, how many times have I told you about asking too many questions?'

'I don't recall you ever saying that. Quite the opposite, you're always telling me I shouldn't take things at face value.'

'For a *tourist*, you're very persistent.'

'And for a *guide*, you're being rather evasive.'

Jabril shot Chandler a sideways glance. 'Okay, a short history lesson.'

'I'm listening.'

'Abrash is an old family friend. He fought alongside my father in '73.'

'Yom Kippur, you mean?'

'Yes, my father was his second-in-command in the Third Armoured Division.'

'Where did they fight?'

'The Golan Heights. The Jews call it the Valley of Tears, though I doubt whether they mourn for any of *our* martyrs.'

'An old friend then.'

'To my father, more like a brother.'

'I don't remember hearing much about the '73 war,' Chandler said. 'I think I was too busy chasing women in London.'

Jabril shook his head disdainfully. 'The history books say we took the enemy by surprise. But I don't think Israeli intelligence was so stupid. In any case, they had American satellites to help.'

'How far did they get?'

'The first day went well. His brigade managed to cross the minefields and were in sight of Kuneitra.'

'What stopped them?'

'Airpower.'

'Israeli?'

'Who else? Most of our tanks were destroyed on the ground. A turkey shoot I think the Americans call it.'

'And your father?'

'He was helpless. Communications were down so he stayed put for three days, waiting for orders.'

'What about Abrash?'

'He lost an eye, so my father looked after him. He probably owes his life to him.'

'So that explains the general's generosity to us at the bridge?'

'You're getting the picture, Mr Chandler.'

'How did they get out?'

'From the Golan?'

'Yes.'

'They had the Egyptians to thank for that. The Israelis

were forced to divert their efforts to the Sinai front. It gave them enough time to get airlifted to Damascus.'

'A lucky escape.'

'I'm not sure my father sees it like that – half the brigade were wiped out.'

Chandler raised his eyebrows. 'But a hell of a tale to tell.'

'A hell of a tale? You haven't a clue, have you?'

'Sorry?'

Jabril rapped his fingers on the dashboard. 'With all your privileges ...'

'What?'

'Coming here ... looking for drama. Maybe something to inspire your next story. A thriller perhaps?'

Chandler bit his tongue. For a few moments he wondered whether his brief relationship with his driver had irretrievably broken down, then let the Arak take the sting out of Jabril's remarks.

'Mr Chandler, I apologise.'

Chandler shot Jabril an uncertain glance.

'Perhaps I'm being too harsh.'

Chandler remained silent.

'But I think we know each other a little better now.'

Chandler took a deep breath. 'Are we back on the same wavelength then?' he asked nervously.

Jabril raised his eyebrows. 'I think we have a way to go before that.'

# Chapter Eleven

*Sharp is the kiss of the falcon's beak.*
Edward Bulwer-Lytton

The hammam lay in the centre of the Old City, between the citadel and the Great Mosque. Stepping into the outer chamber, in Aleppo's oldest bathhouse, Chandler and Jabril stared up at a large domed ceiling. The remains of the day filtered through fine glazed windows. Additional illumination was provided by a lantern hanging from the centre. In the middle of the marble floor an ornate fountain bubbled. They strolled across a bridge of carpets and mats before reaching a broad stone platform at the edge of the chamber. Chandler let his bag drop and began to undress.

Jabril checked his watch. 'It's getting late, but the masseur has agreed to return to the hammam as you're a special visitor.'

'So we just sit here then?'

'It'll be worth the wait,' Jabril muttered.

'Maybe we should leave, find somewhere to get a drink?'

Jabril shook his head. 'I have a better suggestion.'

'There's nothing better than an ice cold beer,' Chandler pleaded.

'Read me one of your stories.'

'What, here – in a bloody bathhouse?'

'It's an unusual setting, I agree, but it might settle your nerves. We can save the drink for later. Please, read.'

*Blind Faith*

*'Hey Ari ... nobody can better Hanna's baklava.'*

Chandler threw Jabril a sideways glance. Jabril remained expressionless. For a moment Chandler was unsure whether he should continue, then returned to his notes.

> *The young boy didn't need an education on the marvels of his aunt's pastries, neatly positioned in his open knapsack. The sweet smell of sliced almonds, crowning a cake skilfully constructed from delicate layers of phyllo, packed with chopped nuts, and drenched in honey, spoke for itself. But as to how little Ari had found himself standing on a crowded train bound for Poland – that remained something of a mystery. A conspiracy of silence, with no clues to shed light on an early morning flight from the family home. No explanation for an untimely frogmarch to the village square. No reasons given for his enforced departure from a homeland that the family had enjoyed, without incident, for generations.*

*Poor Ari, nobody was telling him anything.*

*Approaching his tenth birthday, the boy had grown used to living by his wits. Sure, his Hebrew name, Ari, meaning lion, suggested a destiny shaped by struggle. As his father, Isaac, constantly reminded him, 'Ari, my little lion ...you must keep your strength within – learn to stifle your roar.'*

*And so, he had.*

*Always the butt, never the instigator, of taunts and jeers from other boys in the village, he'd learned to accept, without complaint, the well directed blows from their boots. 'The kiss of leather,' they joked. As a sop to the sensibilities of their neighbours they had even embraced a Greek surname. A desperate need to belong. Why, even Aunt Hanna had joined their endeavours – ostentatiously moulding and baking her baklava in the Greek style. In doing so, she demonstrated, to the whole village, an attachment that she'd hoped would shield them in more troubled times.*

*A yearning to assimilate – to fit in – marked the family tradition.*

*All to no avail.*

*Too young to appreciate the implications of his country's absorption into the Reich, and too naïve to understand the race laws that would determine his future, little Ari accepted his fate.*

*He followed the flow and swam with the tide.*

Looking up, Chandler watched Jabril nod sagely.

*On board the train, space was at a premium. Women and the old guaranteed seats. Standing room only for men and boys. Assuredly third class. As the locomotive picked up speed, whistles blowing and steam belching, Ari clung to his father. He grasped Isaac's roughened fingers tightly. Ari had grown accustomed to the smell that clung to his father's skin and clothes – the strong, meaty odour of the tannery. A trade that bestowed a unique stench. But one that signified craftsmanship and promised high rewards for anyone willing to work the hours. Among the sleepy inhabitants of the village, however, a less generous perspective. Few tears today as Isaac was ejected from a village that once valued his industriousness. Little pity from town folk who, in better times, celebrated his magic in transforming bloodied hide into soft leather.*

Chandler heard Jabril draw breath – hopeful that the tragic drama he was playing out would have the desire effect.

*The journey from Thessaloniki to Cracow took four days. Eight hundred miles travelled. Small fishing villages, hugging the Aegean coast, gave way to unfamiliar mountain and plain. Blazing fields of maize reached out to dense forests of pine and spruce. Outside, the air was colder, fresher. Inside the sealed carriage, a different landscape. Quite simply, the travellers were beginning to smell. Close confinement and poor sanitation exposed as twin culprits in the big stink.*

*Ari was the first to notice the change. He soon picked up the din of unhappy passengers beginning to improvise. Buckets, bowls, cartons and cups were hastily brought into service to capture the rising slurry. Soiled nappies and used sanitary wear were rudely shoved below decks. By day four, the locomotive – pulling eight wagons and their sorry freight, came to a halt at Cracow Central Station.*

*Inside the train, plaintive cries for water and air went unheeded. In an atmosphere now reeking, heaving and breathless, Ari and his family waited. He heard faint murmurings, in Polish and Yiddish, outside the carriage. Noisy couplings of new wagons added to his confusion. With a blast of the whistle, the train left the city, gathering momentum, and arcing eastwards for the final leg of its journey. When the heavy wooden doors were finally unbolted and flung open, the incoming rush of cold air nearly knocked Ari off his feet. For a moment he felt cleansed. But the purification was short-lived.*

*Spilling out of the carriage with all the others, little Ari, as always, relied on his hearing to find direction. But as if the cacophony that confronted him wasn't bad enough – shouts of 'Raus and Schnell', the barks of ferocious Alsatians, the crack of a bullwhip, it was the smell that Ari found most unsettling. An acrid charcoal-like odour hung over the camp. Coppery and metallic, it hinted at burnt skin and hair. Ari had experienced something like this before – the tannery.*

Chandler glanced up at Jabril, who rewarded him with a hard stare.

*With the mushrooming stench taking a firm hold, Ari, his mother and older sisters, shuffled down the ramp towards the entrance of the camp. With his father left marooned at the gates, Ari found himself hauled past electrified fences, searchlights and sullen watchtowers. Behind a neat line of trees the chimneys of Crematorium Number Three issued thick columns of dust and smoke. In the open trenches beyond, the sharp smell of quicklime.*

*Inside the disinfecting room Ari began to undress. He didn't feel the shame and embarrassment afflicting the rest of the party. He was spared their tears and blushes. When the overhead lamps were switched off Ari was unaware of the darkening shroud that began to engulf the chamber. But he could smell the fear.*

*Little Ari – blind from birth – wouldn't see the blue cyanide crystals cascading through the hatches above. But he had no trouble in picking up the scent of bitter almond that infused the deadly vapour. It was a smell that reminded him off his favourite dish … his aunt Hanna's famous baklava.*

'Difficult subject matter, it can't have been easy,' said Jabril.

'It wasn't.'

'Keeping your emotions in check.'

'Bit of a struggle, I'll admit.'

'To carry your readers into the blind boy's predicament.'

'Took a bit of thought.'

'But never losing sight of the protagonist's point of view.'

'Part of the craft, isn't it?'

'A compelling backstory too.'

'I'm glad you—'

'But wholly missing the bigger picture.'

Chandler's face dropped.

'Can't you see? You've left the narrative incomplete.'

'Jabril, the story ... it's only an *episode*, drawn from history.'

'Oh, I see, a one act drama.'

'Well, yes, sort of ... '

'But rather one dimensional, don't you think?'

Chandler took a sharp breath. 'Six million were murdered, Jabril. There's nothing one dimensional about that.'

'I'm not disputing the evidence,' said Jabril, waving his hand dismissively, 'but your tale hasn't run it's full course. It needs, how can I put it, an *epilogue*.'

Chandler scratched his chin.

'A postscript at the very least.'

'You've lost me,' Chandler sighed.

Jabril shook his head. 'Use your imagination – fast forward a few years – try to locate a more *local* catastrophe?'

'I'm guessing you mean the Palestinians.'

'You're guessing correctly,' Jabril replied.

Chandler hesitated. 'You know, I've been working on a piece about them too – I can read it if—'

'How very noble of you – later perhaps.'

Chandler tugged at his shirt buttons. In the rising heat, his muscles ached. But he was unwilling to call an end of play. 'Look, I think we're getting off the point.'

Jabril crossed his arms. 'Really? So what exactly *is* your point?'

'C'mon Jabril, do I need to spell it out?'

Jabril let out a short chuckle. 'That's strange, Youssef is always telling me the same thing.'

'Who?'

'Never mind.'

'Listen,' Chandler continued, 'any writer worth his salt has to present the point of view of his subjects.'

'You mean the Jews, of course'

'I mean the *victims*.'

Jabril licked the sweat from his lips. 'Arabs don't need lessons from Westerners on victimhood.'

Chandler winced. 'I wouldn't presume.'

'Then *don't*.'

Chandler raised his palms in an act of supplication. 'Listen, the whole point of the story is to give voice to the Jewish boy. He didn't deserve—'

'To die in a gas chamber?'

'To die at all,' Chandler roared.

Jabril sucked his teeth. 'The men at the bridge – I suppose you regard them as victims too.'

Chandler remained silent.

For a few moments, Jabril considered his next assault. 'The son you lost ... then the boy at the checkpoint ... little Ari – all this anguish, it's suffocating.'

Chandler lifted the towel to his neck. For a few minutes, they stared at the sea of bubbles breaking the froth of the ornamental fountain.

Jabril was the first to break the trance. 'None of us know what lies ahead, Mr Chandler. If it is written, it is written.'

✧

Chandler heard the dallak push open the heavy door. He spied him pad effortlessly across the marble. The dallak resembled a well seasoned flight attendant. His walnut skin contrasted starkly with his white tunic. He made his way towards Chandler, as he lay on the divan. With Jabril looking on, the dallak rolled Chandler onto his stomach. His broad hands grasped his shoulders, before moving down to his arms and hands. He tugged his fingers with well practiced jerks. Chandler heard the joints of his knuckles crack.

Jabril sat up, then took measured steps across the marble floor, the surface slippery in the rising steam. He whispered a few words to the dallak and left the chamber. The dallak moved his hands under Chandler's groin. Long fingers worked methodically around his anus and perineum.

Chandler pulled himself up sharply. He fumbled for his clothes. The dallak stood still, smiling at Chandler's strong erection.

✧

'Where are you?'

'The hammam,' Jabril replied, shaking his fist theatrically.

'You missed Sami's birthday.'

'I know, but Mr Chandler insists on seeing Krak des Chevaliers. It's a full day's drive and we have to get back to Aleppo by nightfall. Look, I'll make it up to Sami when I get back. I'll buy him a present from the souq.'

'Jabril, it'll take more than a few toys to settle him.'

'I'm sure.'

'Jabril, Sami smashed up all his toys yesterday. Even the tank Qasim painted.'

'What did Qasim say?'

'What does your father *ever* say?'

'Is it fixed?'

'Of course it isn't. Anyway, I can't get out. The police are raiding half the houses in the neighbourhood. Nobody is talking to me. They think you've been passing on information about *them*.'

'That's ridiculous, you know I'd never do that.'

'*I* do Jabril, but that's not how it looks. You need to come home – talk to Sami.'

'Look, it's impossible, Mr Chandler—'

'Fine, you just look after your English friend. Enjoy the hammam.'

'Nadia ... please.'

'*No*, Jabril, you need to decide what's most important, your work or your family.'

✧

Chandler stood smoking outside the entrance of the hammam, waiting for Jabril to finish his call. He watched Jabril drop his phone into his jacket pocket. For a few moments, they watched the passing traffic.

'Mr Chandler, I've been thinking, the men at the bridge ... maybe you're right, it should never have happened.'

# Chapter Twelve

*In all the wedding cake, hope is the*
*sweetest of the plums.*
Douglas Jerrold

'Never here when you need him, is he?'

Nadia gripped Qasim's ankles, took a deep breath, then swung his legs across the bed. A dead weight, he emitted a low groan.

'It can't be right,' she muttered, 'a woman expected to change her father-in-law's incontinence pants. Soiled sheets perhaps, but not *this*.'

She lifted Qasim's trousers. Freshly ironed, following a merciless hotwash, she pulled them up, one leg at a time. Nadia stopped to catch her breath, then buttoned up his shirt and reached for his cardigan. Qasim raised his hand. A salute of sorts, and one, she hoped, that signalled acquiescence.

'Chandler this, Chandler that, it's all Jabril talks about these days. Well, I hope they're enjoying themselves in the hammam.'

Qasim tugged at his belt, oblivious to the sturdy nappy that imprisoned his over-active bladder. But with his mind stuck in reverse gear, he had no trouble recalling the ease by which he had been able to relieve himself in desert sands. Even when directing fire from the turret of a T-62, a piss pot had always remained close to hand.

Nadia lifted her mobile. It registered two unanswered calls to Zafirah. 'I'm sure Theo is a nice enough boy. But what future is there for him here?' She tugged the sheets. 'Then again, Haifa is no place for Zafirah to spend the rest of her days.'

Qasim's eyes followed his daughter-in-law as she took a few steps towards his wheelchair, perched on the far side of the bedroom. With his new quarters, erected hastily after his legs had given up the ghost, the tiny ground floor room acted as a grim reminder of days spent by the old soldier in the close confines of his tank.

'Funny, isn't it? He was the only man I ever had eyes for. Everyone said it was Jabril's looks. Handsome, I'll admit. But, to be honest, it was his *prospects* that really counted. The job at the library, the house in Damascus, never short of money.' Nadia stroked the old man's cheek. 'Does that make me sound like a whore?'

Qasim smiled.

'A marriage made in heaven, they told us. I'm not sure about that. But *he* got what he wanted ... Zafirah ... Sami. One of each. Isn't that what every man wants?'

Flat on his back, Qasim raised his arms. As if communicating in morse code, his forefingers made determined stabbing movements.

'I know he dotes on Zafirah. All this nonsense about putting a bullet in Theo's skull – just talk if you ask me.'

Nadia pushed the wheelchair to the edge of the bed. She leaned over Qasim, then slipped both hands under his shoulders. With a well practiced jerk, she swung her father-in-law towards the wheelchair.

'But Theo has to understand it will never work. I'm sure he could get his pick of Christian girls in Haifa. Maybe I should talk to his mother.'

Qasim's chin dropped. He drifted into a heavy sleep. Nadia squeezed his hand gently.

'A pity it's too late for you to talk some sense into that son of yours – tell him to give Youssef his marching orders. Put a word in with General Abrash. Beg him to get Jabril's job back in the library.'

Qasim began to snore.

'Oh what's the use.'

# Chapter Thirteen

*Build castles in the air*
Robert Burton

'Look at the tits on that.'

Chandler glanced uncertainly at Jabril, then looked towards the girl in the short dress.

'Jabril, where did you learn language like that?'

'Portering in St Pancras station.'

'In London?'

'Is there *another* St Pancras?'

'No, I don't believe so.'

'Before taking up studies in Moscow. It offered an excellent education in the vernacular.'

'Right, it's just, you know, I thought your religion ... '

'You mean the religion that requires me to pray five times a day?'

'Yes, that, and—'

'You think a good Muslim can't appreciate beauty?'

'Well, no, but we hear all this about *modesty*, covering up.'

'Another Western stereotype,' Jabril declared. 'This isn't Saudi Arabia. Anyway, how do you think Scheherazade captured the king's affections?'

'By *story telling*?'

Jabril cocked his head.

'Okay, maybe there was more to it than that.'

'She showed him the *bigger* picture,' Jabril replied, grinning.

'Quite.'

'How long have we spent together, Mr Chandler?'

'Two days.'

'And what have you learned?'

'To expect the unexpected?'

'Precisely. Now go and explore your crusader castle. We need to be back in Aleppo before dark. Will an hour be sufficient?'

✧

*Perhaps the best preserved and most wholly admirable castle in the world.* T. E. Lawrence.

Chandler closed his guidebook and viewed the architecture. Krak des Chevaliers. Outer walls three metres thick. Seven guard towers. An inner ward housing a meeting hall and chapel. Vaulted stone stables. Ramps, arrow slits and shooting galleries at every turn. Enough space to house a full garrison and a thousand horses. Impregnable.

'Excuse me, would you mind taking our picture?'

Chandler turned sharply to face the odd couple. He struggled to suppress a giggle, then studied the middle-aged man holding a camera. Barely five foot, with khaki shorts meeting his knees, he wore a pair of sturdy sandals, with brown socks hugging pale calves. Like an overgrown boy scout on his first date, he stood next to a young woman in a short black dress. She held his hand tightly. *Look at the tits on that.*

The woman was in her early twenties. Her breasts barely restrained by a small red bra, visible above the neckline of her dress, with straps hanging loose on angular shoulders. Her hair was bleached unevenly, held together in a tight bun. Approaching six foot, a true Amazonian. With skin the colour of snow, Chandler wondered whether the concubine was home grown or an expensive import.

'Sorry, if it's too much trouble?' the man ventured.

Chandler reached for the camera. 'No, it's fine. Maybe you should sit on the parapet – take advantage of the ... *elevation*.'

Chandler watched the young woman disappear into a vaulted chamber, then return, holding a small chair. Nonchalantly, she dropped it in front of the parapet. Draping her ivory legs across the backrest, she adopted her finest Christine Keeler pose.

'You're the first Englishman I've seen in weeks,' the man said. 'What the hell are you doing here?'

Chandler took a moment to locate the accent. Home counties with a hint of Bromley. 'I'm here for a few days. We've done Palmyra, but still have to see the rest of Aleppo, and Damascus of course.'

'*We*?' the man asked. 'Who's with you?'

'Just my driver,' Chandler replied.

'Over here, there is no such thing as *just* a driver,' the man whispered.

'How do you mean?'

The man chuckled. 'In Syria, things are never quite what they seem.'

'Oh, not again,' Chandler groaned, 'that's what Jabril keeps telling me.'

'Jabril who?

'Mansour ... from Latakia,' Chandler replied.

The man raised an eyebrow. 'You'll need to exercise some caution with this chap. Be careful what you say'.

Chandler ignored the comment and stayed focused on the girl. She lifted a small make-up mirror from her bag, then applied a fresh layer of mascara. 'Sorry, do you still want me to take some snaps?'

The man in shorts paused. 'I do apologise, I never introduced myself. Rupert Oakshott, from the embassy.'

Chandler steadied the camera. He trained his sights on the girl. 'Sorry, did you say you're the ambassador?' he remarked absently.

'No, nothing so grand,' the diplomat replied, avoiding eye contact. 'Import and export, trade delegations, that sort of thing.'

Chandler ran his eyes along the girl's muscular thighs. Moving north, he detected a narrow triangle of pink cotton shielding her pubis.

'And this is Miss Tuma from St Petersburg,' the diplomat beamed. 'Studying pharmacology ... and a keen historian.'

'Yes, quite,' Chandler said.

'Listen, this Jabril, how did you meet him?'

'A travel agency in Hamra ... Beirut.'

'That's my man. We've had dealings with him before ...

works with his cousin, a chap called Youssef … a nasty piece of work.'

'What sort of dealings?'

'Look old boy, I've probably said too much. Let's just say that Jabril's last passenger was, how can I put it, *taken for a ride*.'

'He's my driver – that's what he's supposed to do.'

The diplomat hung his arm around the girl's shoulder, then whispered a few words in Russian. She began to snigger. Chandler raised the camera – the girl's breasts neatly framed.

'It wasn't the money or missing passport that was really the problem,' the diplomat continued, 'though the poor man was left somewhat out of pocket.'

'So what was it?'

'He wouldn't tell us. Let's just say that taking out health insurance was a wise move.'

✧

Standing in the shadow of the outer gate, Chandler watched Jabril pace erratically across the car park. Grasping his mobile, he appeared unusually animated. The conversation struck Chandler as mostly one way. Every few seconds, Jabril raised his hand and shook his head. Unseen, Chandler edged closer towards him. He strained to listen – Jabril's conversation largely unintelligible. Only *one* word, uttered repeatedly, with a pleading tone, struck home. Like a stone, with sharp edges, cast into a still pond, it bounced perilously across the surface. *Youssef*.

# Chapter Fourteen

*It is a wise father that knows his own child.*
Shakespeare

'How far gone is she?'

'Nearly eight months.'

'And you had no idea?'

'No, she said nothing.'

'Who's the father?'

'How can you ask that? You know it's Theo.'

Jabril pushed the mobile to his ear, trying to shut out the noise of traffic in downtown Aleppo. 'I don't want to hear his name again, Nadia. Have you any idea how I feel about this? Zafirah has *destroyed* us.'

'Don't exaggerate, we're still a family,' Nadia sighed.

'We *were* a family.'

'Jabril, listen, what is done is done – we both have to accept it. Zafirah is going to be a mother. Your first grandchild, and she wants to come home.'

'She what?'

'She wants to have the child in Latakia. Think about it, a little nephew for Sami.'

'She knows the sex?'

'They told her at her last scan.'

'Have you told Sami?'

'Of course not. A *father* should be the first to know.'

Keeping the phone jammed to his ear, Jabril stepped hesitantly into the hotel foyer. He glanced at the young receptionist who watched him closely. 'Have you said anything to Qasim?'

'Qasim? I think it's a bit late for that.'

'Look, you know what the neighbours will say if Zafirah comes back. We're in enough trouble as it is.'

Jabril caught the sound of his wife's rapid breathing.

'This isn't about the neighbours. We can't abandon her,' she exclaimed.

'Like she abandoned *us*. Running off, as if family honour means nothing.'

'Jabril, she telephoned yesterday. Things have gone badly in Haifa.'

'What do you mean?'

Nadia's voice began to break. 'It's Theo's friends. Since the rocket attacks they—'

'What's Theo saying?'

'Apparently, he wants the child brought up as a Christian. Zafirah to convert.'

Jabril clenched the phone. 'That's impossible.'

'I know.'

'Is she getting any support?'

'Are you serious? Even their Arab neighbours are keeping their distance.'

'Nadia, she should have thought of all this before she left. You know, I could have found her a suitable husband.'

'You mean *Youssef*? He's far too old for her.'

'She could do worse.'

'No, Jabril, he *is* the worst. Do you remember what he did to Fatimah?'

'But she cheated on him.'

'Perhaps, but she didn't deserve to be beaten ... to cut off her hair.'

Jabril glanced back to the receptionist. She turned away sharply. 'Nadia, he was simply defending his honour.'

'There's no honour in that. Then to start sniffing around Zafirah, as if nothing had happened.'

'But he's from a good family. You know his mother thinks the world of Zafirah.'

'Youssef can go to hell. And *you* need to decide what's most important – your ambition or your family.'

✧

Youssef stretched his legs, then reached for his cigarettes. The smart boutique hotel, a short walk from Aleppo's Great Mosque, was ideally located. A convenient spot to allow him to spy on worshippers at their daily prayers. A chance to keep a close check on Chandler's movements in the city too. Happily, an opportunity to find entertainment from local whores in the privacy of his hotel room. His mobile began to buzz.

'Now, let's see what we have. This man Chandler. He sneaks across the border while the clerics are preaching sedition at afternoon prayers. Brings four sets of notes, concealed in his baggage. Am I right so far, Youssef?'

'Yes, Colonel.'

'In *Palmyra,* he questions the guide on the city's history of insurrection.'

'Yes sir.'

'In *Homs,* Chandler challenges our methods in dealing with terrorists. Would that be a fair account?'

'Yes.'

'Next stop, Aleppo and a lewd display in the hammam, according to the dallak. Oh, and a discourse sympathetic to the Jews – dressed up as a short story. Am I still on track?'

'I think so.'

'But that's not all, is it?'

'Sorry?'

'Under the pretext of an excursion to Krak des Chevaliers, he arranges a clandestine meeting with the British military attaché.'

'I don't understand, Colonel.'

'Didn't Jabril tell you? You're slipping up, Youssef.'

'How do you know about the meeting?'

'I heard it from the horse's mouth. I'm reading a statement from the attaché's Russian whore. She saw everything. She even had her picture taken.'

'Is she reliable?'

'She has impeccable credentials. She gave me a full account ... even *before* I fucked her.'

'This is a lot to take in, Colonel.'

'Oh, but there's more.'

'What?'

'Did I mention the phone tap?'

'No.'

'Well, this is where it gets *interesting*. Apparently, Jabril's daughter is coming home.'

'But she's living in Haifa with the Armenian.'

'Sadly, it's all gone sour. Anyway, I thought you'd be *pleased*. Didn't you always have an eye for her?'

'Colonel, I'm sure she's not mixed up in any of this, she's too—'

'*Innocent*? Nobody is innocent these days.'

'Are you going to arrest her?'

'Not yet, Youssef. General Abrash won't allow it. He still has the ear of the President.'

'But there must be some way to get at Jabril. Take Chandler too. It would be easy to make them disappear.'

'My thoughts exactly, but as long as *Abrash* is involved we have to be careful. Remember, his men are still loyal and the President thinks he will need them if things get out of hand in Homs.'

'So what do I say to Jabril? He's bound to ring me later.'

'Just be patient. We have plenty of informants who can keep an eye on Jabril and Chandler. When the time is right, we'll reel them *both* in.'

# Chapter Fifteen

*Nobody likes us, we don't care.*
Millwall Football Club
supporters' chant

Burkas, chadors, niqabs, hijabs. A sea of black lapping against the steps of the citadel.

'*Iranians*,' Jabril muttered. 'The only visitors we see in Aleppo now.'

Sitting on a marble platform in the square facing the citadel, Chandler and Jabril watched the women dismount from a procession of luxury coaches. Chandler gazed at their feet. Colourful sandals, shoes and slippers, the sole concession to fashion and femininity. The older pilgrims stopped to rest against a low wall facing the main tower. The younger women hurried to keep pace behind throngs of laughing children who, like miniature Olympians, leaped three steps at a time up the steps of the citadel.

Chandler observed the menfolk. Dressed in short sleeves and slacks, they exchanged cigarettes, before seeking shelter from the sun under the awning of an empty restaurant.

'I've never quite understood the power of religion. Travelling thousands of miles ... you know, Mecca and all that.'

'That's because religion has lost its function in the West. You live in a spiritual vacuum.'

'I'm as spiritual as the next man.'

'Perhaps, but here, religion permeates *every* aspect of life. It is, how you say, *our daily bread*.'

Chandler wiped the sweat from his forehead. Approaching noon and the heat oppressive.

'The original fortifications go back to 330 B.C. but were largely rebuilt in the thirteenth century,' Jabril intoned, with the air of a tour guide.

'Another Krak des Chevaliers then?'

'In a way, but this was built by *Muslims* to defend the city against the crusaders.'

'You make it sound like the citadel is still needed.'

'Probably, but our biggest threat now is the enemy within.'

'An excuse for more repression then?'

'Mr Chandler, all this unrest ... the Arab Spring, as *you* quaintly call it, only brings instability. So we need strong allies.'

'You mean Iran?'

'Naturally. Who else can stop the Americans?'

'What's America got to do with it?'

'Don't be naïve. America has *everything* to do with it.'

'Oh, right ... the sanctions.'

'That, and their irritating lessons in democracy.'

'Isn't that just what people need?'

'Maybe, but not yet.'

Chandler shook his head.

Jabril raised his forefinger. 'Mr Chandler, think of our country as a fragile mosaic – Sunni, Shia, Kurd, Christian, even a few Jews. Tiny pieces held together by a thin layer of cement, like the mosaics you saw in Palmyra.'

'And the cement holding the pieces together is the *President* I suppose.'

'It's not perfect, but it's the best we can hope for. Anyway, the President is above sectarian politics.'

'But he's Alawite, isn't he?'

'So am I.'

Chandler scratched his head, then turned to watch the children prancing along the high walls of the citadel. 'Jabril, if you have such illustrious connections, why are you driving a taxi in Latakia?'

'A long story.'

'So let's hear it.'

'Maybe later.'

'This *mosaic*,' Chandler continued, 'isn't it beginning to crack?'

'All the more reason for remedial action,' Jabril declared.

'Restoration that can only be carried out by a *strong man*, I suppose?'

'The country needs a firm hand.'

'Don't you think it's too late? Did you hear the news? There's talk of an uprising in Hama.'

Jabril nodded. 'So, all the more reason for a determined approach.'

Chandler observed the slow retreat of the burkas down the steps of the citadel. 'Jabril, is *that* what you want – women covered from head to foot – slaves to their husbands?'

'It's not that simple.'

'Is that what *your* wife wants?'

'My wife?' Jabril shot back, feigning surprise. 'She wants what *every* woman wants.'

'You mean children?'

'What else?'

Chandler blew out his cheeks. 'You know, Jabril, it's been three days and you've said nothing about your family.'

'I'm your guide'

'C'mon, I've never met an Arab who didn't talk about his children.'

For a moment, Jabril appeared lost for words. 'You don't have children, do you?'

'No, I told you, my ex-wife miscarried.'

'Then you know what it is like to lose part of yourself.'

'Why ... has *your* wife lost a child?'

'In a way, yes'

'Is she dead?'

'As good as.'

'Is she sick?'

Jabril kept his eyes glued on the women returning to the coaches. 'No, in fact she's never been in better health – she's expecting her first baby.'

'We're back to riddles again.'

'Maybe we should change the subject.'

'Jabril, you talk about your daughter like she's a ghost in some Shakespearian tragedy.'

'Leave it.'

'Listen, you have a *wife* waiting for you. A daughter about to deliver your first grandchild. I'd give anything—'

'You don't understand, Mr Chandler.'

'What is there to understand? Do you think I'd be out here if I had a wife and kids to come home to?'

'Sometimes I think family can be more of a curse than a blessing.'

'*Bullshit*.'

Jabril lit a cigarette. 'It's getting late. We need to go into the citadel. If there's time, you can entertain me with another story. Then, if you wish, I'll tell you mine.'

# Chapter Sixteen

*Daughter am I in my mother's house,*
*But mistress in my own.*
Kipling

'Jabril, where the *hell* are you? I was expecting you to ring this morning.'

'Sorry. It's been difficult.'

'Tell me something new.'

'Mr Chandler is insisting on seeing everything in the citadel. It's a job keeping up with him.'

'You're still in Aleppo then?'

'Yes, until tomorrow. Today, he plans to visit the soap factory.'

'Sounds like an excuse for economic espionage.'

'No Youssef, I don't think so. He wants to bring some home for his nephew.'

'Oh Jabril, aren't you being a little naïve?'

'I don't understand.'

'Can't you see, he's keeping something from us.'

'No, I told you, I haven't let him out of my sight.'

'Don't play games with me. Didn't Chandler tell you about his meeting with the military attaché in Krak?'

'That's impossible, I was with him the whole time.'

'But you're forgetting something. I have it on good authority that you allowed Chandler free rein of the castle. Perhaps you were too busy planning Zafirah's homecoming to notice.'

'How do you know about Zafirah?'

'Jabril, I hope you're not trying to make a fool out of me.'

'No, of course not. But why bring Zafirah into it?'

'Because she's the *key*.'

'I'm not with you.'

'Really? Is it merely coincidental that Zafirah is taking leave of her Zionist associates just as Chandler is beginning to stir the pot here?'

'That's a bit of a stretch, Youssef. From what I can see, Chandler is no more than a tourist trying to impress his friends. And Zafirah simply wants to be near her mother. You know she's expecting.'

'Ah yes, the baby. I'm sure Nadia will be delighted to have another brat to feed. A little Christian into the bargain. Has she thought of a name? Jesus perhaps?'

'Youssef, we don't want any trouble.'

'Trouble? Oh, there'll be trouble alright. You know what we do to female spies? Do you remember the Jewish bitch we lifted in Daraa?'

'I'm hardly likely to forget ... I told you then, the interrogation was excessive.'

'Perhaps, but an interesting challenge for her gynaecologist.'

'Please, Zafirah's done nothing wrong. She just wants to come home.'

'Jabril, listen, you need to help me out here.'

'How?'

'By taking your mission a little more seriously. I want to know everything Zafirah gets up to when she returns – her movements, contacts.'

'Contacts? With who?'

'You know Latakia is crawling with spies. Mossad, CIA, British Intelligence – supplying weapons to local subversives.'

'That's absurd. There's too much security in the city ... the army—'

'The *army?* If you mean General Abrash, you can't seriously believe *he* can be trusted?'

'He's a good patriot, Youssef.'

'Oh, Jabril, my innocent little cousin, always missing the big picture.'

'Look, I've done everything you've asked me.'

'*Except* to tell us about Chandler's secret meeting in the castle. *Except* to inform us about Zafirah's plan to leave Israel. *Except* to explain Abrash's mysterious intervention on Chandler's behalf at Homs. Do I need to go on?'

'Look, you're getting this out of proportion. Chandler's done nothing wrong.'

'No Jabril, Chandler is as good as finished.'

'What about Zafirah?'

'I'm not sure, she's heavily compromised.'

'I don't want her hurt.'

'Okay, I'll talk nicely to the colonel. No promises mind.'

'Please, she's my *daughter*.'

'That's as may be, but the colonel has finally issued orders to arrest her.'

'Can't you stop it?'

'No, I can't. But if you cooperate, the colonel may allow *me* to question her first.'

✧

Reaching the summit of the citadel, Chandler gazed over the city. He was struck by its orderliness. None of the chaotic gridlock he had witnessed in downtown Beirut. Just lines of tiny yellow taxis, patiently waiting their turn at regular junctions. Demonstrating their submission at traffic lights dotting Aleppo's broad avenues.

'There you are,' Jabril called out. 'I thought I'd lost you.'

Jabril took a seat next to Chandler on the empty terrace. For a few moments they absorbed the panorama. Jabril lifted his phone, shook his head, then scrolled for messages.

Chandler held out a cigarette. He spotted Jabril's hands trembling.

'What's wrong ... is it Nadia?'

'No, my daughter.'

'I'm not with you.'

Jabril watched the column of taxis below. 'I'm just your *driver*. I think I've told you enough.'

'*That's* your decision, but, these last couple of days, I think I've become more than just a paying passenger.'

Jabril pulled heavily on his cigarette. 'Zafirah has spent the last year with her Christian boyfriend in Israel. I don't have a clue what she's been doing there. Now, she is pregnant and, without warning, decides to return to Syria.'

'Sounds like she's just a little headstrong.'

'Maybe, but how does it look – to the neighbours – the police? It's easy to put two and two together.'

'And make five, I suppose.'

'In Syria, with the insurgency, *everyone* is making five.'

'Especially your superiors?' Chandler asked.

Jabril stubbed out his cigarette, then lifted another. For the first time, his expression bore none of the superiority Chandler had become accustomed to. As if a veil had been lifted.

'C'mon, Jabril, you must have guessed that I knew you weren't just a tour guide.'

'Is it that obvious?'

'Not at first, but I knew something was up when we crossed the border. That business at the checkpoint, then Homs. You seemed a little too sure of yourself.'

'The mark of a good investigator, Mr Chandler.'

Chandler pulled a bottle of warm mineral water from his rucksack, taking slow, measured sips. 'Investigator or informer?'

'Is there a difference?'

'In England, yes.'

'Mr Chandler, in Syria, the lines are more blurred.'

'Either way, you didn't make much effort to cover your tracks. Those calls to your mobile, I knew they couldn't all be from your wife.'

Jabril raised his eyebrows. 'So, if I am being too obvious, where does that leave *you*?'

'Me? Oh, I'm just an innocent abroad.'

Jabril smiled. 'You know, I'm beginning to think that may be true. But that's not how others might see it.'

'So where do things stand?' Chandler asked. 'Do you still have a job to do, you know, to finish the ... *investigation*?'

'As far as my superiors are concerned, the investigation, as you put it, isn't concluded. And whatever your original intentions were in coming here, they still think you've something to hide.'

'But I haven't done anything.'

'Mr Chandler, what *you* think you have, or haven't done, is beside the point. It's perceptions that count.'

'Whose perceptions?'

'Those in higher authority, I told you.'

'You have me worried.'

'You should be.'

'Maybe I should I call the embassy.'

'No, that would be unwise. The security services are probably tracking every call we make.'

'*We*? Don't they trust you?'

'I'm not sure, after Zafirah ... '

'But you still have Abrash on board – you know, his debt to your father.'

'A double edged sword, Mr Chandler.'

'I don't understand.'

'Look, the general has the trust of the President, but many suspect his real sympathies lie with the rebels.'

'So, where does that leave you?'

'Walking a tightrope, Mr Chandler.'

Chandler checked his watch. 'Shouldn't we get back to the hotel? It's getting late.'

'No, the citadel doesn't close for an hour. But I can think of *one* way to fill the time,' Jabril said, pointing to Chandler's rucksack.

'Another story? You know, I don't think this one will leave you any more reassured.'

'Just *read*.'

*Missing*

*'What do you mean she's missing?'*

*'Patrick, don't make it sound so melodramatic. All I said was that she hasn't been to her classes for a few days.'*

*'So what's wrong with her? Is she sick?'*

*'I haven't the faintest idea, she's not answering her phone.'*

*'Right, so as far as you know she could be lying dead in some dingy squat in Amsterdam. Aren't you just a little concerned?'*

'Amsterdam – such a beautiful city. Have you been there?' Jabril broke in merrily.

Chandler dropped his notes.

'I'm sorry, I didn't mean to interrupt. Please ...'

*'Patrick, we've been through all this before. Remember Glastonbury? Not a whisper for days and then back on the doorstep without a by your leave.'*

*'Your doorstep if I recall, Sarah.'*

*'Well, that's the price of desertion. What did you expect? Your precious little darling begging to crash out on your sofa?'*

*'For Christ's sake, let's not go down that path again. Just give me her address. Somewhere in the Jordaan, isn't it?'*

*'I think so – I'll text you.'*

*

*Dr Patrick Mather. Failed painter. Successful art critic. Aspiring divorcee. He dropped his mobile phone into his dressing gown pocket and shuffled towards the fridge. Yesterday's sauvignon lay wedged between a hardening block of farmhouse cheddar and a bowl of mouldering chilli con carne. It was three in the afternoon and he believed that he deserved a drink. What's needling Sarah? he thought. There had been no delays in monthly payments for Camilla. His quarterly donations, to cover the cost of her travel, accommodation and books, had always been on time. He had even called in a few favours. A quiet word with Professor Wilders at the Rijksmuseum had secured their daughter a six month residency. Now, Camilla had gone AWOL, and all Sarah could do was play the deserted wife card. Mather believed it was time he should become more proactive. That meant booking a flight to Schiphol airport in the morning and securing a face to face meeting with Wilders. Surely the old professor could shed some clues.*

*

*'Jan, was Camilla happy at the Rijksmuseum?'*

*Sitting in a large armchair in his oak-panelled office, Professor Wilders took a moment to consider his reply.*

*'Patrick, let me speak candidly. As an old friend. Camilla never really settled here. The residency, perhaps it was a little premature. Her workshop on the Nightwatch – something of a disappointment. Then the complaints from her students. She's a talented artist of course but, how can I put it, a bit too passionate. I think your daughter's interests lie elsewhere.*

'That's funny,' Jabril blurted out, 'Zafirah is no different – one minute singing the praises of the old masters, the next, obsessed with Picasso.'

'Do you want me to carry on or not?' Chandler snapped.

Jabril nodded apologetically.

*'So why didn't you tell me earlier? I could have come over.'*

*Looking exasperated, Wilders ran his narrow fingers through his handlebar moustache. 'My thoughts exactly, but before I could reach you Camilla was gone.'*

*'Jan, did she say anything before she left?'*

*'Nothing of note,' Wilders said. 'Oh, one thing, she said she wanted to bring her art to real people.'*

*'That's Camilla all over,' Mather murmured. 'I didn't think she'd be content restoring Rembrandts and Vermeers.'*

*'Have you contacted the police?'*

*Mather looked hard at his old mentor. 'I haven't much choice, have I?'*

*

*Leaving the Rijksmuseum, Mather took the short walk across Museumplein towards the leafy tranquillity of Vondelpark. Short sighted and vain, he kept his spectacles tucked firmly in his jacket pocket. The decision nearly cost him his life as he failed to spot tram number 7, at full throttle, hurtle past him. In the park he found an empty bench and reached for his phone.*

*'Sarah, I've been to the Rijksmuseum and they've had no word from Camilla.'*

*'Patrick, I think there's a problem with your standing order.'*

*'Sorry, I thought we were talking about Camilla. It's been nearly two weeks.'*

*'Oh calm down, she'll show up when it suits her. She always does. Anyway, have you sent that money order yet?'*

*'Christ Sarah, that's not going to help find Camilla.'*

*'Just send me a cheque tomorrow, I've got bills to pay.'*

*

*Approaching the police station in Leidesplein, Mather remained oblivious to the sounds and sights of traffic grinding into the square. He was still preoccupied with the call to his wife. He was furious at her lack of concern, but was convinced that his daughter had been in contact. He chided himself at his failure to see this possibility as good news. Mather spotted the entrance to the police station. It lay at the far end of the square, sandwiched between a nightclub and an arts complex. An unassuming grey office block, it denoted a quiet efficiency. Solemn office workers and wide-eyed students glided past on their bicycles. Clutching his briefcase tightly, Mather gave a wide birth to two young men smoking on the station steps. North African, he guessed. Probably dealers. Unobtrusively, he strained to listen to their delicate negotiations about weights and measures. For a moment he considered showing them a photograph of Camilla, then thought better of it.*

*

*'Ah, Dr Mather, you're late.'*

*Inspector Peter Hoogstratten, blond and wearing faded jeans and a creaseless polo shirt, surprised Mather. He had been expecting someone older and more grizzled. Must be a graduate fast-tracked to promotion, he mused. The inspector conformed to every Dutch stereotype, but Mather was relieved to note that he was devoid of a goatee and ponytail.*

*'We had a call from Professor Wilders at the Rijksmuseum,' Hoogstratten said. 'An old friend of the justice minister, so, as you say in England, no pressure.'*

*Mather felt satisfied. His string-pulling had ensured a measure of cooperation, despite the inspector's barbed comment about his punctuality.*

*'I think you have the background,' Mather said.*

*'A few details Dr Mather, but to be honest, we have very little to go on.'*

*Mather felt anger and frustration welling. 'Isn't it enough that my daughter is missing?'*

*'Dr Mather, we have more runaways in Amsterdam than any city in Europe. The drugs, human trafficking, abuse at home ... there are many reasons for a young woman to disappear.'*

'An unhappy sign of the times,' Chandler heard Jabril murmur, before returning to his notes.

*'Inspector, my daughter wasn't ... isn't involved in any of that. A bit of a rebel perhaps, but always very focused. You see, her art ... '*

*'Ah yes, her art,' Hoogstratten broke in, with a thin smile. 'And rather temperamental too ... according to your wife.'*

*'Have you been talking to my wife?'*

*'Yes, I rang her this morning. A pleasant lady. She doesn't seem too worried. She says that Camilla needs, how did she put it ... space.'*

*'Space? From what?'*

*'This is difficult, Dr Mather. What I think she means is space from, well, you. She said your daughter needs to find her own way.'*

*'Inspector, my daughter is missing. Two weeks have gone by and I see no sign of a police investigation. Your only line of enquiry is a telephone call to my bloody wife. I hardly call that pulling out all the stops. Perhaps if you were old enough to have children, you'd be taking this case more seriously.'*

*Hoogstratten lowered his eyes and rapped his fingers on the open file. Mather noticed that it bore a small black and white photograph of his daughter. 'Dr Mather, each missing person in Amsterdam is a cause of great concern to me. Please, be assured, everything is being done to find Camilla. The Commissioner has promised all the recourses I need. We have patrols looking for her throughout the city.'*

*'But you've still found nothing' Mather said.*

*'Not quite. We have one possible sighting in Nieuwmarkt. Tomorrow we concentrate our efforts there.'*

*'Nieuwmarkt? Isn't that the red light district?'*

*Hoogstratten grinned, 'It has a flower market too, but the tulips probably take second place.'*

Looking up sharply, Chandler watched Jabril suppress a chuckle.

*'She needs space. To find her own way. That's how the inspector put it, Sarah. Are they your words or Camilla's?'*

*'Patrick, I think you already know the answer to that. Do you remember dragging the poor girl*

*around all those galleries? She was only twelve for God's sake. Then art college, it was hardly her choice. As for the residency, a clear case of a failed artist forcing his obsessions on an impressionable daughter.'*

*'No Sarah, it was more a case of nurturing natural talent.'*

*'Oh, just look at yourself, Patrick, forcing Camilla to step into your sorry shoes. It's just a pathetic attempt to make up for your own inadequacies.'*

*'She's been in touch, hasn't she? Tell me where she is. If you can't say now, ring me at the hotel tonight. Or text me if that's all you can manage.'*

*'You must be finding this all too hard to take, Patrick. Your little girl, out of your life. Are you feeling abandoned?'*

*'Sarah, stop it.'*

*'Just remember, you're the father who abandoned her. And you're the husband who left me for that slut. Did you hear what I said? Answer me.'*

*

Mather prided himself on his appreciation of the urban aesthetic. The Jordaan, lying west of the city centre, dissected by slender canals and populated with brightly coloured barges, never failed to delight him. The district's contemporary art displays offered a vibrant contrast to the musty collections of the Rijksmuseum. At the same time, his anxiety was rising. There was still no sign of

*Camilla. His daughter's neighbours were unable to shed any light on her disappearance and her landlord was complaining bitterly about unpaid rent. Hoogstratten's words hung over him. She needs space. To find herself.*

*

*Nieuwmarkt. Home to some of the city's finest buildings and oldest churches. But within its embrace, a labyrinth of neon-lit window brothels, sex shops and seedy bars, all competing for space.*

*'You find tissue by shower.'*

*Mather hadn't planned on meeting a whore. Twenty precious minutes that could have been spent searching for Camilla. But if, as Hoogstratten suggested, his daughter had been seen in Nieuwmarkt, his visit to the brothel, he told himself, might be justified. 'Mather observed the young woman pulling at her tight mini skirt. Tanya, so probably Eastern European, he reckoned. Her dark hair was heavily matted. A web of puncture wounds ran along her forearms. He looked at her dead eyes and detected a faint smell of urine.*

*'Tanya, do you recognise this girl? She's my daughter.'*

*The young woman glanced nervously out of the window, then looked back at the photograph. Chandler saw a flicker of recognition.*

*'Maybe I see her here last week,' she replied. 'With man ... Moroccan, I think.'*

*Mather thought back to the north African drug dealers in Leidesplein.*

*'Tanya, please ... have you any idea where she is? Who she's with?'*

*He began to draw a hundred Euro note from his wallet. Tanya turned towards an unshaven middle-aged man thrusting his head through the bead curtains. He was wearing a black leather jacket over a heavy paunch.*

*'You finish now? Everything to your satisfaction?' he asked. 'If you want more time, you pay extra.'*

*'Sorry ... you don't understand,' Mather replied weakly. He held up the photograph. 'My daughter ... she's missing. I think Tanya may know ... '*

Chandler heard Jabril mutter. For a moment he was struck but his change in demeanour – the cocky expression overtaken by a look of self doubt.

*'Ah, your daughter, the artist,' the pimp replied gleefully. 'Very nice, but she make trouble for my girls. She needs more discipline, like Tanya. Maybe I give her good fucking, ja?'*

*'Zeeburg – the campsite at Zeeburg,' Tanya shouted. 'You take train from Central Station, then bus.'*

*For a moment, she looked hesitantly towards her minder before a heavy blow toppled her onto the floor. 'Tell Camilla, she not to worry about me,' Tanya whimpered, reaching for Mather's outstretched hand. 'And tell her she has found good man.'*

*

*Camping had never been Mather's forté. But the site at Zeeburg had its charms. He was struck by the neat rows of tents, smart shower blocks and well manicured play areas. At the perimeter fence he watched a semi-circle of children laughing on the grass. Crayons, brushes and paints were strewn haphazardly on the lawn.*

*He spotted Camilla. She was standing among a group of women. European, Asian, African, all united under the hijab. Perched in front of a rickety easel, Camilla began to apply firm brush strokes to canvas. Splashes of bright ochre contrasted with her shadow on the grass. Lifting large sheaves of paper, the women followed suit. Nearby, a young man, bearded and wearing a white skullcap, looked on. He was smiling. Mather walked cautiously towards the women. To his left he heard low rhythmic whispers from a line of teenage boys. Their heads were bowed and they kneeled on identical prayer mats. He edged forward nervously, unsure whether he should make eye contact with Camilla. Oblivious to his presence, she glided between the women and children. Mather struggled to banish Hoogstratten and his wife from his mind. She needs space ... to find her own way.*

*With a backward glance, he turned to leave.*

'*She needs space* ... it's strange, Nadia said something similar when Zafirah left for Israel.'

Chandler clung to Jabril's words. Relieved that one of his

stories had finally struck a chord. 'Your Zafirah, she sounds strong-willed, perhaps a little like Camilla?'

'If you mean they *both* reject their fathers' values, then they have something in common.'

Chandler listened to the faint hum of traffic below the citadel. 'I'm sure it's not as black and white as that.'

'Mr Chandler, when an Arab girl is found guilty of a sexual indiscretion, her *father* is dishonoured too. Unless she's a prostitute, she must avoid any sexual experience until she marries.'

'Or face fifty lashes?' Chandler grunted.

'Sometimes it's worse than that.'

'Surely, Zafirah doesn't deserve that kind of punishment.'

'Why not? Like Camilla, she's put personal interest before her duty to her parents.'

'Aren't you rushing to judgement? I get the feeling that Nadia has already accepted her decision.'

Jabril's eyes narrowed. 'What unites Zafirah and her mother is that they let their passions get the better of them.'

'You mean only *you* can see things objectively?'

'I'm saying a father knows what's best for his children. He understands the risks.'

'Jabril, there's more than one kind of risk. If you stop Zafirah making what *she* feels is the right decision, she may never forgive you.'

'Mr Chandler, for a man with no children, you've a lot to say about parenthood.'

'You're probably right,' Chandler sighed. 'But it's because I don't have children, I know what it's like to live in a void.'

Jabril rose to his feet. He hung his arm over the parapet. Below, the streets were deserted. He counted the minarets. Like giant needles, they stood silhouetted against the fading light. '*Fine.* So I give my daughter the space *you* say she needs. She returns to Haifa with the baby. Perhaps she decides to marry this ... *Christian.* Have you any idea what's at stake? For me ... for Nadia?'

Chandler joined Jabril by the wall. Above the citadel, a waxing crescent moon promised the sole illumination.

'Do you remember what you said in the car about *A Thousand and One Nights*?' Chandler asked.

Jabril shook his head. 'I'm sure you're about to enlighten me.'

'You said the narrator and the listener have to be alert to fresh signals.'

'Did I say that? It sounds rather grand.'

'Well, maybe it's time *you* tuned into a different signal. Zafirah is pregnant – the narrative frame has just changed.'

Jabril flicked his cigarette over the parapet. 'It's getting late, we need to leave.'

'These last few days,' Chandler said, 'they've been a bit of a roller coaster, haven't they?'

'Yes, Mr Chandler – for *both* of us – and I fear the ride hasn't finished yet.'

# Chapter Seventeen

*On rubbing his magic lamp Aladdin is granted one wish. 'Bring back my dead mother,' Aladdin demands.*

*The jinni replies, 'Impossible, only Allah can bring back the dead.'*

*'OK,' Aladdin fires back, 'then grant me my wish to bring down the President.'*

*The jinni thinks hard for a moment and says, 'now, where did you say your mother is buried?'*

Carpet Dealer in Damascus

'Who took down the curtains?'

'Quiet, I can't talk now.'

'Did you hear what I said? Who took down the curtains?'

'Just five minutes ... please, I haven't even started the introduction.'

'Forget your introduction. Just tell me.'

Looking tired, the President removed his spectacles and placed them on the mahogany table. He pulled a heavy tumbler of Glenfiddich to his lips. In front of him lay a single A4 sheet. He had considered a title for his research at some length. One that would demonstrate his scientific credentials and confound the sceptics.

*Three Blind Mice. The Use of Stem Cells in the Treatment of Macular Degeneration.*

In neat bundles, well-thumbed research papers, from Moorfields Eye Hospital, lay before him. The President rose unsteadily. Clutching his whiskey, he moved towards the First Lady. She had taken centre-stage beside a large window, dominating the south-facing side of the suite. He peered at the vista behind her. Damascus lay shimmering in the afternoon sun – the spectacle cut in two by the narrow figure of his wife. For a precious moment, the President savoured her silence, but he knew it wouldn't last.

'It's *her*, isn't it?' He took another swig of his favourite malt.

'If you mean *Mother*, yes, she said the curtains clash with the carpet from Isfahan.'

'Are you still allowing your mother to make all the decisions?'

'Don't be so disrespectful. Anyway, what's so special about the curtains?'

'They're on limited offer from John Lewis ... your son helped to pick them.'

'So, now you're letting the President's son choose floral patterns for the Executive Suite?'

'He's only *seven* – what do you expect?'

'Perhaps something more masculine.'

'*Masculine*? You've been listening too much to your brother.'

'What's wrong with that? You know he dotes on him. Just wants what's best.'

'If *you* want what's best, allow the boy to enjoy his childhood. If that means decorating our home, so be it.'

The President sighed. He turned to a large portrait of his father. Silver haired and moustachioed, the old man stared back at him. Dressed in a double-breasted jacket, the President's father resembled an avuncular bank manager nearing retirement. The President wished the old patriarch was still around to give him advice.

'Look, I'll talk to Mother, see where she's put the blasted curtains. Just give me an hour to get this finished.'

✧

'Here's the deal. We have a few hundred bandits holed up in the centre of Hama. They've taken over Azem Palace and the Grand Mosque. There are snipers in the clock tower too.'

The President held his head in his hands. He found it difficult to concentrate. He reached for the Glenfiddich.

'I think you're drinking too much.'

'You sound like my wife.'

'Just giving you some brotherly advice. Now, listen, the army is looking for direction.'

'You mean me?'

'Who else.'

The President paused to think. 'Have you ever read Catch 22?'

'No, I never had time for books. I suppose it's one of *her* favourites.'

'Not quite. She has different tastes ... rom' com', I think they call it.'

'I'm surprised she finds the time, between buying fancy curtains and filling the boy's head with foolish notions.'

The President decided against rising to his brother's challenge. 'The situation in Hama, is it hopeless?'

His brother leaned across the table and lifted the President's treatise. He scrutinised the title page, before letting it drop from his hands. 'I could never understand the attraction of being an eye doctor.'

'It beat a career as a surgeon.'

'How's that?'

'Less blood.'

'Look, you're not in London now. You must *focus*. Get a grip – put the interests of the *family* first.'

'You know, I didn't plan any of this ... giving up my work in London ... returning to Syria.'

Turning his back on the President, his brother gazed at the portrait of their father.

The President seized the opportunity to re-fill his glass.

'I'm moving my brigade into Hama soon,' his brother announced. 'We have enough tanks to break their defences. We'll need artillery, of course.'

'The Fourth Armoured Division? Is that really necessary? You know there'll be a massacre.'

'That's not my concern.'

'So, a repeat of '82? The Americans won't wear it.'

'Fuck the Americans! Do you know they've persuaded the British to freeze my accounts?'

'Don't worry, we still have contacts in the City. I'll speak to—'

'She enjoys her little luxuries, doesn't she?'

'Why not, she's worked hard for them.'

'What about the state visits? I doubt whether she receives many foreign invitations now.'

'I know, that's what she misses most.'

'Listen to me, it's not her exotic jaunts that worry me. If we don't get a hold on this insurgency we'll lose everything.'

The President pushed his papers to one side. 'As I was saying, dear brother, it's a catch-22 situation. We're screwed whatever we decide.'

'How do you work that out?'

'Finally, you deem it fit to ask your President for his opinion.'

'I'm listening.'

'It's simple. If we use your Fourth Division to crush the rebellion we'll face further sanctions.'

'And the alternative?'

'The alternative is to give in to the bastards ... yes, and before you say it, this will demonstrate a lack of will and risk wider unrest.'

'Precisely, so we must go for the *first* option – nip this trouble in the bud. We can worry about sanctions later.'

'Maybe there's another option. Move the Third Armoured Division up from Homs. Under General Abrash's control, there may be less bloodshed.'

'Are you serious? That means giving *him* a free rein.'

'Why not, he's a fine patriot. Didn't he get the situation in Homs under control?'

'Perhaps, but he let that British agent slip the net too.'

'What agent?'

'Didn't Colonel Boutros brief you? A British spy was identified outside the city. Posing as a writer apparently.'

'How the hell did he get in?'

'Some fool in our embassy in London granted him a tourist visa. Next, he's spotted in Krak des Chevaliers meeting his handler ... Oakshott, I think his name is.'

'Why wasn't he arrested?'

'You'll have to ask Abrash about that.'

'Where's he now?'

'With one of our operatives in Aleppo.'

'Which one?'

'Jabril Mansour, from Latakia.'

'Can Mansour be trusted?'

'It's hard to say. We recently discovered he has a daughter living in Israel.'

'*Israel*?'

'Yes, and it gets worse. Mansour's father is an old crony of the general. Can you see where I'm going with this?'

'I can't believe Abrash would be so foolish as to betray us.'

'Don't you believe it – he's a Sunni, isn't he? I warned you against appointing him.'

'But we need him to broaden our support. The Sunnis in Hama respect him.'

'Have you lost your mind? The Sunnis in Hama are cutting the throats of every Alawite they can lay their hands on.'

✧

'How could you do that to your sister? Give me the gun and go to your room. *Now*!'

Holding a miniature Walther PPK, the boy's mouth dropped. By his side, his sister remained motionless on her knees. A hand knitted doll, with sorrowful eyes, lay next to her as a silent witness to the mock execution.

The First Lady turned towards her husband. 'Is this your brother's idea of a joke?'

'Sorry, I should have stopped him. He said he wanted to make a man out of him.'

'And I suppose your mother was in on it too.'

'No, she's upstairs, sleeping. Look, I told you, it was just a bit of fun. Where's your sense of humour?'

The First Lady lifted the doll and pressed it back into her daughter's arms. The child continued to sob.

'How do you expect me to keep a sense of humour here. Cooped up all day on top of this bloody mountain. I can't even see my friends in Damascus.'

'My dear, you know that you can visit them whenever you please.'

'Now *you're* the one who's joking. I can't set a foot outside the palace without a full security detail.'

'But it's for your *protection*.'

'Protect me from what?'

'Fanatics.'

'Don't be ridiculous, they're all holed up in Deraa and Hama.'

'Things have changed.'

The First Lady began to straighten her daughter's hair, then turned back to her husband. 'Darling, don't you miss our time in London? The walks in Regents Park ... Harrods.'

Standing next to the window, she gazed down at the fading smudge of light in the city. 'What's *happened* to us?'

The President stared into his empty glass. 'I don't know. Everything has become so ... *complicated*.'

The First Lady placed her arm gently around her husband's shoulder. 'So, what are you going to do about it?'

'About the insurgents?'

'No, about the *Englishman*.'

'You've lost me'

'The writer.'

'How do you know about him?'

'Your brother let it slip this morning, before his stunt with the pistol.'

The President reached for the bottle of Glenfiddich. 'This *writer*, as you call him, isn't my main concern. Anyway, it's out of my hands.'

# Chapter Eighteen

*Needs must when the Devil drives.*
Rabelais

'Are we on the road to Damascus?'

'Yes.'

'When do we get there?'

'We *don't*.'

'What?'

'It's not safe.'

'Why?'

'Because Damascus is where they *expect* us to go.'

'*They*?'

'Youssef ... the colonel – it's complicated.'

Chandler reached for his cigarettes. Jabril's disclosure seemed like a veil had been lifted, only to be replaced by a smokescreen. 'Look, I know you're here to keep tabs on me and that Youssef is part of this but—'

'Things have got out of hand, Mr Chandler.'

'With Youssef?'

'With *everyone*.'

Chandler rapped his fingers on his knees. 'You know why I'm here.'

Jabril shot him a sideways glance. 'To see the sights?'

'Yes, and—'

'Watch history in the making?'

'Well, yes ... '

'But still find time to meet the British military attaché at Krak?'

Beads of perspiration multiplied on Chandler's neck. He struggled to respond. 'The diplomat? Look, he told me he was just involved in import and export.'

Jabril rolled his eyes. 'Mr Chandler, either you are incredibly naïve or you're pulling the wool over everyone's eyes.'

Chandler bit his lip. 'What do *you* think?'

Jabril paused. 'For the moment, I'm willing, as they say, to give you the benefit of the doubt.'

'That's a relief,' Chandler sighed.

'But, that's not how my superiors see it,' Jabril continued.

'Meaning?'

'Let's just say, your *holiday* is officially over.'

They spent the next few minutes in silence. Chandler struggled to take in the full import of Jabril's words.

'So, where are we heading?' asked Chandler nervously.

'Hama.'

'*Hama*?'

'Yes, Hama.'

'You can't be serious.'

'Deadly serious, Mr Chandler. It's the last place they will look for us.'

Chandler leafed rapidly through his guidebook. Pages that celebrated the glories of Palmyra, Aleppo and Damascus, heavily underlined. He had already searched out references to Hama. The diversion to the city wasn't on his itinerary.

'Jabril, the only thing I know about Hama is that it's in full revolt. Didn't you listen to the news?'

'Precisely, so no place for Youssef and his cronies.'

'But you're his cousin – it can't be safe for you either.'

The saloon picked up speed.

'You're forgetting about our guardian angel, Mr Chandler.'

'You mean Abrash?'

'Who else.'

'He's a Sunni, isn't he?'

'Correct,' Jabril replied.

For a few moments Chandler gazed at passing fields of ripe barley and sugar beet. Somehow unwilling to give up her spoils, the landscape appeared unsullied. 'I don't get it, if you are Alawite, how is Abrash able to grant you ... us, safe passage?'

'Because he has *influence*.'

'Over the rebels you mean?'

'Over *some* of them.'

'That doesn't sound too safe to me.'

'I accept, it's a calculated risk, but remember, he took care of us in Homs, and still owes a debt to my father.'

'Sounds like a bit of a gamble, Jabril.'

'You wanted a challenge, didn't you?'

'You make it sound like I have a death wish.'

'Don't you?'

Chandler was stung into silence. Jabril had hit a nerve and knew it.

'What really brings you here, Mr Chandler? And please, no bullshit about Roman ruins.'

'I'm not sure how I should answer that.'

'Try.'

'Boredom, I think.'

'Is boredom such a bad thing?'

'For most people, no.'

'So, what is it? Do you get your kicks from watching other peoples' suffering?'

Like an ailing chess grandmaster, petrified of making a false move, Chandler struggled for the right response. 'Christ, now you make me sound like a bloody voyeur.'

'Oh, nothing so shallow. But perhaps I can offer a better explanation.'

Chandler grimaced.

'You're here to establish your *credentials*.'

'What are you getting at?'

'Mr Chandler, barely a week has passed and already you have a price on your head. A good start for an aspiring writer, don't you think?'

Chandler shook his head.

'A perfect opportunity to impress your readers with tales about our savagery. Try hard enough, cause enough offence, and you may be rewarded with a fatwa – sure to boost sales.'

Chandler lowered his eyes, 'Look, it's probably how I started out. But things have changed.'

'Really, so what drives you now?'

'It's hard to explain. Now, I feel more like ... a *participant*.'

Jabril issued a thin smile. 'Do you think you have the stomach to become a participant?'

'I'm not sure, but I think I'm about to find out.'

> *The Arabic name for the Orentes, running through Hama, is El-'Asi, the Rebel – owing to the fact that, unlike other rivers in Syria, it flows south to north. Its stubborn refusal to freely irrigate the meadows along its borders means that it has to be raised by waterwheels before giving its consent to irrigate the fields. The waterwheels, or norias, are to Hama what her canals are to Venice. All along the curving riverside you see these high, narrow, graceful wheels, which attain the diameter of as much as sixty feet, slowly lifting the river water in their buckets and poring it into lofty aqueducts. Even when you cannot see them, you hear their beautiful noise as they revolve. Each wheel, creaking lazily on its axis, sings its own particular song – the music is mournful and deep – now booming, now moaning, now pleading, now despondent.*

Chandler closed his guidebook. His head throbbed in the heat of late morning. Jabril maintained a steady cruising speed as they headed south towards Hama. On the road, they hardly saw a soul. Just a single truck, monstrously overladen with watermelons, that threatened to cascade onto the empty highway.

Approaching the outskirts of Hama, they hit rush hour. A convoy of human traffic travelled in the opposite direction. Chandler watched a line of rickety buses and beaten-up taxis trundle past. The passengers made up of women and children. The sullen procession lacked the customary fanfare of families leaving the city for a summer outing in the countryside – their expressions, mournful and resigned. Chandler strained to get a clearer view of the children. Like sleeping kittens, they lay curled on their mothers' laps. A few were crying.

'Jabril, where are the men?'

'Still sheltering in the barracks, if they have any sense.'

'Are they Alawites?'

'Mostly, maybe a few Sunni hangers on ... contractors and workmen who look after the military facilities.'

'What'll happen to them?'

'That rather depends on the President and his brother.'

'How do you mean?'

'They have two choices. They can let their men go to hell or they can try to relieve the barracks, probably using the Fourth Armoured Division. The same as in eighty-two.'

'Eighty-two?'

'Didn't you listen to the news back then, Mr Chandler?'

'No, I was too preoccupied with my first divorce.'

Jabril slowed the car, narrowly avoiding a taxi which had skidded across the road with a burst tyre. Its owner, holding a stick, gesticulated to passing drivers, who firmly ignored him.

'The opposition in Hama was crushed,' Jabril added calmly. 'It was the Muslim Brotherhood at the time. They took over the city and kicked out the Alawites – killed quite a few of them too. The government hit back – *hard*.'

Chandler watched the last of the traffic ebb from the city. Reduced to a trickle. Looking ahead, he made out the outline of smart hotels and crumbling apartment blocks. Above the city centre, wispy plumes of smoke gathered. Like unwelcome intruders, they broke up an otherwise cloudless sky.

'Jabril, I was wondering, how the hell are we going to get in?'

'Through good planning.'

'But if you're Alawite, shouldn't you be heading north with all the others?'

Jabril sighed. 'Mr Chandler, how many times have I told you, this is what they would expect me to do.'

'But if the rebels are Sunni, they'll shoot us as soon as they find out who you are.'

'That's why we've taken out insurance, Mr Chandler.'

'Sorry?'

'We are, as they say, a *protected species*.'

'Protected? By who?'

'The general, of course. I rang him this morning.'

'Is he in the city?'

'Not yet, but his shadow hangs over it.'

Jabril pushed on the brakes, then swung the saloon towards the verge. He lifted one of Chandler's cigarettes and searched for his lighter. For a minute, they sat in contemplation.

'Mr Chandler, let me give you a lesson. The insurgents controlling the streets in Hama are Sunni. So is General

Abrash. They respect him. As long as he keeps the army out, the militias won't bother us ... Commander Said has given his word.'

'Who the hell is he?'

'He controls the main rebel force in Hama.'

'Right, Jabril, let's get this clear. Our safety depends on this warlord, Said, telling his men not to tear out our throats. We're also at the mercy of General Abrash, who's playing a double game. And, finally, we're reliant on the good offices of the President, as long as he remains indecisive.'

'Congratulations, you have acquired a perfect grasp of Syrian politics.'

✧

Commander Hatim Said checked his watch. He calculated that the young conscript, lashed to the bleached timber frame of the waterwheel, would take around ten minutes to drown. The prisoner's first baptism in the Orentes would have him gasping for breath. A second immersion, was guaranteed to fill his lungs. But a third dunking in the grimy water would be necessary to finish him off.

✧

*The music of the norias is mournful and deep.*

Chandler watched Commander Said go about his labours. The leader of the al-Farrayya brigade wore a short beard and looked to be in his late twenties. His long thobe, loose fitting undershirt and cotton pants concealed a firm torso. Chandler was surprised to see such a young man in a position of authority. A deep burgundy stain ran from the top of Said's cheek to the nape of his neck. Chandler decided to keep his distance. He hoped the militia leader wouldn't notice him staring at his birthmark.

Said strolled along the thin line of young conscripts, trussed up in pairs on the side of the riverbank. Like Siamese twins, they appeared to be glued to each other. All had their ankles tightly bound. Their wrists were shackled. One prisoner mumbled a verse from the Koran. Another clutched a small family photograph. A smell of stale urine hung in the air.

As a graduate in Islamic Studies, Commander Said was known for his piety. He was also a dedicated student of the human condition. He believed every man should understand his future. To see what was ahead of him. For the conscripts, to focus on the *wheel*. Accordingly, Said told his men to remove the blindfolds from the prisoners, squatting on the riverbank. Next, he ordered that they face the river, with their backs towards him. The last thing Said wanted was for his charges to be distracted by the blemished face of their executioner before he sent them to hell.

Chandler turned his back on the spectacle. He watched Jabril stride purposefully towards the Commander. They shook hands. A few words were exchanged, then, with a murmur of approval, Said lifted his right hand to his chest and returned to his duties at the wheel.

'He has given us two days,' Jabril said. 'If we stay longer he can't guarantee our protection. If he sees you taking notes or photographs, he will order both of us to be shot.'

'I can see why the Commander is so publicity-shy,' Chandler replied. 'The poor sod on the wheel is hardly a glowing advertisement for the Arab Spring.'

'Forget the Arab Spring, Mr Chandler, war is a dirty business.'

'So it's war then?'

'It will be, when the Fourth Division arrive.'

Chandler looked up towards the old citadel. No more than a large earthen mound, reshaped by bulldozers into a rough picnic area. Gangs of small boys, some carrying toy rifles, rummaged among empty shell casings littering the ground.

'Where are we going to stay?'

'It won't be a hotel, I'm afraid. All of them are out of bounds,' Jabril said.

'Can we go into the old town? Find a bar, I could do with a drink.'

'This isn't the time to be seen consuming alcohol – we don't want to upset the clerics. Anyway, it's too dangerous, the town is full of snipers. They're shooting anything that moves.'

Chandler glanced back at the wheel. He spotted the body of a conscript, streaked with slime. Mucus oozed from his nostrils. Two men, muscular and stripped to the waist, sweated to cut him down. They tossed the corpse into the slow moving water, where it drifted downstream, before becoming ensnared between an upturned shopping trolley and a tree stump. He felt nauseous and began to retch.

'I didn't think you would have the stomach for this,' Jabril said.

'I'm surprised you can bare to watch. That lad on the wheel, how old is he?'

'Eighteen, maybe less.'

'Still a boy then?'

'In *your* country perhaps. Here, he's old enough to carry a Kalashnikov.'

'Did he have a choice?'

Jabril paused. 'As a conscript, no.'

'So, he didn't deserve *that*.'

'No, Mr Chandler, he probably didn't.'

Chandler watched the children playing on the citadel. The oldest boy began to clamber down the mound, before cartwheeling towards the edge of the river. A second prisoner was manhandled towards the wheel. Further along the river bank, a group of spectators, mostly women and girls, sat idly in the sunshine, eating ice cream topped with pistachios.

'Jabril, where is this all heading?'

'What do you mean?'

'It doesn't make sense. You're an Alawite, like the men on the wheel. You calmly watch your own people being butchered by Sunnis. The same crowd who would happily put a bullet in *your* head if Commander Said gives the word.'

'Mr Chandler, if you try to make *sense* of it, then you're in the wrong place. Let's go and get some rest. Said says we can bunk down in the staff quarters at the museum. It's not very luxurious but—'

'You haven't answered my question. How can you stand there and ignore what's happening?'

Jabril dug his hands in his jacket pockets. 'Because there is nothing I can do. I don't have a choice.'

'Except to save your own skin?'

'Yes, Mr Chandler, except to save my own skin.'

'*Your* words, Jabril.'

✧

'You can take the mattress in the corner. I'll sleep on the floor.'

Chandler watched Jabril unpack. First, he removed his spare clothes. They included two pairs of grey slacks and four polo shirts – all neatly pressed. His underpants and socks, rolled into tight bundles, had been pushed into a pair of smart walking boots. He removed a leather-bound Koran, then laid out a small prayer mat in the corner of the room.

'There's a fridge in the office downstairs.' Jabil said. 'You'll find plenty of bottled water and some flatbread and cheese. No beer, I'm afraid.'

'Don't worry, I've already commandeered the Arak. Why didn't you tell me you had a second bottle stashed in the car?'

Jabril grinned. 'Well done, Mr Chandler. You must have known I was saving the Arak for a special occasion.'

'Special? You mean sleeping on an old mattress in the middle of a warzone?'

'It's not just special, it's a *privilege*.'

'How do you make that out?'

'Because we are witnessing history in the making, Mr Chandler. Not just out on the streets, but here in the museum too.'

'Really? The museum seems pretty dead to me.'

'On the contrary, the ghosts of the past are very much alive. Next door, you will find gold leaf figurines that date from the eighth century. Downstairs, Byzantine mosaics. The finest depicts an ancient noria.'

'I think I've had my fill of norias today.'

'Did you see the splendid lion at the entrance?' Jabril continued. 'It once guarded an Iron Age palace.'

'So, now I have a statue of a lion to get me through the night?'

Jabril chuckled. 'Oh, I think the Arak will do that.'

Chandler set his rucksack on the mattress. Out of spare clothes, and unable to shower since leaving Aleppo, he breathed in his rising body odour. He unfastened the straps, then ran his fingers along the cluster of polypockets.

'Have I got time, Jabril? I think you may appreciate this one.'

'Later, Mr Chandler, Commander Said is due back at any moment.'

'Bringing more news from the front, no doubt.'

'Probably, but he has a visitor too, a VIP, who's very keen to meet you.'

✧

'Chandler, old boy, good to see you again.'

It took a moment for Chandler to recognise the figure standing at the doorway. Dressed in an olive suit and a Panama hat, his chest was encased in an oversize flak jacket. The man appeared larger than he remembered from their first encounter. Quite the Napoleon.

'*Oakshott* – Rupert Oakshott, don't you remember me? Krak des Chevaliers.'

'Sorry, yes, Mr Oakshott, I wasn't sure.'

'Perhaps you have a better memory of my companion?' Oakshott said, smiling.

'Miss Tuma? Is she still with you?'

'Sadly not. She flew the coup the day after our meeting at the castle.'

'Back to St Petersburg?'

'No, much closer to home.'

'Damascus?'

'No, closer still. She's busy servicing the officers in the military academy in Homs. I should have listened to the ambassador ... *never trust a Russian*.'

Chandler heard the thud of heavy boots. He watched Commander Said push his head through the doorway. Oakshott turned to whisper a few words to the Commander, demonstrating a surprising grasp of Arabic. With a gentle nod, Oakshott signalled his permission for Said, then Jabril, to leave. For a few moments, Chandler and Oakshott stood silently watching each other.

'Strange times,' Oakshott proclaimed.

'Getting stranger by the minute,' Chandler replied, lifting his mobile from his pocket. 'Just checking my messages,' he said, without looking up.

'Mr Chandler, what are you doing here?'

'I was about to ask *you* the same question?'

'It's a complex brief.'

'One that involves you cosying up with rebel militias, you mean?'

'As I said, Mr Chandler, it's complex. In any case, how do you expect our government to proceed without an accurate assessment of what's happening on the ground in Hama?'

Chandler rubbed his chin. 'So you're not here to see me?'

Oakshott offered Chandler a broad smile. 'No, strangely, I'm here at Commander Said's invitation. Engage in a bit of *networking* as my younger colleagues call it. In the larger scale of things, you're still a small fish.'

'Whose swimming against the tide,' Chandler muttered.

'But certainly causing a few ripples,' Oakshott shot back.

Chandler glanced at this mobile.

'Listen, old chap,' Oakshott continued reassuringly, 'whatever Jabril's people think, we both know that our meeting in the castle was unplanned. But it did get me thinking.'

'How?'

'Call it a gut feeling – nobody just pops up in Syria, let alone Hama, without good reason. I can't fathom your motives, but one thing is clear – I won't let a chance encounter go to waste.'

'Quite,' murmured Chandler.

Oakshott paused. 'Your friend, Jabril, says you might be in a position to help us.'

'Really? I was thinking that you might be able to help *me*.'

'Help *you*?'

'Yes, help a British citizen in distress – that's your job, isn't it?'

'Oh, I see, you expect me to provide consular assistance to a chap who's clearly the author of his own misfortune. I'm not sure my superiors—'

'Ever the diplomat,' Chandler replied sourly.

'My dear boy, I'm sure we can find a way around this,' Oakshott continued. 'But you need to help *me* first. I'm not asking very much.'

'What do you want?'

'Jabril says you're a writer, so maybe just the man we're looking for.'

'How?'

'We need somebody with a sharp eye for drama. Someone who can put together a vivid account of what is happening in the city.'

Chandler watched Oakshott lift a crumpled packet from his jacket pocket, pull out a dark lozenge and pop it into his mouth. '*Fisherman's Friend* ... must keep the breath sweet.'

'Are you here to keep *me* sweet?'

'Nothing so vulgar. In any case, her Majesty's government is rather strapped for cash. But I *would* like to arrange a friendly chat with some journalists at the Orentes Hotel. I can take you there now if you want.'

'Journalists? I thought they were barred.'

'Only the foreign hacks, it's impossible to trust them. These ones are *local*. They work with the National Council who are running the show in Hama.'

'So, it's propaganda you're after?'

Oakshott sucked hard on the lozenge. 'Mr Chandler, my department is a great believer in the freedom of the press. They think you may be able to give the boys in Grub Street something to chew on. And assist our efforts in bringing a resolution to this ghastly business in Hama, of course.'

'As long as I toe the official line?'

'Your cooperation could prove mutually beneficial. Jabril told me that you're looking for a *scoop*.'

'Does that mean that I have to come up with a story with the right slant?'

'It means you apply the right emphasis – *rebels call for an end to tyranny, government forces on the run,* that sort of thing. Call it the first draft of history.'

'Sounds like propaganda.'

'On the contrary, it's an opportunity for you to help the opposition in its hour of need. Think about it, a chance to *participate.* Isn't that what you want?'

Chandler edged towards the window. The sun had begun to set. He leaned out and breathed in the cool air. He heard the faint rumble of heavy vehicles, and wondered whether government forces had re-entered the city, or if the soldiers, holding out in the barracks, had attempted a breakout. A bank of dense smoke drifted slowly towards the museum.

'These freedom fighters of yours, did you see what they did to the soldiers on the wheel? Maybe I should report on that?'

'Yes, I saw everything. It was unfortunate.'

'It was *murder.*'

Oakshott cracked on a lozenge. 'That's precisely why we need your assistance – to bring this sorry affair to an end.'

'But I'm supposed to say nothing about the execution of unarmed prisoners?'

'Mr Chandler, the National Council needs all the favourable publicity it can get if it's to make any headway. Hopefully, install a new regime ... one more conducive to our national interest. It's a critical time for the people of Syria. Your help could just swing the balance.'

'Then what, let *these* crazies run the show?'

'These crazies, as you put it, are the only show in town.'

'What about the boys on the wheel?'

Oakshott raised his eyebrows. 'The boys on the wheel? Let's just say that their sacrifice will focus the minds of the men in the barracks.'

✧

Lying face down on the mattress, Chandler reached for his phone. The battery had run low, but enough charge to give him what he needed. For a moment, he experienced a kaleidoscope of emotions. He had put his faith in Jabril, knowing that his unexpected foray into Hama meant that his minder was living on borrowed time. At the same time, behind all the smiles, Oakshott struck Chandler as a wildcard. Yet common sense told him he should accept his offer – take the easiest path out of the city. But where would that leave Jabril?

# Chapter Nineteen

*The difficulty in life is the choice.*
George Moore

'How's the head?'

Chandler pulled the musty blanket over his eyes, shielding him from the sharp rays of sunlight streaming into the room. He had a crick in his neck. His head was fit to burst. Jabril crouched next to him, then reached for the empty bottle of Arak, lying at the end of the mattress.

'I've never fully understood the appeal of alcohol. It brings out the worst in men, loosens their tongues, and always a sore head in the morning.'

Chandler groaned and rolled onto his stomach. His right leg dangled outside the covers, exposing the frayed edge of his underpants.

'Drink this,' Jabril said, holding out a bottle of chilled mineral water.

Chandler's arm appeared from under the blanket and snaked towards Jabril's outstretched hand.

'Did *I* have a loose tongue last night?'

'Too many expletives to count.'

'Sorry, did I embarrass you?'

'Oh, nothing I haven't heard during national service.'

'And no worse than the porters in St Pancras station, I imagine.'

'No, probably not,' Jabril sighed.

'So what was I babbling about – the executions on the wheel?'

'Strangely not. You seemed more concerned with Mr Oakshott's proposal to meet the journalists.'

'A stupid idea.'

Jabril's eyes narrowed. 'I disagree ... look, it was probably foolhardy bringing you to Hama ... just to keep Youssef off my tail. But it could be your free pass out of the city.'

'You think?'

'Why don't you talk to them? It's a sure way to get Oakshott on side. He's a lot of influence over the National Council.'

'What has he got to offer *them*? He told me his department is strapped for cash.'

'It's not money they're after, Mr Chandler.'

'So, what is it?'

'*Recognition*, and weapons, of course.'

'I don't see any shortage of guns around here.'

'That's true, but the opposition in Hama only has access to small arms. It's heavy weapons they want – mortars, rocket-propelled grenades, surface-to-air missiles. They'll need them when the President sends in the tanks and helicopter gunships.'

'How are they going to get their hands on that kind of firepower? Anyway, isn't the city surrounded?'

'Not entirely,' Jabril replied. 'General Abrash's forces still hold the road from Homs.'

'What difference does that make?'

'It means he can siphon off heavy armour from the Third Division and arm the rebels – for a price, of course.'

'Jabril, if the general thinks he'll be richly rewarded for all this, he's likely to be disappointed. I don't think Oakshott does handouts ... he said as much himself.'

'I agree, but money isn't Abrash's primary concern.'

'So what is?'

'The general wants your government to put in a good word for him at the Hague.'

'The International Criminal Court?'

'Yes, they want him extradited for war crimes.'

'Sorry, isn't Abrash one of the *good guys*?'

'In the eyes of London perhaps, but Washington is pushing the court to take a stand. You saw the executions in Homs.'

'Maybe it's time for Abrash to face the music?'

Jabril smiled. 'I thought that you didn't believe in retribution.'

'I believe in *justice*.'

'Mr Chandler, justice is a relative concept in Syria.'

'There was nothing *relative* about Abrash's men gunning down unarmed civilians.'

Jabril examined the empty bottle of Arak, then tossed it towards a basket at the far side of the room. 'You shouldn't trouble yourself about the civilians in Homs. They will deliver their own justice.'

'While London lets Abrash off the hook?'

'It's *realpolitik*,' Jabril fired back. 'Oakshott knows that Abrash has a strong hand. If the British play ball, Commander Said will get all the weapons he needs.'

'Enough to keep the Fourth Division out of the city?'

'Nobody can guarantee that, but if the gamble pays off, enough to prevent a massacre.'

'You mean Said gets the guns and Abrash escapes a charge of war crimes.'

'Precisely.'

'Oh, I can see it all now, Jabril. *General Abrash ... saviour of Hama ... champion of democracy*. If he plays his cards right, a bloody knighthood.'

Jabril grinned. 'I have no doubt that the general will accept any honours that London wishes to bestow upon him.'

'And everyone's a winner ... except the poor bastards on the wheel.'

'Isn't it time you set aside your lofty ideals, Mr Chandler? Abrash has no more choice in this matter than you or I.'

'I think the only decision *he* is making is to save his own skin.'

'He has family too.'

'So do the prisoners by the river, but the executions go on.'

'They will continue for as long as Commander Said deems necessary,' Jabril replied, frowning. 'We can't stop them.'

Chandler searched for his shoes.

'You should consider Oakshott's offer seriously,' Jabril said. 'Talk to the journalists – give them what they want to hear. Then *leave*.'

'You make it sound so easy.'

'It is. Just one interview and you get your exit papers. Oakshott's even offered to place his personal driver at your disposal. Nobody will bother you.'

'What about you?'

'Me? I'm afraid Oakshott's generosity doesn't stretch that far. In any case, Commander Said has other plans.'

'What has he in mind?' Chandler asked doubtfully.

'I'm to act as link man to General Abrash – *Liaison Officer*, I think he called it.'

'Very impressive, Jabril, but is it wise to put your trust in the rebels?'

'Mr Chandler, we *all* have to compromise. I can no more alter the course of events in Hama, than the Orentes can decide to change direction.'

✧

'Courtesy of Her Majesty's Government. Go on, tuck in.'

'A gift from Our Man in Damascus?'

'The very same.'

Chandler examined the confection spread before him. *Sweet Hama*. It struck him as strangely decadent. Sitting on two dishes, a dozen cylinders of thick, sticky dough. Stuffed with a creamy filling that Chandler didn't recognise. Drenched in honey and sprinkled with pistachios, they nestled between generous scoops of vanilla ice cream.

'*Halwat al-jibn*. A Hama speciality. Try some,' said Jabril.

'Do you think that Oakshott's still trying to sweeten me up?' Chandler asked.

'Probably.'

Chandler held a plump column between his thumb and forefinger. He hesitated as the Arak, lurking in his gut, began to repeat on him. He pushed the dough into his mouth, then resisted the impulse to gag.

Leaning against the window ledge, Jabril watched him lick the cream from his fingers. 'Well, are you going to talk to the journalists or not? And please, no more lectures on morality.'

'Is that what you got last night?'

'Yes, Mr Chandler, but I think it was the Arak talking.'

Chandler joined Jabril at the window. He looked down at the courtyard. Oakshott's driver, dressed in a pale tunic and wearing a black peaked cap, was busy wiping layers of dust from the windows of a silver Range Rover.

'How long have we got before Oakshott returns?'

'An hour at most,' said Jabril.

Chandler moved towards his rucksack, wedged between the mattress and the wall. He lifted one of the polypockets. Like a nervous actor, facing his director at a first rehearsal, he held up his story. 'Ready?'

*The Choice*

*Squatting in the dust over a cup of black coffee, Ahmed lit his first cigarette of the day.*

*He looked about him. Al-Shati camp. Home to the dispossessed.*

'*Finally*, Arabs are given their voice,' Jabril broke in, jubilantly.

'Simply restoring the balance,' muttered Chandler, without looking up.

'A wise decision,' Jabril grunted.

*Ahmed should have felt like a refugee, but, as a qualified mechanic, he had a future of sorts. His busy garage offered rich rewards.*

*Ahmed should have felt like a prisoner. Like all the other camp dwellers, cut off from an older, half remembered Palestine. The Strip offered no escape. Its life blood drained from a shrinking, failing state.*

*Ahmed should have felt diminished. He reflected on the success of his brothers – forever saluted by their doting parents for the distant generosity they demonstrated, through monthly donations from Boston, Damascus and Beirut.*

*In his uncle Tarik's opinion, Ahmed should have followed a different path. Accept promotion, as an engineer no less, in the furtive squads assembling the Qassams. To gaze at the spiralling streaks of silver, and whispering vapour trails, from the rockets sure to bring fear and uncertainty to the Jewish settlements in the south.*

*But, for Ahmed, grease monkey remained the safest bet. He had made his choice.*

*Then the storm.*

*First light ushered the murmur of sleepy drones. Clear afternoon skies blackened by swooping F-16s and thunderous Apaches. Nightfall brought a deluge of sullen regulars, and nervous, trigger-happy reserves.*

*Ahmed, his wife Jasmine, and their unborn child hunkered down. They had no choice. A pause in the bombardment offered them brief respite. Ahmed clambered uncertainly into the open. He surveyed the garage. A tangle of metal and glass, fractured pipes, a child's shoe. Below, the hint of burning flesh. Noxious.*

*He sat alone, amid the rubble, drawing stiffly on a cigarette, Ahmed considered his options. What to do?*

For a few moments, Jabril and Chandler sat quietly, distracted by the revving of engines and the clump of heavy boots in the courtyard. Neither wanted to be the first to speak.

'*What to do*? It's an infuriating cliffhanger,' Jabril finally declared. 'You will have your readers demanding an immediate sequel!'

'I'm not bloody Scheherazade,' Chandler shot back. 'And I don't do cliffhangers.'

'Really? So where is the *resolution*?'

'Now you're sounding like old Sharkey.'

'Come on, Mr Chandler, you can't leave poor Ahmed dangling on a precipice.'

'I don't think I have. *He* knows what to do.'

'You mean he should take up his uncle's offer to join the Qassam brigades?' said Jabril, smacking his lips.

'No, he must rebuild his garage.'

Jabril hesitated. He hadn't expected Chandler to be so definitive. 'But sometimes the odds stacked against us are too great. We have to decide what's possible and take the most practical course.'

'To build rockets you mean?'

Jabril stubbed out his cigarette on the window ledge. He glanced at Chandler's unfinished breakfast. Five uneaten cylinders lay stacked side by side. The sight reminded him of his son's bedroom, adorned with little platoons of toy soldiers awaiting inspection by the boy's grandfather. 'Yes, Mr Chandler, Ahmed must build his rockets and defend his honour.'

'What's honour got to do with it?'

'The honour of his family, of course – the group, the tribe, if you like. We call it *sharaf*.'

'Won't that make matters worse?'

'That's not the point. If an injury has been done to Ahmed's property, it must be avenged, or else he'll be permanently dishonoured.'

'So, what you're saying is that his only option is to resort to violence? Maybe fire a few rockets into Haifa – that's where Zafirah lives, isn't it?'

'What I am saying is that he doesn't enjoy the luxury of free will.'

'I'm not with you,' Chandler sighed.

'Do I have to spell it out?'

'Looks like you're going to anyway.'

'Mr Chandler, you've always enjoyed freedom, haven't you? You select, then discard, a wife. You leave your job when it proves tiresome. You come to Syria on a whim. Do you want me to continue?'

Chandler held his tongue – reluctant to fire off another platitude.

'*Your* life is full of choices,' continued Jabril. 'Freedoms that Ahmed can only dream of.'

Chandler heard distant gunfire coming from the river. For a moment, he wondered whether Commander Said had employed a firing squad to make shorter work of the conscripts by the wheel.

'You know, *my* future was decided the moment Zafirah left for Haifa,' Jabril said.

Chandler picked up his notes, then rehomed them to the rucksack. 'No Jabril, *your* future will be determined by whether you forgive her. Maybe it's time to rebuild your relationship.'

'As Ahmed must rebuild his garage, I suppose.' Jabril declared.

'Precisely,' Chandler replied.

Jabril cocked his head. 'So, Oakshott's offer ... it seems that you've already made your choice.'

'Yes, Jabril, and maybe it's time to make yours.'

# Chapter Twenty

*The die is cast.*
Julius Caesar

Eyes neatly framed by her niqab, the assistant led Jabril down a broad staircase to the museum basement. Jabril peered inside. Poorly lit but bombproof. Sidestepping a heap of crumbling mosaics, he caught sight of the Commander of the al-Farrayya brigade. He was seated behind a large desk, flanked by a stack of mortar shells and an open wooden chest. Commander Said kept his head lowered. In front of him sat a tangle of wires and a scattering of mobile phones. Jabril watched him lift, then crack open one of the phones, before removing its sim card.

'Isn't it curious how the conscripts are happy to be entertained by whores at night, but always find time to ring their mothers in the morning,' Said muttered.

Jabril looked towards the open chest. It housed an assortment of arrowheads and broken spears. Said caught his eye.

'Neolithic?' Jabril ventured, to break the silence.

'Probably,' Said replied absently.

'It's the shape of the arrowheads. They're—'

'You seem distracted,' Said broke in. 'Perhaps you're spending too much time with the writer.'

'No, Commander, I told you, I'm here to liaise with General Abrash. He's promised—'

'Promised exactly what?'

'Promised to move his heavy armour up from Homs.'

'Fine intentions, Jabril. The question is *when*?'

'He says it should reach you in three days, four at most.'

'That will be too late. In case you haven't noticed, the Fourth Division is at the city gates. The President's brother only has to give the order.'

Jabril wiped the perspiration from his forehead. 'Shall I give Abrash another call?'

'No, we don't have time. We need to re-evaluate the situation – look at our assets.'

'What assets?'

'*Chandler*, of course.'

'I don't think he's much use to us, Commander. He's still refusing to speak to the journalists.'

'I know that. Oakshott has already briefed me. Something about an aversion to propaganda.'

'He's worried about his reputation ... as a writer.'

'An inflated sense of his own importance?'

'Probably – it's a common failing among the English.'

'So I believe. But we can still use him.'

'How?'

'Think about it. Chandler is British. An unbeliever perhaps, but a *British* unbeliever.'

'I don't understand.'

'Oh, Jabril, stop playing the innocent. How much do you think he is worth?'

'To the National Council?'

'No, to *us*.'

'Well, he's of no value to me, Commander. More of a hindrance.'

'Then we will just have to sell him off.'

Jabril stiffened.

'I have friends in Baghdad who are sure to be interested. Their money will oil the wheels with Abrash, get us the weapons we need – though I'm sure they will drive a hard bargain.'

'Does Oakshott know about this?' asked Jabril hesitantly.

'Of course not.'

'And if the Salafis kill him?'

Said pursed his lips. 'Oh, the British will publicly mourn the loss. Then they will forget about him.'

Jabril watched Said pop open another mobile. 'What do I say to Chandler?'

'Does he trust you?'

'He has *come* to trust me.'

'Good, so give him all the reassurance he needs. Tell him there's still time to talk to the journalists.'

'And then?'

'When the time is right, probably tomorrow, my men will lift him and I will arrange delivery.'

# Chapter Twenty-One

*A little less conversation, a little*
*more action please.*
Mac Davis and Billy Strange

'Do you want me to stop?'

'No, keep going.'

'Won't it hurt the baby?'

'Don't be silly, it's fine.'

Theo crooked his leg over Zafirah's narrow thigh. He eased his arm under her waist and cupped her breast. He was worried that full penetration might induce premature labour. Worse, that their unborn child would resent his unwelcome intrusion.

With the window of their sixth floor apartment pushed open, they listened to the steady rumble of the evening traffic grinding its way up the twisting road into Haifa. The air conditioning was turned to maximum. Only a strong sea breeze, and the downdraft from Mount Carmel, combined to make the room temperature bearable.

'Are you still determined to have the baby in Damascus?' Theo asked. 'I'm worried about you travelling alone.'

Zafirah patted her belly gently. 'But I won't be on my own, will I?'

Theo sat up and scratched his neatly trimmed beard. He lifted Zafirah's wooden comb, then began to run its teeth through his thick hair.

'Don't you just *love* yourself,' Zafirah said.

'*Somebody* has to.'

Zafirah pulled herself up on the pillow. In her eighth month of pregnancy, she found it difficult to understand why Theo still found her attractive. Her breasts were sore and she had suffered severe cramps. Only one thing remained undiminished – her libido. She felt blessed. Throughout their tentative lovemaking, Zafirah, as always, took the lead. In her third trimester, her orgasms were more intense than ever.

'*Dr Goldstein* says that a partner's semen is an effective prevention against pre-eclampsia – it boosts the immunity apparently.'

'Too much information,' Theo shot back.

'*Dr Goldstein* says we can fuck like rabbits, providing we select the right position.'

'Zafirah, don't push it.'

'*Dr Goldstein* says it's possible to make love until the last day.'

Theo shook his head and set down the comb. He lifted a bottle of Zafirah's moisturiser and squeezed it onto his hands.

He massaged the cream vigorously around his forehead and Roman nose. Zafirah watched him with a broad smile.

'The last day? But you won't be with me on the last day,' he said.

Zafirah pulled a face. 'Theo, we talked about this last night ... you know that Mother wants me at home for the birth.'

'I thought *this* was your home.'

'It is, but it's not where I should be when the baby arrives.'

Theo pressed another helping of cream into his hands. 'Listen, the facilities in Haifa are better – the doctors can deal with any complications.'

'There won't *be* any complications. You heard what Dr Goldstein said, everything is perfect.'

'I don't see anything perfect about you heading off to Damascus on your own. You won't even have your father there to help you.'

Zafirah sat on the edge of the bed. Her long hair lay generously across her shoulders. 'I've done without his help since we left Aleppo,' she murmured.

'I know, but maybe it's time I contacted him?'

'Not a good idea! He would shoot you as soon as look at you.'

'My family haven't been much help either, have they?' Theo said.

'Can you blame them? I think they had you lined up for a nice Christian girl.'

'What about your mother – what's she saying?'

'Not much, but I know everything will change when the baby is born ... you know, when my father sees his first grandchild.'

Zafirah watched Theo dress. She envied his taut figure, silhouetted against the pale wall of the apartment.

'What time are you leaving?'

'Around six, I want to miss the morning rush and the security checks at the border.'

'I'm still not happy with you travelling alone. It will be a full day before you reach Damascus.'

'Don't worry, Alima is meeting me there. She has a room made up. Hanif has promised to drive me to the hospital when I'm ready.'

'Zafirah, this is madness, depending on aunts and uncles you hardly know, doctors you've never met.'

'They know what they're doing. Anyway, I'll only be away for a few weeks.'

'It should be *me* who's with you. It's not too late for me to ring Dr Goldstein.'

Zafirah stood up and stepped across the carpet. She slung her arm across Theo's wide shoulders. She moved his hand towards her stomach.

'Can you feel it kicking? Maybe a footballer? He can play for Armenia.'

'I think we should aim higher than that,' Theo chuckled. 'Centre forward for Barcelona! I won't accept anything less.'

Zafirah turned towards the open dresser. She stared at her collection of narrow jeans, draped redundantly on hangers, then looked back at Theo.

'Don't worry,' Theo announced, 'you're still the most beautiful woman in Haifa.'

# Chapter Twenty-Two

*Be motivated like the falcon, hunt gloriously.*
Rumi

Flying at a low altitude, tracking the shoreline above Latakia, a trio of ageing Mig-21s drew together in close formation. Like middle-aged executives on a lads' night out, they engaged in a series of turns, loops and barrel rolls above the surf. Rewarded by a ripple of applause from office workers seeking the shade, and whoops and yells from a thousand patriotic sun worshippers jamming the sands. And then they were gone.

Watching the last of the vapour trails disappear into the blue, Nadia was pleased to have caught the arial theatrics. She kicked off her shoes, enjoying the sensation of sand between her toes. But a part of her resented Jabril's absence. Another missed opportunity for Sami to enjoy time with his father. For all that, she refused to allow this to dampen her spirits – determined to make the most of her brief respite.

Leaving the strand, she made her way through the ornamental gardens, fronting the National Museum. She stopped to check her mobile. A missed call from Zafirah. Nothing from Jabril. *Where the hell is he?*

✧

Youssef thumbed methodically through Jabril's collection of library journals. Each edition neatly sequenced, they charted his incremental rise through the ranks of the library department. They ended abruptly at the point of his enforced retirement. Some pages marked by indecipherable scribblings, others littered with post-it notes. Youssef scratched his head. Where to start?

A fishing expedition followed by a full inventory – that's what Colonel Boutros had instructed. Gazing at the bookcase, populated with compendiums of Arab folk tales, volumes of satirical poetry and the complete works of Kipling, Youssef felt uneasy. More at home with army training manuals and his burgeoning collection of European pornography, he was unsure how to carry out a full forensic examination. He comforted himself with the thought that, for all Jabril's intellectual chatter and grand qualifications, his cousin, ultimately, had nothing to show for it.

'Head in the clouds – that's always been his trouble,' murmured Youssef.

Qasim sat dozing in his wheelchair. A sour geriatric odour hung in the air.

'I suppose you've wondered whether all the sacrifice has been worth it. A son who sires a whore of a daughter. Then she returns the favour by bringing a little Christian into the family. A poor reward, don't you think?'

Youssef placed his hand gently on the old man's shoulder. 'Poor Qasim – maybe it's a blessing that you've lost your marbles.'

✧

Nadia adjusted her head scarf, taking full advantage of the cool Mediterranean breeze. Leaving the tranquillity of the museum gardens, she picked her way through the mass of shoppers spilling into the city centre. She paused opposite the Moscow Café. Crowded with young customers, wearing designer summer outfits, she thought back to happier days spent with Jabril in Damascus during their courtship. For a moment, she imagined Zafirah sitting centre-stage among the smiling twenty somethings.

Nadia switched her gaze to a group of older revellers. They were clustered beneath a large canopy fronting the restaurant. They struggled to make themselves heard above the din. Light skinned and surprisingly muscular, the group raised half-filled glasses in drunken salutes. Bleary eyed, one of the men rose to attention. He began to make a toast. Probably Russian, Nadia thought.

✧

'Not a bloody word – what is your son playing at?' Youssef muttered, pushing Qasim's wheelchair towards the breakfast table. 'And the Englishman telling anyone willing to listen that he's only here to see the sights – what do you make of that, Qasim?'

The old soldier's eyes lay open. He stared forlornly at a dish of flatbreads sitting inconveniently out of reach.

'It's not as if I haven't given him every opportunity to progress – putting a word in all the right ears ... pulling out every stop.'

Qasim tugged at his trousers, then pushed his palm against his crotch.

'Let it flow,' sighed Youssef.

For a few moments, the invalid sat motionless, before raising his forefinger, as if he had remembered something important.

'The country in chaos and your Jabril decides to do a flit – what's do be done?'

Qasim's head dropped. Youssef watched his eye lids twitch.

'Back in the Golan?'

✧

Nadia searched for loose change. She found enough to pay the bus driver who would return her to Sharia 14. Ten minutes to wait but sufficient time to buy a carton of dates. Qasim's favourite and, hopefully, a remedy for his constipation. For a moment, she chided herself for leaving the old man on his own, wondering what her neighbours would make of her selfish excursion. She lifted her mobile – still no word from Jabril.

✧

'What do you mean, nothing?'

'Colonel, I checked every room – cupboards, drawers, even under the damned floorboards. Like I said, *nothing*.'

'Okay, leave everything as you found it. I'll need a full report in the morning, mind.'

'What about Jabril?' Youssef begged.

A long pause. Youssef pushed the phone closer. He detected a dry snigger.

'Just be patient, Youssef, there are plenty of ways to skin a cat.'

✧

Nadia pulled open the shutters. She had another hour before Sami was due to come in from school. She was starting to prepare dinner when her mobile buzzed. Number unknown and a voice she didn't recognise.

'Mrs Mansour?'

'Who is this?'

'Nadia?'

'Yes ... '

'It's Theo.'

# Chapter Twenty-Three

*Unto us a child is born, unto us a son is given.*
Isaiah

'Jabril, why haven't you been returning my calls?'

'Sorry, it's been difficult, I tried to—'

'You have to get to the hospital.'

Jabril tightened his grip on the mobile. 'What's wrong? Is it Qasim?'

'No, it's *Zafirah,* she's had the baby.'

'*What*? Is she in Haifa?'

'No, Damascus.'

'I don't understand.'

Nadia sighed. 'She left Haifa yesterday, but her waters broke as soon as she crossed the border. Theo rang to tell me.'

'Is she alright? What about the baby?'

'They're both fine. General Abrash has everything sorted out.'

'*Abrash*? What the hell has *he* got to do with it?'

'Jabril, there was nothing I could do. You weren't answering your phone, so I got his private number from Qasim's old diary. The general arranged for an army ambulance to get to her. The baby was born at the side of the road.'

Jabril took a deep breath. He detected the twin odours of stewed lamb and kerosene emanating from the museum courtyard. 'Where's she now?'

'I told you, Damascus, in the general hospital. Alima is with her. I'm trying to get out of Latakia but the roads are full of Youssef's men.'

'I thought your sister didn't want anything to do with Zafirah.'

'No Jabril, it's *you* who disowned her. *My* family believe in sticking together.'

'Nadia, she is *still* my daughter.'

'*Finally*, the words I've been waiting to hear. When can you come?'

Jabril watched Chandler stir from his sleep. 'I can't leave just now. It's difficult—'

'Still singing the same old tune. What's most important, your damn work or Zafirah?'

'You sound like Mr Chandler.'

'What?'

'It doesn't matter. It's a long story.'

# Chapter Twenty-Four

*It is a double pleasure to deceive the deceivers.*
La Fontaine

'Can you see him?'

'No, he's been gone since twelve.'

'Strange, isn't it? How he disappears for ten minutes every hour ... like clockwork. What's he up to, Jabril?'

'Probably sharing a pipe with the guards. Or maybe seeing a woman.'

Chandler moved towards the sink and cupped his hands under the tap. The water resembled pea soup. He splashed it liberally on his face, then lifted his razor. 'Does he leave his keys in the car?'

'Yes, every time, his cap and tunic too. He probably doesn't need a uniform for what he has in mind.'

Chandler joined Jabril by the window. 'What about your own car – don't you mind losing it?'

'The BMW? It belongs to the agency. Anyway, it seems a fair exchange for the attaché's Range Rover.'

'It looks like we're *both* burning bridges today,' Chandler muttered.

Jabril shook his head. 'More a case of shifting priorities – call it early retirement.'

'As a police informer?'

'As an *investigator*,' Jabril shot back.

'I suppose that's down to me,' Chandler said sombrely.

'This isn't just about *you*,' Jabril continued.

'Meaning?'

'*Youssef*, of course. The only reason we've been hiding out in Hama in the first place ... I can't go on working for the bastard and protect Zafirah as well.'

Chandler tugged at the straps of his rucksack. 'You know, Oakshott isn't going to like this.'

'Stealing his car?'

'Yes, that and missing my interview with the journalists.'

'I wouldn't worry too much about him. Oakshott will suffer a temporary embarrassment, but he'll keep his pension.'

'What about Said?'

'The Commander won't be so forgiving,' Jabril said. 'He will feel dishonoured.'

'Sharaf?'

Jabril chuckled. 'You learn fast. Remember, you're his prize possession.'

'It's a long time since I've been called that.'

'He'll be sorely disappointed when he hears you've slipped the net.'

'My heart bleeds.'

'Mr Chandler, you're not reliving a work of fiction here. The decision you're making carries severe consequences.'

Chandler began to pack. Averting Jabril's gaze, he stuffed his soiled underwear beneath the bundles of stories. He dropped his rucksack by Jabril's case at the foot of the door. Like a dishevelled older brother, the bag sat apologetically next to its smarter sibling.

'What about *you* Jabril? Said won't be too impressed when he finds out you've flown the nest.'

'Probably not, but I think the Commander already suspects I'm not such a big fish.'

'That's no reason for *both* of us to cut and run.'

Jabril looked hard at Chandler. 'Let's just say, I'd hate to see you made a hostage to fortune.'

✧

Jabril stepped gingerly between the conscripts on the riverbank. He was surprised that they had been left unguarded. Carrying a large blade, he looked like a medieval executioner. He leaned down to whisper a few words to the lost souls, before cutting through their plastic shackles. Every few paces, Jabril looked over his shoulder – relieved that there was no sign of Commander Said or yesterday's picnickers. Five minutes until his rendezvous with Chandler. Any longer, and Oakshott's driver would be sure to reappear, and the game would be up.

One by one, the prisoners picked themselves up and limped away. Most headed towards the citadel. A few tumbled down the riverbank towards a narrow barge, tied to the wheel. One prisoner refused to budge and buried his head in his hands.

Furious that he was unable to control the shake in his hands, Jabril threw down the knife, then moved cautiously along the potholed road leading to the museum. He resisted the urge to run. A group of militia stood sullenly in front of a ramshackle barricade, made up of a burnt-out car and refuse bins filled with breeze blocks. They eyed Jabril suspiciously. He muttered a few words and strolled swiftly past.

He reached the perimeter of the museum. A minute's grace. He walked quickly through the entrance of the courtyard. The diplomatic car stood at the far end of the square, but no sign of Chandler. *Don't do this to me.*

Jabril heard a distant shot coming from the direction of the river. Then, more sustained bursts of gunfire. He increased the length of his stride, careful not to stumble on the uneven path. He heard somebody shouting behind him.

'*Mr Mansour ... Mr Mansour.*'

He glanced behind and spotted Oakshott's driver hurry across the courtyard. The driver's trousers were unbuttoned and his belt dangled limply by his side.

'Your cutting it a bit fine, aren't you?' Chandler snapped, throwing himself into the passenger seat.

They watched the driver tug at his trousers and break into a trot. Jabril jumped into the vehicle.

'The *keys* – where are the fucking keys?' he screamed.

The driver launched into a gallop across the cobblestones.

'Here they are. I was looking after them for you. You can't be too careful these—'

'Shut up and hand them over. Where's his cap?'

Chandler leaned over to the backseat. He grabbed the driver's cap and jacket. Jabril hurriedly threw on the uniform, then switched on the ignition. The engine revved uncertainly, lurched forward, and stalled.

'Jabril, use the bloody gears, it's not an automatic.'

The car moved forward and began to pick up speed. Jabril watched the driver in his rear view mirror. He appeared distracted. His trousers began to slip down to his knees. Like a Buster Keaton movie in reverse, the driver turned on his heel and beat an erratic retreat across the courtyard.

'Who's doing the shooting?' Chandler asked.

'Said's men – I created a small diversion.'

'What?'

'I freed the prisoners by the wheel. It'll buy us time.'

'How long have we got?'

'A few minutes at most. The conscripts won't last long.'

'A stay of execution then.'

Jabril's eyes narrowed. 'Mr Chandler, would you prefer to be martyred by a bullet or take your chance on the wheel?'

✧

Driving through the checkpoint, controlling the intersection between Jam al Abdul Nasser Street and al-Bulhuri Street, proved a breeze. Three bored militiamen, carrying old carbines, quickly mustered. With exaggerated salutes, they waved them through. At Ahliah bus station, Chandler looked past Jabril's shoulder towards the Orentes. He observed a barge, partially submerged, floating gently downstream. Three escapees lay waist deep in water. Chandler couldn't see a mark on them. Like tiny hatchlings, their mouths gaped open, frozen in a steely grimace.

They maintained a steady cruise along the road flanking the river, skirting past boarded-up coffee houses and empty restaurants. Reaching the Four Norias Restaurant, five hundred metres east of the city centre, they caught their first sight of the Fourth Armoured Division. A dozen soldiers, heavily laden with ammunition belts, sat brooding at the side of the road. Outriders. Beside them, squatted a camouflaged troop carrier. A dozen Kalashnikovs, arranged like a miniature tepee, stood in front of the vehicle. Jabril watched a middle-aged officer lift his beret and leap from the vehicle. He took position in the centre of the road, then raised his hand. Jabril dropped into first gear and threw down his cap.

'How's your Russian, Mr Chandler?'

'What?'

'Your *Russian* – it's our best chance of getting through. They're used to visits from Russian advisors from the military academy in Homs.'

'Jabril, you know I don't speak bloody Russian.'

'You don't need to – just *look* as if you do.'

With one hand gripping the wheel, Jabril pulled at his tunic, before bringing the car to a halt in front of the troop carrier. Chandler watched him stride authoritatively towards the officer on the road. They exchanged a few words. Jabril held out a packet of cigarettes. He gestured towards a helmeted sniper stirring in the undergrowth, then clapped his hand warmly on the officer's shoulder.

The officer smiled and directed Jabril towards an unmanned trailer, housing rocket launchers and mortars.

'A fellow alumnus at Moscow University and a distant

cousin, I believe,' Jabril said, as he pushed himself back into the driver's seat. 'The class of '88 ... we had a lot in common.'

'Jabril, how long can we keep up this pretence? Oakshott is bound to have got wind of our escape by now.'

'It's not just Oakshott I'm worried about.'

'Who then?'

'I told you, Commander Said. I think that you may have spoiled his day.'

'And travelling in Oakshott's staff car – *wonderful*.'

'Don't worry, we'll get the plates changed soon.'

'Is that before or after we reach the border?'

'What border?' Jabril replied.

'The *Lebanese* border, of course. Isn't that where we are heading?'

Jabril shot Chandler a sideways glance, then pulled into fifth gear. 'No, we're taking the road to Damascus.'

'Damascus?'

'Yes, Mr Chandler, *the road to Damascus*.'

# Chapter Twenty-Five

*Keep your friends close, and your enemies closer.*
Sun Tzu

'Well, Jim, what's the view from the bridge?'

'*My* view or the Pentagon's?'

'Give me your *own* opinion.'

'Bill, you know I've never been a believer in the domino effect. I learned that in 'Nam.'

'What's your point, Jim?'

'My *point* is that I was wrong. The Arab Spring is proving that.'

'How?'

'Cos they're going down like ninepins. Just look at Ben Ali, Gaddafi, Mubarak.'

'Mubarak, now that *was* a surprise. He was a good friend of the States.'

'Sure, but I'm confident that we'll come to an arrangement with his successor.'

'Maybe, but hey, let's forget about the broader picture. How are things on the ground?'

'In Egypt?'

'No Jim, in *Syria*.'

'Looking good. Our guys at the Pentagon are picking up reports of unrest in Homs, Deraa and Hama. Yesterday there were protests in Aleppo and the suburbs of Damascus.'

'Sounds like we've got 'em on the run.'

'No Bill, the situation isn't yet critical, but I think we have an opportunity.'

'To go in and kick ass?'

'Hell no, the days of sending in the marines have long gone.'

'What about private contractors?'

'That's not an option ... not since the Blackwater fiasco.'

'That's a pity.'

'I agree, but you know as well as I do that this administration doesn't have the stomach for direct intervention.'

'You're right, Jim. Too many bleeding hearts in the White House.'

'There's another way to tackle this, Bill.'

'How?'

'We strengthen our links with the opposition.'

'You mean cosy up with the Free Syrian Army?'

'No Bill, they're just a rag tag.'

'So who are we talking about – the regular army?'

'You got it in one.'

'But aren't they still loyal to the President?'

'The elite divisions are, but we've a contact on the inside.'

'Who?'

'He commands the Third Armoured Division – a guy called Abrash.'

'So what's his beef – is he unhappy with his pay cheque?'

'No Bill, it's a little more complicated than that.'

'Go on.'

'He wants us to put pressure on the court in the Hague ... to get him out of a fix.'

'What do they want him for?'

'Shooting civilians.'

'C'mon, when did we lose sleep over a bit of collateral damage?'

'That's not all he wants, Bill. He's asking us to help him get a friend's son out of Syria. He feels he owes the old man.'

'Is that it?'

'No, there's more.'

'*Jesus.*'

'There's a man travelling with him – an Englishman, posing as a tourist.'

'Wait a minute, I got an email about this guy from our embassy in London. The Brits say the motherfucker blew one of their covert operations in Hama. MI6 isn't impressed.'

'That's all the more reason we should act fast, Bill. Have you spoken to the President?'

'Yeah, I briefed him this morning. He's still nervous about ruffling diplomatic feathers.'

'Do you think he'll talk to Abrash?'

'I wouldn't count on it. America has burnt its fingers too often with fucking warlords.'

'Bill, you need to tell the boss that Abrash is the best chance we have.'

'But what's in it for the President? He doesn't need any more screw ups before the primaries.'

'Tell him about the gas.'

'Don't they have any oil?'

'No, they got Jack shit.'

'That's a shame.'

'Yeah, a fucking tragedy.'

'Jim, you didn't hear me say this. Keep talking to Abrash. Tell him Uncle Sam will do what he can. But keep this under the radar. We can't afford another row with London. Now, get me a goddam drink.'

# Chapter Twenty-Six

*They say late thanks are ever best.*
Francis Bacon

The traders in the Old City refused to take no for an answer. From all directions, the souq screamed for Chandler's attention.

'Please ... only one minute ... come in and have tea,' pleaded the shoemaker, pressing a pair of bright red slippers into Chandler's unwilling hands.

'All handwoven ... for you, I give two for the price of one,' boomed the carpet seller.

'Everything genuine,' whispered the smiling antique merchant, casting his hand towards shelves stocked with fake Ottoman cavalry sabres.

Chandler inhaled the powerful aroma of spices, tobacco smoke and incense. He lingered next to a stall selling erotic underwear. He watched a grinning trader hold up a pair of musical knickers. 'Extra batteries free of charge.'

'Harrods it *isn't!*' Chandler shouted to Jabril, above the din.

Jabril took no notice. Clutching a bundle of dollars, he continued to haggle with a stallholder over the price of baby clothes. He winked at Chandler with a conspiratorial smile.

'Okay, I'll give you ten dollars for the lot,' he said.

'Are you crazy?' roared the stallholder. 'Do you want me to live on the *streets*?'

Jabril spun ostentatiously on his heel and marched back into the thoroughfare.

'Wait,' called the stallholder, 'twenty dollars ... my final price.'

Jabril grinned broadly as another carrier bag was greedily packed.

'How long have we got?'

'We've an hour before we need to be at the hospital. Have you any spare dollars?'

'Jabril, I gave you my last cent a minute ago. Haven't you bought enough?'

'No, I need money for the plates.'

'*Plates*? I didn't realise you were buying for Nadia too.'

'No, Mr Chandler, new plates for the *car*. Registration documents too.'

Chandler raised his eyebrows. 'You surprise me. I thought, with your contacts, you might be able to call in a few favours.'

'Things have changed in Damascus, Mr Chandler. Do you see any tourists? All the traders want now is dollars and *more* dollars. Now, give me your credit card.'

✧

The bric-a-brac store lay at the far end of the souq. Its narrow frontage barely two metres wide. Chandler followed Jabril down a winding stairway. He lowered his head below a small archway, before entering a surprisingly cavernous interior. The walls were lined with wooden shelves, filled with dirty bottles, copper kettles, and discoloured brassware. Carpets, divan covers and embroidered prayer mats hung haphazardly from beams. In the corner of the cellar, he spotted a 1940s gramophone, playing Edith Piaf.

'Do you have *milk*?' Chandler asked.

The Bedouin shopkeeper looked nonplussed. Heavily bearded, with a mountainous paunch, he shifted unsteadily on a plastic chair. His check keffiyeh nestled snugly around his face, secured to his forehead with a thick agal made of goat's wool. His dark skin was creased and leathery. Chandler tried to estimate how many years the old man had spent under burning desert skies. Jabril sat next to him, wearing a thin smile.

'It's polite to address him by name – Raslan, an old family friend,' Jabril whispered.

'Does he understand what I said?'

'This isn't high tea at the Savoy,' Jabril said sternly. 'When a Bedouin offers you tea, the only concession is extra sugar.'

Chandler lifted the glass. He felt the tips of his fingers burn. The shopkeeper pushed a small bowl of sugar towards him, before reaching for Jabril's cigarettes.

'Did I tell you about Raslan's grandfather?'

'No, Jabril.'

'He fought with T. E. Lawrence. They were the first to liberate Damascus.'

'Is that why Raslan is here?'

'Yes, but the rest of his family were forced to leave the city after partition.'

'Partition?'

'The Sykes Picot agreement – perhaps it was omitted from your history books. It gave France control of Syria and Lebanon. The British got the rest.'

'Where are his family now?'

'A few live near Homs. They work for wealthy farmers. They don't have any land of their own.'

'Hard times.'

'It's worse than that, Mr Chandler. To earn your living through hard labour is considered the worst fate to befall a Bedouin. Working the soil, instead of demonstrating your skill and courage on a horse or camel, is seen as degrading.'

'So, where does that leave *me*, Jabril? I've not got much to shout about – redundant and unpublished.'

'The Bedouin would regard *you* as highly privileged.'

Chandler pulled a face. 'It doesn't feel like it. There have been times when I would have given up everything for the simple life.'

'Life is never simple.'

Chandler sipped his tea. 'What about the rest of Raslan's family?'

'They are scattered along the mountains between Syria and Lebanon. They herd sheep and goats. Raslan is their only connection with Damascus.'

'So what's Raslan's connection with you?'

'It's a long story – I'm not sure we have time.'

'Jabril, you've listened patiently to *my* stories. Isn't it time *you* took up the mantle of narrator?'

Jabril stubbed out his cigarette and, for a moment, closed his eyes. 'It was the drought of '58, the worst for a century. My father had just graduated from the military academy. It was his first posting.'

'Is that when he met Raslan?'

'Yes, but the meeting was never planned. His platoon were chasing Bedouin smugglers along the border – that's when he came across Raslan. He was visiting his family outside An Nabk. The Wadi had run dry and most of the livestock were dying of thirst.'

'Did he stop to help?'

'Let's say he disobeyed orders.'

'You've lost me.'

'My father had strict instructions to shoot anyone suspected of smuggling.'

'A difficult choice then?'

'Not for Qasim. His radio, how you say, suffered a *malfunction*, so he was unable to follow orders.'

'Russian technology, you can never trust it,' said Chandler, chuckling.

'He commandeered the first water tanker he could find. It was too late for the animals, but Raslan and his family survived.'

'This is sounding all too familiar, Jabril. Qasim is nothing short of a saint! Saving General Abrash in the Golan and Raslan in the desert. Your father must be owed a mountain of favours.'

'It's not a question of favours. The Bedouin are our brothers. The only debt we owe is to Allah.'

Chandler finished his tea. The conversation between Jabril and Raslan continued to ebb and flow. It ran from low whispers to colourful hand gestures and unrestrained laughter, punctuated by thoughtful silences.

'Raslan says that Youssef was spotted in the souq this morning. He's been asking questions about Zafirah.'

'Does he know she's in the hospital?'

'No, I don't think so, but it's dangerous for us to remain in Damascus for too long – the mukhabarat have informers on every street.'

'Jabril, you can't leave without seeing her.'

'I know, but we mustn't overstay our welcome. We can get a taxi to the hospital, then pick up the car later, as long as we leave the city before dark.'

'Perhaps you should stay as long as it takes ... you know, to make amends.'

'Mr Chandler, the time has passed for apologies. Anyway, Nadia—'

'Jabril, this isn't about Nadia. It's your *daughter* who needs you now. Isn't it time you listened to her side of the story?'

'I have a sinking feeling that you're about to tell me. *Give her space*. Wasn't that the message of your story in Aleppo?'

'So you *were* listening, Jabril.'

'Of course, I told you, Camilla and Zafirah have a lot in common.'

'What about Camilla's father? Can you identify with *him*?'

'Yes, we're both long-suffering.'

'But now you'll give Zafirah room to breathe?'

'For the moment, I will respect our differences.'

'*You're all heart.*'

'Don't push it, Mr Chandler.'

Chandler watched Raslan stuff a wad of dollars into a small camel-skin pouch. 'More Bedouin hospitality?'

'Call it a belated thank you. We'll need the money once we cross the mountains.'

'*Mountains?*'

'Don't worry, Mr Chandler, I'll explain later.'

# Chapter Twenty-Seven

*Vengeance is in my heart, death in my hand.*
*Blood and revenge are hammering in my head.*
Shakespeare

'Keep your mouth shut until we get to the hospital.'

'Aren't you getting a little paranoid? It's only a bloody taxi.'

'These days, in Damascus, there is no such thing as *only a taxi*.'

'C'mon, Jabril ... '

'Think about it, Mr Chandler. When I collected you from the hotel in Beirut, did you seriously believe I was simply your driver?'

'Well, yes, at first.'

'And how long did it take to suspect I was something more?'

'I told you, that first checkpoint, on the road to Palmyra. You seemed rather over confident.'

'Quite. So there's is no reason for you to be so naïve now.'

'I feel another lesson coming on.'

'In Damascus many drivers are well educated,' Jabril continued. 'They include engineers, accountants and teachers. But there are no jobs for them, so they must supplement their income.'

'By chasing fares?'

'Of course. And some also act as the ears and eyes of the security services.'

'You mean they're police informers?'

'They don't have much choice. It's the only way to get by when business is bad.'

Chandler helped Jabril push another carrier bag into the boot. 'Okay, I get the message. Don't worry, you won't hear a peep out of me until we're inside the hospital.'

✧

The journey across the centre of Damascus took longer than Chandler expected. The little yellow taxi moved cautiously through the heavy traffic. They passed the Four Seasons Hotel, towering over the still waters of the Baroda River, and picked up speed along the highway leading into the administrative district. Chandler gazed at the drab edifice of the city hall. But reaching the commercial centre, he was struck by the cityscape's modernity. Traffic police, with starched white shirts and dark gloves, waved them through one junction after another, along broad tree-lined avenues. It reminded Chandler of Paris. For a moment, he resented his missed opportunity to stay in the city longer. What had the guidebook said? *Damascus – the oldest permanently inhabited city in the world, home to the remains of John the Baptist and the site of Paul's miraculous conversion.* Chandler wondered whether he would ever return. But, for now, history would have to wait.

✧

'I've spoken to Dr Sadek – I told him we were coming. He says Zafirah is tired, but is otherwise doing well.'

Chandler struggled to keep pace with Jabril as he bounded up the hospital steps. 'You *rang* him? I thought you said that we shouldn't be using our phones.'

'I know, it was a little foolhardy, but it was only for a minute,' Jabril replied.

'Can you trust him?'

'Of course, he's a good friend.'

'And a good doctor I hope.'

'The best in Damascus. He learned his trade in the army medical corps. The old man should have retired years ago but his patients won't let him.'

'Don't tell me, another friend of your father?'

'Not directly, but he's close to General Abrash. He removed a cataract from his good eye last year and didn't charge him a penny.'

'Are you expecting a similar dispensation for Zafirah?'

'The doctor has already demonstrated his generosity, Mr Chandler.'

'How?'

'By not informing the authorities that Zafirah is here.'

'Is that being generous?'

'It's *more* than generous. Opponents of the government are routinely dragged from the wards by the police. He's taking a big risk. If he is caught, he'll lose more than his pension.'

'Jabril, wait a minute. Where did you put the bags?'

'What bags?'

'The ones with the baby clothes. Didn't you lift them?'

Jabril's cheeks began to redden. 'Damn, they're still in the boot of the taxi. Mr Chandler, you'll have to go back, the driver may not have left.'

'Maybe *you* should go back. I can wait for you here.'

'No, I need to see Zafirah. Please, you'll need to run. *Hurry*!'

✧

'Tiny, isn't he? Your mother's eyes,' said Jabril.

'But Theo's nose,' Zafirah sighed, forcing a smile.

Jabril gently squeezed his daughter's hand, then glanced at the monitor keeping watch over the open box incubator. The baby lay on his back, his twitching feet the only sign of movement. Above, the low hum of the ceiling fan.

'A near miss, wasn't it?' Jabril said forcefully.

'I should never have left Haifa – a stupid idea,' replied Zafirah.

'For once, I agree with you.'

'Theo should be with me,' Zafirah whispered.

'Yes, he *should*.'

Gripping the bed rails, Zafirah pulled herself upright. She reached for the wooden comb that Theo had secreted in her travel bag. 'I look a mess.'

Jabril's eyes widened. 'No, it's the *situation* that's a mess – your mother stuck in Latakia ... your grandfather on his last legs.'

Zafirah groaned.

'Oh, and it gets worse. I heard from a friend in the old quarter this morning – Youssef has been spotted in Damascus – if he knows you're—'

'I don't understand, he's still your boss isn't he?'

'It's not as simple as that, he—'

'I'm sure you can put in a good word for me?' Zafirah said, acidly.

Jabril blew out his cheeks. 'No, it's too late for that.'

'But you *are* still working for him?'

Jabril bit his lip. 'For the moment, let's say I'm off the payroll.'

Stung into silence, Zafirah continued to run the comb through her hair.

'In Hama ... I decided to burn my bridges,' added Jabril, sombrely.

'What the hell were you doing *there* – the city's in revolt isn't it?'

Jabril turned his head away. 'As strange as it sounds, going to Hama seemed the safest course ... for me *and* Mr Chandler.'

'Then why did you *leave*?'

'It's complicated,' Jabril declared.

Zafirah dropped the comb. For a few moments she appeared distracted.

'Your mother tells me the boy will be brought up a Christian, that you may convert,' Jabril continued.

'I'll do what I have to do,' Zafirah said.

Jabril released his grip from his daughter's hand. 'That's not the answer I'm looking for.'

Zafirah narrowed her eyes. 'It's the best you're going to get. Anyway, there's no time to explain.'

Jabril hesitated. 'She needs space.'

'What?'

'It's not important – just something from one of Mr Chandler's stories.'

✧

Zafirah lay on her side and listened to the intermittent bleeps of the monitor. She wondered how long it would take for her father to return to the maternity suite. 'I need to check on Mr Chandler, he should have been back by now,' Jabril had told her. Zafirah smiled when Dr Sadek pushed open the door, then detected the outline of a taller man standing behind him, grasping the doctor's shoulders.

✧

It took nearly a full minute for Jabril to make sense of the drama being played out in the maternity suite. He watched his old handler stroke Zafirah's neck with the muzzle of a handgun. Youssef was unshaven, with a greasy stubble that did little to conceal his pockmarked skin. With one hand, he held her narrow wrist in a tight grip. She kept her eyes firmly lowered and quietly sobbed.

The last time Jabril had witnessed a nine millimetre Makarov being held to a woman's temple was in Tudmor prison. He could still recall Youssef's words to the pretty Israeli backpacker with poor map reading skills.

'Settle yourself, Sarah.'

'I promise, this won't take long.'

'A little more cooperation please.'

'Now, lie still and lets have some fun.'

On the far side of the private suite, Zafirah's newborn lay on his back sleeping peacefully in the incubator. Hardly a whimper, just his chest rising and falling with an even rhythm. Dr Sadek rocked unsteadily on the edge of Zafirah's bed. His nostrils streaked with blood. He carried a heavy bruise on his left cheek. One of the lenses on his spectacles was cracked.

'You disappoint me, Jabril. All that training and you still manage to break the first rule.'

Jabril watched Youssef from the doorway. He strained to make out whether the weapon's safety catch had been switched off.

'I honestly believed that you had slipped the net,' Youssef continued. 'Then you're foolish enough to make that call ... we had you tracked in seconds.'

'Youssef, your argument isn't with Zafirah. Please, move the gun away.'

'Once again, you're missing what's in front of your nose. Didn't Zafirah tell you about our little romantic encounter in Tartus? ... before she hitched up with her Armenian friend.'

'I don't understand.'

'Really? Perhaps Zafirah should tell you herself?'

Youssef lowered the pistol, then hung his chin on Zafirah's shoulder. 'Do you remember – behind the harbour walls, with old Qasim snoozing next to us on the rocks? A poor chaperone, don't you think?'

'You're lying,' Jabril screamed.

'I don't suppose your slut of a daughter has said anything about this to poor Theo. It would make for a bad start – maybe enough to cause a rift?'

'Youssef – put down the gun.'

'Naturally, Zafirah put up stiff resistance. I would expect nothing less from a Mansour.'

'Shut up, Youssef.'

'She needed some persuasion, as you might imagine. But I never take no for an answer.'

'Youssef, leave Zafirah out of this. I told you, your quarrel is with me.'

'No, Jabril, my quarrel is with *both* of you. Don't you understand the cost of betrayal?'

'Please, do what you like with me, but leave Zafirah out of this.'

'Oh, Jabril, now you're forcing *me* to choose. You or Zafirah? It hardly seems fair, but *somebody* has to be punished. Perhaps we should let Zafirah make the final decision.'

Zafirah tore her hand from Youssef's grip and swung round to face him. Her cheeks wet, and her hair matted. Her vision was obscured by the Makarov pointed between her eyes.

'Do what you have to do,' she murmured.

Youssef let out a short chuckle and reached for his pocket. 'That's strange, isn't that what you told me in Tartus?'

He lifted himself from the bed and edged slowly towards the incubator. He shot a backward glance at Zafirah. 'You've always been a poor decision-maker, haven't you?'

'Please, Youssef, not the baby.'

For a moment, Jabril was unsure what to make of Youssef's gentle seesawing handstrokes across the baby's neck. It took a few seconds before he detected the glint of hard steel beneath his fingers. Then, a tiny gasp, and a rush of air.

Jabril launched himself from the bed. In a flurry of fists, he caught Youssef off balance. Both men found themselves in a heap, breathless on the floor. Youssef thrust a hand into his trousers, then realised that the Makarov he had shoved under his waistband was now lodged inconveniently beneath his crotch. He managed to land Jabril a heavy punch to the neck and scrambled for the door.

✧

As a veteran of the Golan campaign, Dr Sadek counted himself as something of a specialist on battlefield trauma. Shrapnel injuries, severe burns, burst eardrums – he had seen them all. The doctor moved swiftly across the suite. He knew he had only seconds to spare. Staunching the flood of crimson with his plump fist, he calculated that the infant had a minute at most. Dr Sadek reckoned it was a blessing that Youssef had opted to sever the jugular vein instead of the carotid artery. The difference between a determined trickle and a violent spurt – with the baby's heart as final arbiter. On the *downside*, he was unsure whether the staff at the nurses' station would pick up the automatic alert from the child's monitor. They always seemed to be at their tea. He knew it would take more than a stent, and some nifty needlework, to repair the damage caused by the boxcutter. Dr Sadek leaned over the incubator and glued his face to the baby's mouth and nose, then pressed two fingers against his chest. Between gentle compressions, he observed the child's eyes dilate. He felt the pulse begin to slow and watched the baby's skin lose its colour. Thirty seconds passed, and still no sign of the crash team.

'*Where the hell are they?*'

✧

Weighed down by carrier bags, Chandler quickened his pace along the hospital corridor. The rooms all looked the same and he struggled to locate the private suite. He was surprised at the level of activity in the maternity ward. On the panel behind the deserted nurses' station, a red light was flashing. Three medics and an overweight nurse, carrying a defibrillator, rushed past him. They nearly collided with a middle-aged man, with a pockmarked face, walking calmly in the opposite direction. The man stopped when he made eye contact with Chandler. For a second, his yellow teeth bared in a rictus smile. Then, he resumed his stroll along the corridor.

Chandler dropped the bags as soon as he heard screaming coming from the private suite. He pushed himself against the wall as a convoy of breathless doctors wheeled an incubator furiously past him. Chandler saw sheets of reddening gauze dangling from a baby's neck.

Stumbling into the suite, Chandler first caught sight of Jabril. He was huddled behind Zafirah with both arms wrapped tightly around her waist. Alongside, Dr Sadek, appearing pale, rocked unsteadily on his feet.

'This is all my fault,' Jabril groaned. 'Why did I have to make that bloody call?'

Chandler looked at Dr Sadek. 'What the hell is going on?'

The doctor wiped the sweat from his forehead. 'Mr Chandler, the baby is badly hurt. It doesn't look good. You must tell Jabril to leave now. Youssef is sure to return.'

'What about Zafirah? We can't leave her here.'

'She can stay with my sister tonight,' the doctor replied, 'then she has to leave. It's not safe for her in Damascus.'

Moving swiftly across the linoleum, Chandler placed his hand on Jabril's shoulder. 'We can't stay here,' he muttered.

Jabril remained glued to his daughter. Neither appeared willing to budge.

'Listen, you heard what Dr Sadek said, we have to leave. *Now*!'

Jabril released his grip on Zafirah's waist. Tasting blood rising in the back of his throat, he moved round to face her, then cupped her face in his hands, before kissing her hair.

Chandler led Jabril into the corridor. The bags, stuffed to the brim with baby clothes, sat forlornly in the spot where he had dropped them. They walked in silence to the carpark. Late afternoon, and the air starting to freshen.

✧

'Jabril, I can't do this on my own. How do we get back to the car? You didn't tell me where we are supposed to collect it.'

Jabril remained speechless.

'Please ... *say some*thing. We don't have much time.'

Jabril lifted his wallet and removed a faded business card. Chandler checked the address – a body repair shop in the old quarter.

'That's all I need – this time let *me* do the talking.'

With arms linked, they shuffled out of the carpark into the slow moving traffic. 'I know this isn't what you want,' Chandler said softly, as he raised his arm to hail a taxi, 'but we can't stay here. We don't have a choice.'

# Chapter Twenty-Eight

*Since you have no aversion to our manners;*
*since you know how to use the lance, and manage*
*a horse like a Bedouin, stay among us.*
Constantin-François Volney

'Move to the left. Did you hear me? Give him room to pass – no, not that far, you'll have us in the bloody ditch. Okay, stop the car, I'll take the wheel.'

Jabril struggled to bring the vehicle to a halt. He lowered his head and stared blankly at his knees. Chandler watched the lorry zigzag up the highway, then regain control of the road, its hazard lights flashing angrily.

'I know this is difficult,' Chandler sighed, 'but we have to get to An Nabk in one piece.'

Jabril shot him a sullen glance before returning his gaze to his knees.

'Look, I appreciate that getting us to the mountains is probably the last thing on your mind, but there's no point getting us both killed on the road. You know Zafirah wouldn't want—'

'How do you know what Zafirah wants?' Jabril snapped.

'I *don't*, after what happened in the hospital, I wouldn't presume ...'

'Then *don't*.'

Chandler leaned back in his seat. He struggled to find the right words.

'Mr Chandler, my grandson has his throat slit in front of me and his mother. I am responsible for what happened. Nadia will never forgive me.'

'Jabril, you don't know how the baby is. You said yourself, Dr Sadek is the best surgeon in Damascus – you should ring him.'

'Are you serious?' Jabril roared. 'That's what caused all this – how could I have been so stupid?'

'Listen, you mustn't give up. When we get across the mountains I'll make some calls, see if I can get Zafirah out, the baby too if—'

'Make some calls? Who do you intend to ring? Your MP? Nothing *you* do can influence what happens to Zafirah.'

Chandler stepped out of the car. The sun began to set. An hour before nightfall, but thirty miles before they would be within sight of An Nabk. A strong breeze whistled through the gorse, lining the edge of the deserted road. He walked over to the driver's side and nudged Jabril firmly into the passenger seat, then rehearsed the gears and switched on the ignition.

'Jabril, I may be a *nobody*, I don't have any generals in my address book, but there's more than one way to skin a cat.'

'What are you trying to say?'

'What I'm saying is that you should give me a chance.'

'There's nothing you can do.'

'You're wrong – I've something we can use.'

Jabril raised his eyebrows. 'Go on, surprise me.'

'I have a *recording*. I made it in Hama.'

'That's impossible. I didn't see you use any recording equipment. I was with you.'

'Not all the time, Jabril. Do you remember leaving me alone with Oakshott in the museum? I voice recorded everything he said. It's on my mobile.'

Jabril shook his head. 'I don't understand – how will that help Zafirah?'

'I'm not sure yet. I need to work it out, but what he told me is going to seriously embarrass the Foreign Office, Downing Street too.'

Jabril lit a cigarette and watched wisps of smoke spiral towards the window.

✧

A mile before An Nabk, and with a jab from Jabril's thumb, Chandler took a sharp left and followed the rough dirt truck taking them towards the baby slopes of the mountains. With lights set at full beam, and added illumination from the stars, the vehicle maintained a firm grip on the winding incline. Chandler felt his ears pop.

'Stop over there, next to the drop,' Jabril said.

'Are we here? I can't see anyone.'

'That's why we're stopping. We can't afford to give him any sudden surprises.'

'Who?'

'The sheikh, Raslan's cousin. He has a bad heart.'

'Isn't he expecting us?' Chandler said.

'Yes, but Raslan didn't say when. In any case, for the Bedouin, the concept of punctuality doesn't exist.'

Chandler studied the clearing. 'The place seems deserted.'

'Mr Chandler, the mountains are never empty – this is the busiest smuggling route in Syria.'

'Guns?'

'No, weapons come through the border with Turkey. Here, it's mainly hashish, though there's less call for it now.'

'So not such a big deal for the security forces.'

'On the contrary, army patrols have been sent from Homs – they're trying to catch deserters planning to join the Free Syrian Army.'

'I can't see how a few deserters will give us much trouble,' Chandler muttered dismissively.

'You're forgetting, they're also hungry and desperate, so we need to stay clear of them.'

'Okay, smugglers and deserters – is that it?'

'No, the mukhabarat will be close by – they're chasing anti-government activists escaping from the towns. Assisted by the *shabiha* – Alawite paramilitaries. They get rewarded for each one they catch.'

'Bounty hunters? It's getting more like the Wild West by the minute.'

'With one crucial difference, Mr Chandler.'

'What's that?'

'There will be no ninth calvary coming to our rescue.'

'So, let's get this straight – bandits, deserters and rebels behind every rock. The army, police, militias, even my own bloody government, after my scalp – all in less than a week.'

'Yes, Mr Chandler, for a *nobody*, that's quite an achievement.'

Chandler grimaced, then reached into the back of the glove compartment. He lifted a bottle of Arak and set it on the dashboard.

'You should save that for later – it's the last bottle. Anyway, the smell of liquor will offend the sheikh.'

Jabril began to fumble under the driver's seat. He lifted three empty cigarette packets, before pulling out a heavy revolver. He examined the weapon for a few seconds. It had a long barrel and a dark Bakelite handle. He snapped open the muzzle and checked the cylinder, counting six copper cartridges.

'Where on earth did you get that?'

'It belongs to Oakshott, a Webley Mark VI. Pre-war, I think. You know, the Arabs have a particular fondness for antiquity.'

'Like your attachment to the T-62, I suppose.'

Jabril smiled. 'We have a traditional resistance to change. Anyway, it's rather elegant, isn't it?'

'Did you carry that into the hospital?'

'No, I wish I had – perhaps my grandson would be alive if—'

'I told you, you don't know how the baby is ... Dr Sadek—'

'The doctor isn't a miracle worker,' Jabril fired back.

Chandler watched Jabril flick on the roof light, then squint down the barrel. 'That's strange, I don't think the gun has ever been fired, not recently anyway.'

'Perhaps we won't need it,' suggested Chandler.

Jabril paused. 'You've never killed anyone, have you?'

'Funnily enough, that's not how we usually settled disputes in the rates department.'

Jabril leaned towards the window and lined up the gun sights. 'Don't worry – after the first, it gets easier.'

'The first?'

'The trick is never to look into your target's eyes.'

'You're making me nervous.'

'You *should* be – nerves sharpen the senses. Now, let's lift the bags and get rid of the car.'

'Won't we need it to get through the mountains?'

'Mr Chandler, you can't be serious. No vehicle can handle this terrain. In any case, the car makes us too conspicuous. From now on, we travel on foot.'

Jabril gestured Chandler towards the door.

'Wait till I release the handbrake, then push hard from behind. Ready? *Heave*!'

✧

The Bedouin encampment sat incongruously in the middle of a narrow plateau. On one side, flanked by a steep gulley. On the other, shielded from the wind and rain by a forbidding limestone rockface. Chandler watched Jabril walk slowly towards a circle of low tents. They were constructed from rough goat skin, supported by thick wooden poles. Some had been crudely patched with cardboard and sacking which flapped lazily in the breeze. In the centre of the camp, showers of sparks danced above the embers of a dying fire.

'Wait here,' Jabril ordered, before moving hesitantly towards the largest tent.

To his left, Chandler spotted a large German Shepherd take a few paces towards him. His heart began to race, then he noticed that the hound was tethered to a long metal chain. The dog fell on its haunches a metre before his feet. Its expression struck Chandler as strangely mournful. For a moment, he contemplated the wreckage of the Range Rover lying at the bottom of the ravine. No going back. Shivering in the night air, Chandler watched Jabril disappear into the tent. The dog pushed its enormous head onto its paws, closed its eyes, and let out a sleepy groan.

✧

'A few ground rules,' Jabril said sternly. 'You must confine yourself to the area reserved for *men*. You are forbidden to speak to the women unless invited to do so. You may talk to the children, though they will not understand a word you are saying. You—'

'I think I get the message.'

'It's for your own protection. Now, if you get hungry, there is bread and cheese. When you get cold, you will find extra blankets.'

'Is that it?'

'No – one more thing. If you need a shit, you must go outside. You will find the view of the mountains is splendid – it will assist your bowel movements.'

Chandler stretched his legs on the hard mat. It reminded him of the nights he had spent on his first wife's Japanese futon in the spare room. 'You know, all this putting on a brave face, you don't need to try so hard.'

'You're right, Mr Chandler, it's a curse I inherited from my father.'

'Really? I thought some of my British stiff upper lip might be rubbing off on you.'

Jabril reached under his jacket and pulled out the Webley. 'Here, take this. It will ward off evil spirits.'

'No, Jabril, you keep it. If it's alright with you, I'll stick to the Arak.'

✧

Chandler woke to the sound of children. He listened intently to their laughs and yells outside the tent. Still fully clothed, he slithered off the mat and pushed his head awkwardly through the cardboard catflap. The rush of heat took his breath away. On the far edge of the plateau, Chandler observed a small herd of mountain goats struggle to evade the attentions of the dog. They found sanctuary on a craggy rockface overlooking the camp. The dog sniffed unenthusiastically at their droppings, then pricked up its ears and bounded towards a commotion next to the campfire. Chandler hauled himself out of the tent. The smell of woodsmoke began to fill his nostrils. He spotted Jabril.

'Meet the enemy,' Jabril announced jubilantly, pressing his boot firmly on the young man's throat.

Wiping the sleep from his eyes, Chandler looked at the figure lying face up in the sand. 'What's going on?'

'He's been sent by Youssef to spy on us.'

'How do you know?'

'We caught him close to the sheikh's tent early this morning,' Jabril went on. 'The idiot fell over an oil drum and woke half the camp. Didn't you hear anything?'

'No, the Arak is a strong sedative.'

Jabril shook his head.

'You still haven't told me – how do you know he's with Youssef?' asked Chandler.

'Because he's the bastard's nephew. His name is Ali. Ugly specimen, isn't he?'

Chandler turned his back on Jabril and watched the women and men of the clan. They had arranged themselves in concentric circles. Furthest away, a group of young women sat silently weaving. They wore long embroidered dresses over cotton pantaloons. Their faces delicately tattooed. They appeared to be taking directions from an older woman. Her face was covered with a veil, studded with gold and silver coins. Closer to the centre of the camp, a group of young men sauntered between upturned drums of kerosene and empty water containers. Wearing loose white robes and chequered headcloths, they watched Chandler closely. A few carried rifles. Next, he caught sight of the sheikh, shuffling towards Ali. He prodded the young man's stomach with his walking stick.

'What are they going to do with him?' Chandler asked.

'Normally, it's the Bedouin custom to welcome strangers,' Jabril answered. 'But in *this* case, it's more complicated, after what Youssef did to my grandson.'

'So, what do you have in mind?'

'We don't have a choice, Mr Chandler. If we let him go, we are all finished.'

'There's always a choice, Jabril.'

'And what would you suggest?'

'Perhaps we could tie him up, then move on – it would buy us time.'

Jabril waved his hand dismissively. 'No, the sheikh would see that as a sign of weakness.'

'Or compassion?'

'Mr Chandler, the only compassion this pig deserves is a bullet.'

Chandler watched the young man gasp for breath. Two children raced over and tugged at his shoes. 'Have you forgotten what you said about the conscripts in Hama? You agreed the executions weren't justified.'

'That was *before* the hospital,' Jabril declared.

'But if we kill him, it makes us no better than Youssef.'

'No, Mr Chandler, if we kill him, it makes us *even*.'

Jabril lowered himself across Ali's chest. He pushed his knee onto his neck. Drawing out the revolver, he placed the muzzle against the young man's cheek.

'I'm having no part of this,' Chandler spat out.

'It's too late, you're *already* part of it. Don't you remember what you told me on the road to Hama? You said you wanted to be a *participant*. Now's your chance to prove it.'

Jabril spun the revolver on his forefinger and held out the weapon. 'Go on, put Ali out of his misery. If *you* don't, I'm sure our Bedouin friends will be able to assist – though they may want to take their time.'

Chandler watched the sheikh lean towards Jabril and whisper into his ear.

'The sheikh has offered us a compromise that will satisfy everybody – one that won't offend your delicate sensibilities,

Mr Chandler.' He pointed towards a mound of pebbles, assembled by the children to mark the entrance to the camp.

'If Ali can reach the far side we will let him run on. You know the gun is old, so his odds are promising.'

'This is *sick*,' Chandler hissed.

'It's the best offer on the table.'

With a kickstart from Jabril's boot, Ali launched into a lightening sprint across the plateau. Amid deafening ululating from the women, and shouts from the children, he covered twenty metres before Jabril had time to aim the pistol. Chandler watched the men with the rifles exchange grins and cash. Ali took the first bend around the sheikh's tent with ease, then picked up speed on the final straight towards the pebbles. The spectators fell into a tense silence. Jabril steadied the revolver with both hands. Taking a last backward glance, the barefoot runner was within a metre of the finishing line, before he was felled by a single shot. He staggered a few paces, dropped to one knee, and tumbled face down.

Jabril smiled and tucked the gun under his belt. He opened his arms to accept an embrace from the sheikh. Chandler watched the German Shepherd amble towards the body, then sniff a dark patch of blood spreading over the sand.

'Don't worry, Mr Chandler, your hands are still clean. Now, it's time to pack. We have a long day ahead of us.'

# Chapter Twenty-Nine

*Up lad; when the journey's over*
*there'll be time enough to sleep.*
A.E. Housman

'Take these,' Jabril ordered, dropping Ali's boots at Chandler's feet.

'*Dead men's shoes*? I'm not sure I should wear them.'

Jabril frowned. 'You're not used to climbing, are you?'

Chandler's mind rewound to documentary footage of Everest and K2.

'Don't worry, Mr Chandler. We will be travelling *through* the mountains, not over them.'

Chandler looked up doubtfully. 'The guidebook says the Anti-Lebanon range reaches a height of two thousand metres. The closest I've been to a mountain is watching my nephew abseil down the climbing wall in Milton Keynes.'

'This will be a little more challenging,' Jabril said. 'The

border lies on the far side of the crest of the mountains. After that, Baalbek, and we're home and dry.'

'Baalbek? I hear it has the best ruins in Lebanon.'

'You're forgetting, it's *Hezbollah* country too – I don't suppose your guidebook told you that. That's where Raslan's money will ease our passage.'

'You mentioned a *crest*,' Chandler said nervously. 'I thought you said we wouldn't be climbing?'

Jabril chuckled. 'Let's call it *advanced hill walking*.'

Chandler held up his flimsy jacket for inspection.

'You will need more than that. I'll ask the sheikh if he has any spare clothes. It's going to get a lot colder.'

'Isn't he coming with us?'

'No, his mountain days are over, but he's willing to lend us his sons for the journey. They're good marksmen and expert navigators.'

Chandler turned to the women, hauling large camel-skin panniers, stuffed with flatbread and cheese, out of the tents. Young children danced among them. Then he switched his attention to the men. Three stepped forward and exchanged their cotton garments for thick woollen robes.

'To keep out the cold,' Jabril explained.

'I can already feel it. You know, I don't think I'm fit for this.'

'Stop complaining, Mr Chandler. You should consider yourself privileged – the sheikh is giving up his only sons. Do you understand the risk they are taking?'

'Oh, I get it – more Bedouin hospitality.'

Jabril's eyes flashed with anger. '*A lot more* – the gift of his sons is in honour of my father.'

Chandler thought back to Jabril's testimonial at the souq in Damascus. 'Oh, I forgot, the drought. Are these debts ever paid off?'

Jabril rolled his eyes. 'Is the concept of *duty* really so alien to you?'

For a few moments, Chandler reflected on his two decades in the rates department.

'No, but duty means something different at home. My colleagues were always exchanging favours, of course. It's just that the stakes were never so high.'

'Then you should feel honoured.'

Chandler reached for a cigarette. 'Did I tell you what they called me?'

'No, I don't believe you did,' Jabril sighed.

'The invisible man.'

Jabril licked his lips. 'Why did you put up with it?'

'I've never really thought about it. It was only a job after all.'

'It sounds like you took the easiest route.'

'No Jabril, I took the *safest* route.'

Jabril frowned. 'Haven't you have been chastising *me* for doing just that?'

'Sorry?'

'Do I have to spell it out? Your stories – you've used them to question every choice I've made.'

'That's funny – I thought it was the other way round,' Chandler muttered.

'And attacked me at every opportunity.'

'Look, Jabril – they're just stories.'

'And an excuse to lecture me at every step. *Show pity ... understand ... forgive*, the list goes on.'

'No, there's more to them than—'

'Forget the stories, Mr Chandler, it's *you* I'm interested in. Who really *are* you? You come here looking for cheap thrills but are desperate to emerge the returning hero. Isn't *that* the *real* story?'

Chandler recoiled from the sting of Jabril's unexpected challenge. After leaving the hospital, he had anticipated a change in Jabril's mood. But he had hoped the setback would be temporary. He'd welcomed Jabril's belated condemnation of the executions in Homs and Hama. Drew comfort from his desire for reconciliation with Zafirah. Chandler had even convinced himself that his stories, so full of moral urgency, had somehow played a part in Jabril's conversion. But, like the twists and turns on the road, everything had, once again, changed.

'I suppose you think I'm rather pompous,' Chandler murmured.

Jabril forced a smile and continued to pack.

✧

'Beautiful, isn't it?'

The peregrine falcon hovered above the ridge, then wheeled across the rock face, before disappearing into the scrub. Spellbound, Chandler and Jabril watched the bird of prey.

'There are very few left,' Jabril declared after a few moments.

'An endangered species – like the Bedouin, I suppose.'

'No, Mr Chandler, the Bedouin will be here long after we've gone. And probably the falcons too.'

Chandler observed a lizard perched on a flat stone, its grey speckled skin matching the hue of the rock.

'My grandfather told me there were once leopards and lynx in these mountains, bears and jackals too.'

'And now?

'Nothing so exotic. You would be lucky to find a wild hamster.'

Chandler watched the sheikh's sons sitting, smoking cigarettes, at the edge of the gulley. Like jellyfish suspended in plankton, their narrow legs dangled in the scrub as their robes billowed in the breeze. 'Jabril, what you said earlier – when we were talking about *duty*, I didn't mean to—'

'The government don't trust the tribes,' Jabril broke in. 'They can't understand their need to be independent – never to play by *their* rules.'

'My dig about obligation, you know I didn't—'

'He's eating your food, Mr Chandler.'

'What?'

'The dog, he's got your lunch.'

Chandler watched the dog finish off the last of the flatbread. 'Fuck, I was saving that for later.'

Jabril chuckled, then pushed his knapsack towards Chandler.

'Here, take some of mine. I have plenty.'

'He's not getting away with it,' Chandler yelled, reaching for a stone.

In a flurry of fur, and wagging its tail, the dog continued to bury its jaws into Chandler's rucksack, causing an explosion of empty chocolate wrappers. Chandler raised his arm.

'Leave him,' Jabril pleaded, 'he's just a creature of habit.

He can't help himself. I told you, I have plenty left.'

Chandler let the stone drop. 'You seem to have more patience with the dog than with me.'

'Of course,' Jabril said. 'The animal is just following his instincts – he hasn't a choice.'

'Bloody choices – I thought we were trying to stay off the subject.'

Jabril drew his forefinger to his lips, his eyes still glued to the dog. 'He's lucky, isn't he?'

'Who is?'

'The dog, of course – he has nothing on his mind except where to find his next meal.'

Chandler watched the German Shepherd sniff at a bleached tree stump, before lifting his hind leg to irrigate it with a fine spray.

'Maybe he's searching for a mate,' Jabril said.

'I hope he has better luck than me.'

Jabril pursed his lips in a moment of contemplation. 'Is finding a mate still important to you?'

'I don't know,' Chandler muttered. 'Living alone isn't easy. Sometimes the house is so bloody quiet.'

'Silence can be a blessing.'

'I agree, it gives me time for writing, but you can have too much of it.'

Jabril finished the last of the flatbread. 'You said you have a nephew. Do you still see him?'

'Not much. He's growing up fast and doesn't want his old uncle hanging onto his coat tails.'

Jabril smiled. 'In Syria, we cherish the family. When times are difficult, it's all we have.'

'It was easier when he was younger,' Chandler continued. 'I would call round, take him to the park, then go for a burger.'

'So what happened?'

'My sister thought we were getting too close – told me I was trying to find a substitute for the child I had lost, that the boy felt suffocated. Then the shutters went up.'

'Leaving you to your own devices?'

'Leaving me with *nothing*.'

'Then maybe it *is* time you find a new mate,' Jabil declared.

Chandler pushed his boots closer to the fire. 'I'm not sure. I'm probably too used to following my own routines.'

Jabril clapped his hands. 'So you and the dog have something in common after all.'

Chandler watched the German Shepherd lick the remaining traces of chocolate from its paws. 'I've been wondering, isn't the *Saluki* the hound of choice for the Bedouin? The Royal Dog of Egypt and all that.'

'It is, but this one has an even more distinguished pedigree.'

'How?'

'It's a long story,' said Jabril.

'Then keep it short, and, please no cliffhangers.'

'The last of an illustrious line,' Jabril began. 'His forebears were a male and a female pup. Otto and Helga. They were donated to General Dentz, the Vichi High Commissioner in Damascus – a personal gift from Reich Marshall Goering. The Heinkel they were travelling in came down during a storm near An Nabk. The sheikh's father, he was only a boy then, found them wandering in the sand.'

'And took them in – another example of Bedouin generosity, I suppose.'

'Call it a sense of duty,' replied Jabril.

For a few seconds, Chandler watched the German Shepherd, now dozing at his feet. His breathing was punctuated by whimpers and grunts. 'Let's hope the dog has a sense of duty too.'

✧

The air grew fresher the higher they climbed. Pine, juniper and beech gave way to barren limestone. Wildflower hung tenaciously to the edge of the path. The sheikh's youngest son, Ibrahim, believed in leading from the front. As a natural athlete, he had always impressed his family with his prowess on horse and camel. Among the tribe there was an unspoken consensus that he was the sheikh's favourite. Ibrahim took measured steps along the unforgiving track. He seemed oblivious to the weight of three ancient shotguns slung over his broad shoulders. Amir, the sheikh's middle son, lacked the ambition of his brothers. Nor had he ever been known to express an opinion. He was content to act as quartermaster. Without complaint, Amir carried his brothers' provisions in two large barbaries, yoked across his neck. Habib, the oldest, took up the rear. College educated, he wished he was elsewhere. Every few metres, he stopped to straighten his spectacles, before glancing over his shoulder towards Chandler who, gasping for breath, struggled to keep up with him.

Treading carefully along the escarpment, Ibrahim came to a sudden halt. Without turning, he raised his arm, then began to shout.

'What's he saying?' Chandler called to Jabril.

'He's telling us to keep back – something's not right.'

Chandler watched the German Shepherd race over to Ibrahim. The dog edged forward along the cracked earth. Chandler spotted a length of black flex cushioned under Ibrahim's right foot. The wire snaked a few metres across the path, then joined forces with a grey cylinder, wedged between two rocks. A booster charge was lodged beneath its tailfin. Jabril observed Ibrahim's foot tremble over the pressure plate.

✧

Chandler felt the air sucked out of his lungs well before he heard the blast. Seconds later, clumps of earth began to rain over his head. He was unsure if he should dive for cover, but realised that there was now little point. Clawing grit from his eyes and hair, he could barely make out the figure of Jabril, lying curled up in a tight ball. No sign of Ibrahim. A cloud of dust hung over Amir. He had thrown himself across Habib in the second before detonation. Amir's robe was shredded. His smouldering skin reminded Chandler of mincemeat.

'Be careful, Mr Chandler – there may be more,' Jabril moaned, as he picked himself up and stepped gingerly towards the crater. He kept his eyes glued to the ground. When he was satisfied there were no further booby traps, he beckoned Chandler to move forward.

'What was it?'

'A mortar round ... 60mm I think. I should have seen it.'

'Where's the dog?'

'*Fuck* the dog,' Jabril shot back. 'Help me with Amir – he's losing a lot of blood.'

Uninjured, Habib lay spread-eagled under his brother. Jabril began to tug at his wrists, while Amir emitted a low groan.

✧

Jabril and Chandler set about burying what they could find. Ibrahim had taken the full force of the blast. Chandler chose to ignore his sandal, housing the stump of his foot. Chandler watched Jabril pick tiny shards of hot metal from Amir's scorched back. He wished Dr Sadek was here to assist. The light began to fade and both Jabril and Chandler concluded that Amir would never last the night.

'We'll collect some stones in the morning and bury him next to Ibrahim,' Jabril muttered.

'Is he dead?'

'Not yet, but he only has a few hours.'

'What about Habib? Should we tell him to go back?'

Jabril looked at the young man weeping softly on the rocks. 'I'm not sure.'

'But he's the sheikh's last son,' Chandler pleaded. 'We have to let him return to his father.'

Jabril paused to think. 'No, Mr Chandler, the sheikh made a promise. Habib stays with us.'

'Hasn't his father made enough sacrifices? I don't think I could live with myself if—'

'Listen, this isn't about what the *sheikh* wants. It's a matter of honour. My father saved the sheikh's life. None of his sons would have been born without his intervention. He doesn't have a choice.'

'Abrash ... Raslan ... the sheikh, so many bloody obligations.'

'The *Arab* way, Mr Chandler ... but it's also a question of *survival.* We don't have a hope of reaching Lebanon without Habib to guide us through the mountains.'

'Ever the pragmatist,' Chandler said sourly, lifting his rucksack.

✧

'I need a drink.'

'You'll find water in my bag.'

'No, a *real* drink – where's the Arak?'

'You took the last bottle last night.'

'C'mon, Jabril, you must have one hidden somewhere – my nerves are shot.'

Jabril pulled the woollen blanket across his shoulders and warmed his bare feet on the fire. 'You'll have to feed your addiction with a different spirit.'

'This isn't the time for a lecture on abstinence.'

Jabril ignored the rebuke and tossed a stick into the fire. 'Before their conversion to Islam, the tribes believed in spirits – jinnis. They're still convinced that jinnis are around us – in the mountains ... rivers ... trees.'

Chandler shrugged. 'Oh, it's *spirits* now. And how the hell are they going to help *us*?'

'Some of them are benevolent. But others are devils.' said Jabril. 'Did you notice the women in the camp wearing the amulets? They use them to ward off demons. They even dress the young boys like girls, to ensure that the *evil eye* won't notice them.'

'So how do you know which jinnis are malevolent?'

'You don't,' Jabril shot back.

Chandler licked his lips. 'Talking of help, are you sure you're not holding back on the Arak?'

Jabril sighed, then reached into his bag. He lifted a bundle of dark green leaves, secured with twine.

'What the hell is that?'

Jabril pulled out two of the leaves. He lifted a small knife from his pocket. 'Khat.'

'It's a drug, isn't it?' Chandler asked hesitantly.

'Yes, but it also has *medicinal* qualities, according to our Bedouin friends,' Jabril replied, continuing to hack at the leaves.

Chandler looked over to Habib. The young man was lying face up, staring blankly at the stars.

'Take some, Mr Chandler, but chew it slowly. Then get some sleep.'

# Chapter Thirty

*This world nys but a thurghfare ful of wo.*
*And we been pilgrymes passing to and fro.*
*Deeth is an ende of every worldly score.*
Chaucer

'Hurry up Ari, the doctor is waiting.'

Chandler watched the boy's aunt pull him briskly to the head of the line.

'Please, give him room,' Hanna shouted, 'can't you see the boy is blind?'

Her pleas to make way were drowned by the noise of coaches converging at the entrance of the camp.

Chandler watched the passengers disembark. In their late teens, wearing brightly coloured puffa jackets, and clutching mobile phones, they leaped, one by one, onto the tarmac. Chandler observed one young man study his guidebook, then argue about directions with his companions.

'The Little Red House ... we should visit that first.' His friend looked doubtful.

'I think we are in the wrong place,' she said. 'Perhaps we should check with the driver?'

Chandler turned back to Ari and Hanna as they wove their way through a sullen row of men wearing clogs, and dressed in long striped overcoats. Their heads were lowered and their bodies appeared rigid. None of them noticed Chandler jump the queue.

Chandler spotted Ari standing beside the young physician. Handsome and wearing a dark uniform, the doctor stared directly over Ari's diminutive figure towards the striped overcoats. Beckoning the men to step forward, he sized them up individually, before deciding their future with a wave of his hand. Chandler tried to catch the doctor's eye but remained firmly ignored.

'On behalf of the camp administration, I bid you welcome,' the doctor announced.

Chandler watched Hanna stroke Ari's hair.

'You see my little lion, it really isn't so bad,' she said softly. 'Now, be a good boy and listen to Herr Doktor. Remember what your father said – you must learn to stifle your roar.'

The doctor caught her words, then paused. 'We have a lot to get through. With so many visitors from the city, we must move quickly.'

Hanna nodded enthusiastically.

'Now, a few formalities,' the doctor continued. 'Do you have the admission fee?'

Chandler watched Hanna thrust her hand into the pocket of Ari's shorts. She held up a few green and brown coins while the doctor looked on disdainfully.

'Do you have anything else?' he asked.

Hanna groped the lining of Ari's jacket, before removing a small silver coin. Chandler lunged forward to snatch it, then lost his footing in the mud. Neither Hanna nor the doctor seemed to notice.

'This one is better,' the doctor remarked.

Hanna held Ari's arm tightly as they were led into a wide clearing at the rear of the camp. Chandler followed them. He watched Ari and his aunt negotiate a mountain of suitcases and steep piles of shoes. Women and young children sat quietly sorting through the detritus. Occasionally, a commotion erupted as jewellery and gold were ripped from the stitching of a coat or skirt. Hurrying after Hanna and Ari, Chandler saw a young woman leaning against an easel. He watched her apply liberal smears of yellow paint to a blank canvas. Her audience followed her demonstration intently. Chandler caught the strains of an orchestra beyond the gates. A slow rain began to fall.

'Canada,' the doctor enthused, casting his arm in a wide arc across the site. 'It has enough room to meet everybody's needs. Just look at Camilla. A refugee from Amsterdam. A difficult childhood. Her father abandoned the poor girl in her prime, then tried to impose his values on her when she reached womanhood.'

'Hypocrite!' cried Hanna.

'Be assured madam, Camilla is now free to pursue her passion for art without interference.'

'She needs space. Find her own way,' Hanna chirruped.

Chandler pursued Ari and his aunt along the perimeter of the barracks. The paths, intersecting the huts, now filled with groups of chattering students being hastily corralled by the blockführers. They paused beside the execution wall. A dozen corpses lay on the rough ground.

'It's a tragedy,' the doctor commented. 'If only they had behaved themselves.'

'Do you hear that Ari?' Hanna said.

'We are such a diverse community here,' the doctor continued. 'We must learn to get on with each other. This means we must be willing to compromise.'

'There can be no room for troublemakers,' Hanna intoned.

'Indeed. And that is why we must respond to unrest firmly – to nip it in the bud. Never to be afraid to set an example.'

'Or else the mosaic will crack?'

'Precisely. Now, we need to move on- there is so much more to see.'

Climbing the wooden steps of the camp hospital, Chandler tried to place himself between the doctor and Ari, who, oblivious to his presence, looked right through him. Sidestepping a female orderly, carrying a tray of empty syringes and blood soaked swabs, he entered a suite, marked private, at the end of the corridor. On a white wooden table, in the centre of the room, he contemplated a neat row of eyeballs. They ranged from pale yellow and blue to dull green and piercing violet. Some were tagged with numbers. Others had handwritten notes lying next to them.

'A fine collection, but can it help Ari?' Hanna asked softly.

The doctor smiled. 'We must never give up hope.'

The slow trudge to the metal works, on the edge of the camp, took longer than Chandler expected. He watched coaches, crammed with students, speed by. The workshop, a hive of activity. Chandler observed men, in sandy-coloured fatigues, and wearing protective glasses, bustle around a forest of angle grinders and lathes. The machines belched smoke and issued wide showers of sparks.

'The trick is to keep them busy,' said the doctor.

'Yes, leave them no time to engage in sabotage,' Hanna added.

Chandler watched the visitors make their way towards a young man crouching in the corner of the workshop. He was assembling a mortar. A jumble of steel tubes, silver tailfins and loose wire sat next to him.

'The Palestinian is our best operative,' the doctor boasted. 'Ahmed was nothing more than a grease monkey until he arrived at the camp. Now, he is our finest rocket engineer – our best hope of turning back the Bolsheviks.'

'Did you hear that, Ari?' Hanna gasped. 'Your father could have done with men like that in the tannery.'

Chandler struggled to keep up as they retraced their steps back into the camp. A fine dust hung in the air. He found it hard to breathe.

The ante-chamber of the crematorium was bursting with discarded shoes, mingled with bundles of clothing. At the far end, he spotted a row of artificial limbs. Men, blackened with soot and wearing only shorts, sweated over trolleys. Chandler watched the doctor place himself between Ari and his aunt, then kneel down to speak to the boy, their faces inches apart. He cupped Ari's chin in his smooth hand.

'My little lion, too often we delude ourselves that life is full of choices,' he whispered. 'But I think you already understand that we must go with the flow and swim with the tide.'

'We have to learn to fit in,' Hanna said.

Chandler felt his arms and legs stiffen. He opened his mouth to speak, but no words came out. He struggled to get Ari's attention, but remained unseen.

'The Gypsy children find my philosophy difficult to understand,' the doctor went on. 'They complain that they see too little of Uncle Pepi, and resort to mischief when I am not present to guide them. But every time they misbehave, I give them a second chance. What about you, Ari? Are you willing to gamble on my generosity?'

Chandler watched Ari dig into his knapsack, then produce a thick slice of baklava. The doctor clapped his hands rapturously. 'Look at that – little Ari sees better than any of us! The boy may be blind, but he has an eye for the main chance.'

Lifting the silver Roman coin from the pocket of his tunic, the doctor held it firmly between his thumb and forefinger. Chandler watched Augustus spiral into the air. He tried to shout a warning but Ari remained deaf to his screams. He felt the air rushing from his lungs and a crushing weight on his chest.

✧

Blinking rapidly in the darkness and gasping for breath, Chandler pulled tightly at the covers. Locked under the giant paws of the German Shepherd, the blanket refused to budge.

# Chapter Thirty-One

*He that dies pays all debts.*
Shakespeare

With his feet slipping on the scree, Habib led his followers up the foothills. Scrambling over boulders and wet limestone, they gathered up on the first crest at noon, before descending, one slope after another, into a shallow ravine. An unassuming drizzle turned swiftly into a thunderstorm, followed by intense lightning. The party were forced into a hasty bivouac. As blue skies were restored, Habib led them along paths blocked with the debris from rock falls. Under his instruction, Jabril and Chandler constructed improbable fords over streams with ambitions to become rivers. With the German Shepherd padding cautiously ahead of them, the group, once again, pushed upwards. Clasping each other for support, they traversed a narrow ridge, covered with a fine dusting of snow.

'Jabril, these boots are too small, I've a dozen blisters about to burst.'

'Your boots are the least of our problems.'

'I thought you said we were going *through* the mountains, not bloody over them.'

'I wouldn't call these mountains, Mr Chandler. They are more like *Munros*. You have them in Scotland. There's an important distinction.'

'One damn climb after another.'

Jabril grinned. 'You must feel like the Grand Old Duke of—'

'Leave it out, Jabril.'

'And when they were up, they were—'

'I told you – that's enough ... how much further?'

'As far as it takes.'

'Not the answer I want to hear.'

Jabril called Habib to stop. The guide lifted the bags from his shoulders.

'Okay, a ten minute rest break ... but no more. We've a long way to go.'

'Marvellous, base camp one, and still a fucking mountain to climb,' Chandler grunted.

'Perhaps you should have declined the khat last night.'

'You're right – why didn't you warn me?'

'About the drug?'

'No, about the *dreams*.'

Jabril shrugged. 'It must have been all our talk of jinnis and demons. They have a habit of coming back to bite you.'

'The jinnis didn't feature, Jabril. It was all the *other* stuff.'

'What stuff?'

'Stuff from my stories – mixed in with things that have happened since we got here. I can't make sense of it.'

'Dreams are never meaningless, Mr Chandler. We should *listen* to them. It's an old Arab tradition.'

'I told you, it was a jumble.'

'Probably, but you must remember *something*?'

Chandler paused. 'Shit happening ... mainly to the Jewish kid.'

'Anything else?'

'Being unable to help him, I suppose.'

Jabril frowned. 'It sounds demonic – maybe we shouldn't discuss it.'

'C'mon Jabril, you can't stop now.'

'Mr Chandler, look at Habib. His name was given to the sheikh in a dream. Good dreams usually bring glad tidings. Sadly, yours isn't one of them.'

'It feels like the jinni has been fucking with my head.'

'Quite possibly – a case of the devil toying with the sleeper. The more you think about it, the worse it gets.'

'Best to forget about it then?'

Jabril chuckled. 'If you were to ask my neighbours, they would tell you to spit three times and pray.'

Chandler eased off his boots, then massaged the raw skin on his heels. His blisters began to weep.

'There is *another* type of dream, however.'

'Go on,' sighed Chandler.

'The type that arises from within – brought on by our daily worries.'

'No shortage of those, Jabril.'

'Maybe we should leave the last word to Scheherazade.'

'I wondered when *she'd* come up,' Chandler snorted.

'Why not? Her stories are—'

'Childish and vulgar – isn't that what you said?'

'I also told you not to take them at face value.'

'I stand corrected.'

'Her tale about the poor man of Baghdad. Did you read it?'

'No, but I'll put it to the top of my list.'

'He leaves his wife and home to seek a hidden treasure, simply on the command of a dream.'

For a few moments, Chandler reflected upon his impulsive foray into Syria – searching for a reputational treasure that remained as elusive as ever. 'A fool then,' he muttered.

'Perhaps, but wise enough to take fresh instructions.'

'Who from?'

'From another man's dream, of course. Telling him to return home.'

Chandler rolled his eyes. 'Okay, so how does it end?'

Jabril raised his hand dismissively. 'I'll leave it to Scheherazade to fill you in on the outcome. It's time we moved on.'

'You know, between *A Thousand and One Nights* and my night terrors, I think I've had my fill of symbolism. Now, throw me a cigarette.'

✧

'It's still hot – they can't be far off,' Jabril said, digging his boot into the dying embers.

'Who's been here?' asked Chandler.

'It's difficult to tell. From the shoe imprints, I'd say they are military, perhaps scouts sent after us from Homs.'

'Or the Free Syrian Army?'

'That's a possibility. Then again, it could be the mukhabarat.'

Chandler watched Habib slide his hunting rifle out of its camel-skin sheath. 'What about Youssef? Could he have overtaken us – did *he* set the booby trap?'

'That's also possible, Mr Chandler. He has the expertise. What is certain, is that whoever it is, they can't be far off. We should keep moving.'

Chandler pulled up the hood of his cagoule and watched the German Shepherd paw briskly into the snow. Habib walked slowly towards the animal, then dropped to one knee. He unearthed a dark coloured lozenge. Sniffing the stiff turd for a few seconds, he snapped it in two, like a twig. Jabril edged towards him and, after a minute's examination and a quiet exchange of words, he nodded enthusiastically.

'Habib says the shit is not the product of army rations. It's too rich. It's also recent. Whoever made this has been dining expensively ... probably in Damascus.'

'*Youssef?*'

'That would be my guess.'

'Looks like extra rations for Sherlock,' Chandler said, patting the dog's head and lifting a lump of cheese from his pocket.

'If it *is* Youssef, he won't be alone. His men will be well armed.'

'But all we have are a couple of rifles.'

Jabril patted his jacket. 'Don't forget the Webley. I have five rounds left.'

'Fine. So if Youssef turns up with his cronies, armed to the teeth, we have a couple of antique shotguns and an old pistol to defend ourselves.'

'You're forgetting, Mr Chandler, Habib is a fine marksman.'

'He had better be.'

✧

They reached an open clearing, flanked on one side by a large rock face. It reminded Chandler of the Bedouin encampment. Dusting the snow off his shoulders, he watched a thick cloud scudding past, then peered towards a shimmering peak on the horizon.

At the far edge of the clearing Habib set down his rifle and rolled his shoulders. He sat with his back to Chandler. Habib lifted a notepad from a leather pouch secured to his belt. Unseen, Chandler took a few steps towards him. He watched the young man flip open the pad. Precise line drawings, featuring a variety of mountain goats, populated the pages. They were accompanied by handwritten commentaries. Probably constructed by the young man himself, he guessed. Chandler had, from the start, recognised that Habib was different from his brothers. Jabril had told him as much. As if retelling a tale from Arabian Nights, Jabril had spoken about Habib's obsession to break free from the narrow constraints of Bedouin existence. And of his attempt to cut the family's umbilical cord. When, despite his father's doubts, he had seized upon a government bursary promoting social inclusion for nomadic tribes. The money had allowed Habib to finally jump ship, then study zoology in Homs. He had felt blessed. No surprise, Jabril informed Chandler, that the young man had bitterly resented his father's insistence to return home, barely six months into his course – the *Koran* being the only text required to keep body and soul together, according to the sheikh.

✧

'Mount Herman,' Jabril announced, raising his arm. 'At its highest point, it's two and a half thousand metres. From the summit, it offers fine views of the Bekaa Valley. Turn the other way, and you'll see all the way across the eastern plateau to Damascus.'

'Jabril, if you think I'm going to climb—'

'Shut up!'

'What?'

'I said *shut up*.'

Chandler watched Jabril jerk his head skywards. For a moment, he wondered whether he had spotted another falcon.

'We need to take cover, I think it's a drone.'

'But I can't see anything.'

'Use your bloody eyes – there, beneath the cloud.'

Chandler narrowed his focus. Hovering below the cumulus, he made out the rectangular outline of a silver object coming closer into view. It resembled something between a plane and a glider. It hung over them inquisitively.

'Is it American?'

'No, it's made by our friends in Iran. Used for reconnaissance. But this could be armed. The Fourth Division are the only ones with access to them.'

'Have they spotted us?'

'Without a doubt,' Jabril replied, waving furiously at Habib.

The first missile crashed into a bank of snow, where it failed to explode. The second had more success, erupting beneath overhanging rocks to their left. Chandler watched an enormous boulder slip its mooring and begin its descent. With ground breaking speed, the rock hurtled towards Jabril. With yards to spare, it careered to the right, then regained its course and slammed into Habib's chest.

✧

'Take his gun,' Jabril ordered.

Chandler peered under the boulder. He saw Habib's fingers twitching. Jabril's eyes remained glued to the skyline. Chandler saw no sign of the drone or the dog.

'Jabril, what about—'

'I don't want to hear about the fucking dog!' Jabril yelled.

For a moment, Chandler wondered whether he should rebuke Jabril over his insistence that the Bedouin meet their obligations ... point out that the sheikh's last son had finally paid off his family's debt, even as Habib lay shaking in his death throes.

'*We're screwed*,' Jabril announced, tossing over the rifle.

Chandler ran his fingers over the weapon. Apart from a few scorch marks, running along its stock, the rifle appeared intact. He wondered whether he should hold onto it, then told himself that the closest he had come to firing a gun had been to spectacularly miss his target at the funfair, while his embarrassed nephew looked on.

'Without Habib to guide us, we have no chance of reaching Lebanon,' Jabril said.

'Aren't we nearly there?'

'Listen, Mr Chandler, the border is a good ten miles away. You are barely able to walk and Youssef is still on our tail. I'm sorry, I think we have finally run out of luck.'

# Chapter Thirty-Two

*Common people do not pray; they only beg.*
G.B. Shaw

'Robert, have you any idea how late it is?'

'Sorry, I wasn't thinking. Look, I need to talk.'

'Where are you?'

'Syria.'

'Oh yes, the er ... holiday.'

'You've got to help me.'

'What's up?'

'I haven't got time to explain – all I can say is that I'm in a bit of a predicament.'

'Really? Sounds like the start of a good story.'

'Cut the crap, this is *serious*.'

'What have you been doing – taking photographs where you shouldn't?'

'You could say that, but not photos. I made a voice recording ... it's on my mobile.'

'I don't understand, is that why you're in trouble?'

'No, the recording is the only way I can get *out* of trouble. I'm going to send it to you.'

'I've lost you Robert – what has any of this got to do with me?'

'I can't go into detail now. Let's just say it puts the government in an embarrassing position.'

'Aren't you letting your imagination get the better of you?'

'Listen, I recorded a senior official from our embassy in Damascus. He was trying to cut a deal to keep me quiet about rebels executing unarmed prisoners in Hama.'

'Is that so? Could be good fodder for my next piece. Can I use it?'

'You're not taking this seriously. I want you to send the recording to the Foreign Office – tell them it will be distributed to every news editor in the country unless they agree to my terms.'

'Robert, I think you're getting a little beyond yourself. What makes you think they're going to take any notice of small fry like you?'

'That's just it, I don't think they see me as small fry. I've already hacked off the embassy in Damascus, and the local security services are after my blood.'

'Where are you now?'

'I'm with my driver in the mountains, near the Lebanese border. His name's Jabril Mansour. Have you got that?'

'Can't *he* help you?'

'No, he's in trouble too.'

'Sounds complicated.'

'Just tell the Minister that he has to apply some pressure ... maybe pull a few strings with the Americans.'

'Robert, I think you're asking me to punch above my weight. The closest I've been to a politician is to write to my MP about the hunting ban.'

'Fine – get on to *him* too.'

'What makes you think they're going to listen?'

'They will, once they've talked to General Abrash.'

'Who the hell is he?'

'They'll know who he is.'

'Is that it?'

'No, Jabril also has a daughter. She needs to get out too. There can be no deal unless they agree to that.'

'Robert, this is a pretty big ask. You know I'm not one for sticking my head above the parapet.'

'Really? Is that why you've been telling the writers group to take more of a *moral* stance? It's time you put your money where your mouth is.'

'No, I'm sorry, you're expecting too much. I need time to think this through.'

'*Time*? That's a luxury I don't have. Just do what I'm bloody asking and get back to me. I'll keep my mobile on.'

'Robert, do you remember me telling you how to demonstrate more narrative tension?'

'Yes.'

'Well, you *have* now.'

# Chapter Thirty-Three

*Alack, the night comes on, and the bleak winds.*
Shakespeare

'Where have you been?'

'Call of nature.'

'Wake me if you decide to go wandering again, Mr Chandler.'

'Sorry, what time is it?'

'It's past midnight, you should get some sleep.'

'How can I with Youssef looking down on us.'

'Youssef will be as tired as we are. Anyway, he's never been much of a night fighter.'

'Don't tell me – he needs daylight to see the whites of his victims' eyes.'

'This isn't the time for jokes. Get some rest.'

Chandler pulled his knees to his chest. Wearing a three day stubble, he raised a cigarette to his cracked lips.

'Shouldn't you get in touch with Nadia, find out about Zafirah and the baby?'

'I told you, it's no time for jokes.'

'I don't understand.'

Jabril shook his head. 'If *you* had a wife, you wouldn't be asking me to contact mine.'

'Sorry, I didn't mean—'

'Mr Chandler, what do you suggest I say? That I've only a few hours to live, that she can look forward to the rest of her life as a widow?'

Chandler sat quietly in the darkness. Looking skywards, he watched the tail of a shooting star fizzing across Ursa Major. 'You know, Jabril, that's all the more reason to ring her.'

# Chapter Thirty-Four

*They who are in the highest places and have the most power, have the least liberty because they are most observed.*
John Tillotson

'Mr President, I have the Prime Minister on the line.'

'This early? Okay, put him through.'

'Prime Minister, you're through to Washington.'

'Mr President?'

'There's no need for formalities – what's the problem?'

'Sorry, I know it's early.'

'It's fine, but you've woken the dog.'

'How is the new mutt? I hear he's creating havoc in the Oval Office.'

'Damn right, the kids keep letting him in. Anyway, that's not why you rang, is it?'

'No, I wish it was. Listen, we have a problem in Syria.'

'Are you telling me something new?'

'No, this is more of a *local* difficulty.'

'Go on.'

'One of our nationals smuggled himself into Hama ... you know, where the conscripts were massacred. Now he's gone AWOL. We're worried he's going to blow the lid on our operations in the city.'

'Is that it?'

'No, it's more complicated. He's threatening to distribute a voice recording of one of our diplomats trying to buy him off, then tell the press that the government is in cahoots with the rebels executing prisoners in the city.'

'Is that a problem?'

'Not for me personally, but it could be for our partners in the Coalition. You know how steamed up they get about human rights.'

'Who is this guy?'

'His name is Robert Chandler – he's some kind of writer. His Syrian driver is with him. They seem to have become a team.'

'Where are they now?'

'Somewhere in the mountains between Syria and Lebanon.'

'What do you expect *us* to do about it?'

'Take him out.'

'What do you mean, kill him?'

'No, send your people in – arrange a rescue mission. If you can get him as far as Beirut, we can deal with him face to face.'

'I'm not sure about this. Wouldn't it be wise to leave this

one to the Arab League – a little quiet diplomacy can go a long way.'

'No, we don't have time. The Syrian security services have them cornered. We've a few hours at most.'

'But we don't have anyone on the ground.'

'What about the Israelis?'

'Are you kidding? If we get *them* to mount a cross-border mission, we'll have the Russians shouting down our necks at the Security Council.'

'Okay, so use the navy seals, it worked with Bin Laden, didn't it?'

'Yeah, and we're still getting flack for that. Anyway, the nearest guys we have with that kind of firepower are holed up in Baghdad.'

'You know, there's a wider dimension to this.'

'How?'

'We had a call from a General Abrash. He commands the Third Armoured Division in Homs. He's on our side, but he's threatening to withdraw support for the rebels in Hama if we don't agree to Chandler's terms.'

'Is he the real deal?'

'I think so. Our embassy in Damascus says he's a major player.'

'Why does the general give a damn about Chandler ... are they connected?'

'No, it's more about the *driver* – well, his father to be precise. The general told us something about having to honour an old debt.'

'If Abrash is such a big shot, can't he sort it out himself?'

'It's not that simple, there's something else.'

'Shoot.'

'We got a message from the First Lady.'

'Are you serious? I thought she was in Florida.'

'I mean the *Syrian* First Lady. She has a soft spot for the literati, especially writers from Britain. She met quite a few when she lived in London and doesn't want to queer the pitch if she has to return to Britain in a hurry.'

'Is there much chance of that?'

'There is if the whole shooting match goes belly up. She's already put out some feelers.'

'What's in it for us?'

'Well, she has the ear of her husband. You know, she might be able to apply a woman's touch. Get the President to back off.'

'I'm not convinced. The whole region is one hell of a tinderbox. Look, you said yourself, this is a *local* difficulty. You need to find a *local* solution.'

# Chapter Thirty-Five

*Let us, then, be up and doing,*
*with a heart for any fate.*
Longfellow

Jabril had a choice to make. An important one. He had to decide whether Chandler could be trusted with an ancient breach-loading rifle or whether to allow the writer, with an aversion to guns, to hold off Youssef's hordes with a vintage Webley. He spent the first hour after dawn cleaning the Martini-Henry. Weighing in at nine pounds, the rifle felt like a dead weight in his hands. The sheikh had assured him that the antique was capable of hitting a man at four hundred yards, but would be deadlier at closer range. He had also heard that, in hot climates, the weapon was prone to seizing up. Perhaps the cold mountain air would improve its performance, he thought. Inserting a brass cartridge into the firing chamber, Jabril wondered whether

Chandler's slack shoulders would cope with the rifle's heavy recoil. Remembering Chandler's account of his lacklustre performance with his nephew at the shooting range, Jabril's mind was made up.

✧

Chandler emerged from a broken sleep. He sat up and rubbed his eyes. Then, for a few minutes, he caressed the soles of his blistered feet, before easing them gently into his boots. Jabril watched Chandler toss the last crumbs of cheese towards the German Shepherd, then passed him the revolver.

'You have *five rounds*, so make each one count. Oh, and save the last bullet for yourself.'

Chandler grimaced. 'Wonderful, a prehistoric pistol and a clapped-out shotgun against Youssef's Kalashnikovs. I think we have them outgunned.'

Jabril forced a smile and dropped the spare cartridges into a small pouch fastened to his belt. '*Rudyard Kipling* – are you familiar with his work?'

'Jabril, this really isn't the time.'

'His poem, *Fuzzy Wuzzy*, is one of the earliest literary references to the Martini-Henry. Do you want to hear it?'

'No, but I've a sinking feeling you're about to give me a rendition.'

Jabril rose to his feet and assumed the position of master orator.

*'Then 'ere's to you, Fuzzy Wuzzy, an' the missis an' the kid.*
*Our orders was to break you, an' of course we went an' did.*

*We sloshed you with Martinis, an' it wasn't 'ardly fair;*
*But for all the odds agin' you, Fuzzy Wuzzy, you broke the square.'*

Chandler tucked the Webley into his rucksack. 'Is that supposed to make me feel better?'

'Of course,' Jabril shot back. 'For all the British army's superiority, a force of poorly equipped Sudanese warriors proved victorious.'

'No, Jabril, I think you'll find it was force of numbers that did the trick.'

Jabril ran his fingers along the Martini-Henry. 'Perhaps, but it wasn't just that. What counted most was their willingness to accept martyrdom. Think about it.'

✧

Chandler and Jabril spent the next hour in silence. Overhead, wispy clouds gave way to blue skies. The sun rose and the thin layer of snow began to melt. The German Shepherd sniffed under rocks for signs of life, while Jabril maintained his gaze on the ridge, running along the top of the rock face. Chandler took a tally of secure firing positions at the edge of the clearing.

'I think I owe you an apology,' Chandler said.

Jabril raised his eyebrows. 'What on earth for?'

'For being such a pompous ass.'

'Aren't you being a little hard on yourself?'

'Not hard enough. I've spent the last few days spouting nonsense about making the right choice, when I'm the first to run away from tough decisions. You must think I'm a bit of a fraud.'

'Mr Chandler, I haven't seen you run away too often.'

'No, Jabril, I'm not talking about now ... I mean *before* we met.'

'How?'

'Remember when I told you about my second wife ... losing the baby, things becoming impossible?'

'Yes.'

'Well, there was more to it than that.'

Jabril rubbed his hands briskly. 'Maybe this isn't the best time for confessions.'

'After she miscarried, I found it impossible to be with her,' Chandler went on. 'Her moods, the bloody silences, never wanting to get intimate.'

'It's difficult to understand what goes on in a woman's mind,' Jabril said softly. 'Take Nadia, I remember when—'

'That's exactly it, but I never really tried. I thought we should just, you know, *move on*. Maybe try again when things settled.'

'And did you?' Jabril asked.

'Did I what?'

'Try again.'

'No, all I could do was to spend every waking minute checking her supply of tablets – in case she, you know ... '

Jabril raised his hand.

'The funny thing is ... when the break finally came, it wasn't mutual – I just walked out on her, as if the baby ... *our* baby, had never existed.'

'And that was the end of things between you, I suppose.'

'Pretty well. But guess what? She remarried two years later. I didn't mind that so much, but her new man came fully equipped with a son of his own from a previous marriage. Ironic, isn't it?'

'Have you met him?'

'Her husband?'

'No, his son.'

'Not a chance – I totally blanked her and the kid.'

Jabril nodded. 'I would have done the same.'

Chandler hesitated. 'I don't think you're being totally honest.'

'What are you saying?'

'I'm saying *you've* been man enough to put a pointless feud behind you.'

'Zafirah?'

'Yes.'

'There's an important difference, Mr Chandler – she is my flesh and blood.'

Chandler watched the German Shepherd sink on its haunches, then lick its paws.

'It's strange.' Jabril sighed, 'a week ago I didn't care if Zafirah was alive or dead, and believed that all Theo deserved was a bullet to the head.'

'So you've moved on – you've accepted her right to make a new life for herself.'

Jabril bit his lip. 'I wish I had told her that in the hospital – I wanted to but ... '

'You went to see her – I think that speaks for itself.'

'I'm not sure I had much choice. Think back to your story – Camilla's father. At the end of the day, he didn't have a choice either.'

Chandler took a deep breath. The cold mountain air stung his nostrils. 'You know, I've never had much difficulty telling *other* people what to do through my bloody stories. But when it comes to the crunch ... when I have to take a decision that really counts, I always bottle it.'

Jabril lifted the rifle and blew a layer of dust from the breach. 'You're no better or worse than the rest of us. Remember Homs? You asked me to intervene when the men were executed. I did nothing. In the hospital, I watched my grandson have his throat cut and failed to protect him.'

'Nobody is going to judge you for that.'

Jabril shrugged. 'They might try, but it would make no difference.'

'How do you work that out?'

Jabril set down the rifle. He scanned the ridge. 'Remember Beirut? You joked about being fluent in Arabic by the time you returned.'

'Not much prospect of that now,' muttered Chandler.

'Probably not ... but have you learned a *single word*?'

'No, I don't think so.'

'Think hard, Mr Chandler ... a *single word?*'

'*Insha' Allah*?'

'*Good,* now tell me what it means.'

'I think it translates as *God willing,* doesn't it?'

'*Excellent,* you're not such a poor student after all.'

'I've a good teacher.'

'We have another expression that's worth remembering ... *if it is your day, it is your day*'.

'Trust in fate, you mean.'

'Exactly. In Arabic, we say *qismah* – the English call it kismet.'

'What's your point, Jabril?'

'My point is that we can both fulfil our destiny without the need to justify our every action.'

'But, surely, we have to accept *some* personal responsibility.'

''That's very true, Mr Chandler – providing you remember that Allah is the final arbiter for all our decisions. Now, isn't it time you cleaned your gun?'

✧

A ricochet from the first shot severed the front leg of the German Shepherd below the knee. The second round, fired from the ridge, struck the dog squarely between the eyes. Chandler dropped his rucksack, then sprinted across the clearing. He flung himself behind a boulder. Breathless, he waited. From the security of the rock, he glanced behind for any sign of Jabril. If Jabril had opted to remain in the open he would have no chance, Chandler reckoned. But the firing had ceased, and he thought it likely that Jabril had either sought the protection of the gorge, or had decided to head for the rock face below the ridge. He heard a single shot from behind and guessed that Jabril had chosen the former. Squinting under the glare of the sun, Chandler located his rucksack. It lay on its side in the middle of the clearing. He spotted the muzzle of the Webley protruding from the open flap. He remembered what Jabril had told him. *Save the last bullet for yourself.*

Chandler forced himself to his feet and raced across the open ground. He hoped Jabril might give him covering fire, then reminded himself that the Martini-Henry could muster no more than twelve rounds a minute. Reaching the bag, he turned on his heel for the return run. A volley of gunfire from the ridge kicked up tufts of earth around his feet. Chandler dropped to his knees. He looked up and watched a figure, clad in khaki and wearing a baseball cap, slip a fresh magazine into his AK-47. He waited for him to administer the coup de grace, before a shot from Jabril sent the gunman toppling over the edge. His companions appeared to stall. A freeze frame moment that allowed Chandler to complete his dash to the boulder.

'Mr Chandler – they're leaving the ridge,' yelled Jabril. Chandler slowly raised his head above the boulder and watched three figures, with rifles slung across their shoulders, shimmy down ropes. A round from Jabril's Martini dropped the first. Chandler heard a sharp crack as the man's skull made contact with hard limestone at the foot of the rockface. His two companions paused, unsure whether to haul themselves back up, or continue their descent. Their indecision proved costly as a further two rounds from Jabril sent them hurtling to oblivion.

Chandler heard shouting from the ridge.

'Mr Chandler, my name is Youssef. I have no argument with you. Please, throw down your gun, stand up, raise your arms.'

Chandler was unnerved by Youssef's conciliatory tone. He lay motionless for a few moments. He needed time to think.

'Mr Chandler, I have promised your embassy that your safety is guaranteed. Please, this is my *only* offer.'

Chandler pulled his mobile from his pocket. Still no word from Sharkey. For a few seconds, he considered Youssef's assurances. For all Youssef's misdeeds, Chandler had no evidence that *he* had ever been his main target. He toyed with the notion that *Jabril* had perhaps been the author of his own misfortune. He had, after all, deserted his post in Hama and had been foolhardy enough to take flight to Damascus. Then murdered Youssef's nephew for sport.

Seizing the revolver from his rucksack, Chandler raised the weapon a few inches above the rock. Keeping his head firmly down, he let off four rounds, in quick succession, in the direction of the ridge. Chandler heard Youssef's men laughing above him. He curled into a ball as a burst of machine gun fire peppered his sanctuary. The muscles in his chest tightened and his breathing grew more rapid. Chandler loosened his grip on the Webley. With one hand holding the barrel, he lifted the pistol above his head and tossed it clear of the boulder.

From his kneeling position, at the top of the gorge, Jabril flung down his rifle. A scattering of spent cartridges lay at his feet. He was unsure whether the Martini-Henry had given up the ghost through overheating, or whether the firing mechanism had decided to jam. Either way, he knew the game was up.

Standing shoulder to shoulder, Jabril and Chandler looked up towards the ridge. They watched Youssef take centre-stage among his men, then draw a large hunting knife from a sheath hanging from his fatigues.

A thousand feet above them, a peregrine falcon engaged in a display of loops, spirals and pirouettes. Dropping steeply towards the plateau, the mature female caught the glint from Youssef's blade, before spotting three corpses lying at the foot of the rockface. She had never tasted human flesh. But denied her customary fare of hamsters and small reptiles, now lying low in the scrub, her menu was about to change. Sensing that the body count was going to rise, all she had to do was wait.

'You should have hung on to the revolver,' Jabril said.

'I'm sorry, I was unsure, I've let you down.'

'Try to remain still, it will be over soon.'

'Jabril ... please.'

'Kismet, Mr Chandler, kismet.'

# Chapter Thirty-Six

*Let's roll.*

Todd Beamer,
United Airlines Flight 93

Youssef didn't know whether to laugh or cry. The unexpected sound of rotor blades, and the approach of an attack helicopter, with Syrian army markings, promised a swift end for Jabril. Watching the hunter-killer from his vantage point, he savoured the expression on Jabril's face. It spoke a mixture of surprise and consternation. With four anti-tank missiles mounted on stubs behind the cockpit, and a rear gunner ready to open up with a general purpose machine gun, Youssef reckoned that Jabril's fate would be decided in seconds.

At the same time, he felt disappointed. He had relished the opportunity to finish Jabril off himself. *Slowly*. Time and again, Youssef had, in his mind, run through the scene.

To draw the blade of his hunting knife across his cousin's smooth shaven throat. To give Jabril's English companion a chance to bear witness to Syrian rough justice. The sudden arrival of the helicopter heralded a rude upset to Youssef's plans – just as the party had begun to get going.

✧

'What's happening?' Chandler shouted, above the roar of the engine.

Jabril didn't answer. He kept his eyes fixed on the Gazelle. He watched it discharge a small canister. In seconds, the hovering beast was enveloped in a grey smog. Jabril tried to work out why it required a defensive smokescreen when it was obvious that he and Chandler had abandoned their weapons. It didn't make sense.

Youssef was asking himself the same question. He was at a loss to understand why the rear gunner, still visible among the smoke, now had *him* in his sights. A burst of machine gun fire, spewing up a cloud of limestone at the edge of the ridge, confused him further. A poor marksman, he reckoned.

As the fog began to clear, Jabril focused on the split-screen fronting the cockpit. He didn't recognise the pilot, whose head was obscured by a scarf clinging to his face in the slipstream. But he had no problem identifying his passenger. Crowned with a green star-spangled beret, and wearing a heavy moustache, he carried a general's rank.

Youssef had been equally observant. As soon as he spotted the dark patch covering the passenger's left eye, his suspicions were confirmed. *Abrash.* A second burst of gunfire sent Youssef's men diving for cover.

'Looks like old Sharkey has come up trumps,' Chandler proclaimed.

'Sharkey? What the hell has *he* got to do with this?' Jabril shouted, through the din of rotor blades.

'He finally did what he was told,' declared Chandler, beaming.

Frustrated at being denied a balcony seat to watch the turkey shoot, Jabril and Chandler could only listen to the symphony of gunfire and screams. Youssef watched his men crawl like lemmings towards the edge of the ridge. They had nowhere else to run. Peering down at the broken bodies, lying at the foot of the rockface, none of them fancied their chances as jumpers. A final burst of machine gun fire drew a few desultory shots from Youssef's Makarov. Then silence.

✧

Chandler ducked under the downdraft as the Gazelle came to rest in the centre of the clearing. He saw the pilot swivel in his seat and give the thumbs up to the gunner. Jabril sprinted towards the open door, now framing the portly figure of the general. Abrash straightened his beret and stepped out.

For a few seconds, Jabril and Abrash stood motionless, neither wishing to be the first to speak. Then they fell into a warm embrace.

'Mr Chandler, the general apologises for his late arrival. Sadly, he has to leave soon – he has unfinished business in Homs. Oh, and he hopes the rest of your journey proves less eventful,' Jabril declared, with a wide smile. 'The general trusts that his next meeting with you will be in more convivial surroundings – London, perhaps.'

'Is Youssef dead?' Chandler begged.

Jabril glanced up towards the ridge. The sky had turned silver and snow began to fall. 'God willing. Now, it looks like we have a clear run to the border. It's just a few miles on foot. When we reach Baalbek, I have friends who will take us to Beirut.'

'I hope it's that simple,' Chandler grunted. 'My feet are killing me ... and I haven't the stomach for another cliffhanger.'

# Chapter Thirty-Seven

*What will it profit a man if he gains the whole world, but loses his soul.*
Mathew 16:26

'Baalbek – City of the Sun – named after Baal, the god of fertility. What do you think?'

'Well, it beats anything I've seen in Syria.'

With his back against a lump of granite, in a shady corner of the hexagonal court, Chandler absorbed the vista. On one side, the Temple of Jupiter, its six columns standing seventy feet, rudely dissected the skyline. Behind him, sat the Temple of Bacchus. Decorated with intricate carvings of lions and bulls, honouring the victories of Mars, Diana and Vulcan, the immense structure dwarfed anything he had witnessed on his travels. It was all too much.

'Remember, Baalbek *was* once part of Syria, the premier city in the Roman empire,' Jabril boasted. 'Everything built with the express purpose of demonstrating the might of the emperor.'

'Does that include Augustus?'

'Of course, the Great Court was completed under his reign.'

Chandler reached into his pocket and lifted the silver coin. Glinting in the sunlight, Augustus appeared to be smiling.

'I wish I could manage a hike through the ruins, Jabril, but my feet are in bits.'

'That's not a problem. Anyway, I'm not sure that you'd be safe on your own.'

'Oh, I was forgetting, this is *Hezbollah* country, isn't it?'

'It's not Hezbollah I'm worried about,' Jabril replied drily. 'Syrian influence is still strong here. It wasn't long ago that Baalbek hosted their army headquarters.'

'You're making me nervous, Jabril. I thought we'd escaped all that.'

'I don't think escape is the correct term. It would be more accurate to say that we've found *temporary respite*.'

Chandler pulled up his legs. His mood began to darken. After a sleepy intermission at the Hotel Jupiter, following their arrival at the border, he again felt vulnerable. 'If the Syrians have agents in Baalbek, shouldn't we leave now? There must be taxis to Beirut.'

'No, that would draw too much attention. Youssef may be gone, but others will be watching us. In any case, I've arranged a small reception.'

'A full honour guard of balaclaved Hezbollah militants, I suppose.'

'Nothing quite so formal. The Commander will be on his own, but don't worry, he's not armed – he doesn't need to be.'

Chandler kicked his cigarette butt under a shard of granite. 'You're full of surprises.'

Wiping the sweat from his forehead, Chandler watched a battered Toyota kick up dust as it traversed Rue Abdel Halim Hajjar. It made its way towards the entrance of the ruins. Midday, and the sun unforgiving.

'He's taking a big gamble meeting you,' Jabril continued.

'Who is?'

'Farik Najibullah. His father has a cabinet seat in the national unity government. His older brother runs Hezbollah's social assistance programme in Sidon.'

'So what makes *him* so important?'

'He's in charge of Hezbollah's military branch, between here and Zahle.'

Chandler raised his eyebrows. 'A terrorist then.'

'No, Mr Chandler, *a resistance fighter*. He earned his stripes in the war with Israel. He personally took out two of their Merkavas with anti-tank missiles. Since then, he's been placed in charge of imports.'

'Importing what?'

'Katyushas and Scuds, mostly from Syria. Some of the rockets can reach as far as Haifa, even Tel Aviv.'

'Jabril, if Hezbollah have such a cosy relationship with Syria, what the hell are they doing meeting us?'

'I told you, the Commander is taking a gamble, but maybe I should leave it to *him* to explain.'

✧

Chandler expected someone fiercer, more battle-hardened. A man bearing the scars of his heroics against the Israelis perhaps. A little *gravitas* at the very least. He observed a slightly built figure step from the pickup, loaded with crates of tobacco leaves. He was kissed on both cheeks by Jabril. In his mid-thirties, he wore open-toed sandals and three quarter-length shorts. His long hair tied loosely in a pony tail. More like a backpacker than a seasoned resistance fighter, Chandler thought. The Commander took measured steps towards Jabril, before placing his hand on his chest. His expression appeared almost apologetic.

'Are you sure this is the right man?' Chandler whispered.

'*Quiet* – his English is perfect. He understands every word you say.'

'Welcome to Baalbek,' Najibullah announced. 'I trust that Mr Mansour is looking after you. Have you had time to see the sights?'

'Jabril has been doing his best Mr Na ... *Commander,* but I'm still finding it hard to get around ... my feet.'

Najibullah grinned. He pulled a packet of unfiltered cigarettes from his pocket, then offered one to Chandler.

Chandler glanced uncertainly at Jabril.

'Don't worry,' Najibullah said, 'we no longer rely on the hashish trade. You will be safe enough with the local tobacco.'

Chandler resisted the impulse to gag as thick smoke assaulted his throat and lungs.

'I took a call from General Abrash this morning,'

Najibullah said. 'He commends you on your fortitude in such trying circumstances. He wishes you a safe return to London.'

Chandler cast a sideways glance at Jabril, then returned his gaze to Najibullah. 'I'm sorry, I may be a little naïve, but I thought that Hezbollah and the Syrian government were allies. Aren't you going out on a limb talking to me?'

'Times are changing, Mr Chandler. Of course, the President remains a good friend – we will give him our support for a while yet. But you must appreciate the *larger picture*.'

'I think we're talking in riddles again,' Chandler muttered, his face turned steadfastly to Jabril.

'Remember what I told you about the river,' said Jabril, grinning, 'its course always changing.'

'Our friends in Damascus,' Najibullah went on, 'have many faces. Some will continue to support the President at any cost – I cannot blame them – their lives depend on it. Others, like General Abrash, are looking for a way out – to find a compromise that will preserve the integrity of the nation and also ensure their own survival.'

'Then there are the Salafis, of course,' Jabril broke in. 'Foreign fighters – here to stir the pot.'

'So what's in it for you ... sorry, for the *resistance*?'

'Well, that's where *you* come in,' Najibullah chimed.

Chandler let his cigarette drop. He looked at Jabril. 'Now, where have I heard *those* words before?'

'I don't understand,' Najibullah said.

'*Oakshott* – he was looking for favours too.'

Najibullah chuckled, then slapped his chest. 'That's odd, he's just been in touch with us. He mentioned some sensitive information in your possession. He's concerned you might, how you say, let the cat out of the bag.'

Chandler watched Jabril break into a mischievous smile.

'Don't worry, I don't think the Commander plans a full body search.'

'Mr Chandler,' Najibullah continued, 'I am here to guarantee your personal safety – to arrange transport for you and Mr Mansour to Beirut. I expect nothing in return.'

'Nothing?'

'Nothing of any *material* value. Our movement is already flush with donations. All our brothers require are a few friendly words. I hear you're a great storyteller ...'

'Listen, I've already told Oakshott, I'm not willing to become anyone's apologist.'

'I have no time for apologists either. All I expect from you is that you tell your friends in London that Hezbollah has treated you well, and that we have no quarrel with Washington.'

'Is that it?'

'Perhaps to ask your government to respect our territorial integrity – to cease their interference in the internal affairs of Lebanon. Maybe use their influence on Israel to release our prisoners.'

'The list seems to be getting longer by the minute.'

Najibullah pulled hard on his cigarette. 'We have our local difficulties, of course. But these can be easily overcome with goodwill and a little give and take. Just ask your government to give us space – and allow us to get the job done.'

'Commander, I think you're overestimating my importance – I don't have much say in government policy.'

'But you have the recording. That makes you a big fish in the diplomatic pond.'

Chandler turned back to Jabril. 'What do you think?'

'Mr Chandler, it's the best offer we've had all week.'

Chandler took a step towards Najibullah, whose face remained expressionless. In that moment, he decided that the deal being offered seemed a small price to pay for his freedom.

'So, have we reached an accord?' asked Najibullah.

Chandler stroked his chin, then nodded his assent.

✧

Breathless in the heat, Chandler climbed the monumental staircase up to the propylaea, its portico flanked by two towers. At the base of the supporting column, he struggled to retrieve his old school Latin in order to read the inscription: *For the safety and victories of our lord, Caracalla.* He wondered what the hard-nosed Roman emperor would have thought, as he sat down to nurse his swollen feet.

'Did you know that Baalbek played host to a thriving trade in prostitution?' Jabril said gleefully.

Chandler tried to ignore him, but gazing at the swollen granite columns, holding up the Temple of Jupiter, he struggled to banish their phallic associations.

'The city was known for human sacrifice too,' Jabril went on. 'Anath, the wife of Baal, is said to have tied the heads of her victims as ornaments across her back, and their hands to her belt.' He spotted Chandler wince. 'Don't worry, Hezbollah have long given up the practice.'

Chandler watched the yellow and green flag fluttering

in the gentle breeze above the visitor centre. He sat down, moved the rucksack beneath his head, and closed his eyes.

'Is that any way to spend your last hour in Baalbek?'

'What are you worried about?' Chandler said dismissively, 'do you think a short nap is going to anger the gods?'

'It's a possibility, after all, they *have* been looking after your interests since you arrived.'

'Really? I thought my survival had more to do with blackmail and backroom deals?'

'Once again, you're only seeing part of the picture,' Jabril shot back.

'What have I left out – divine intervention?'

Jabril chuckled, then lifted a silver hip flask from his jacket pocket. 'You'll be pleased to see that I've managed to secure a fresh supply of Arak from the Commander. It's produced locally, so, sadly, not a patch on its Syrian cousin.'

'I thought Muslims abhor liquor,' Chandler said, holding out his hand for the flask.

'They do, but the Commander thinks this might provide a sweetener, while you work out how to deliver his message.'

'Whether I get to deliver his message or not is in the lap of the gods' Chandler declared.

'Very true, but for now, the gods are telling me that they want you to provide them with a little *taster* ... a small sacrifice.'

'Meaning?'

'A final story, of course – Baal has been waiting patiently to hear it.'

'Fine, but there's one condition attached,' Chandler said, reaching for his bag.

'Go on,' answered Jabril uncertainly.

'That you don't upset the gods with any of your damned interruptions.'

*If You're Reading This*

*Stealth had never been Jason's strong point. Whether stashing well-thumbed pornography under his bed, or concealing mouldering hashish beneath the floorboards, his father was certain to find it. A contrived discovery and mock parental disapproval sure to follow. Jason had always been an open book.*

*Since being notified of his son's death at precisely 2.15 on the first day of July, Derek waited for the return of his son's army kitbag. When it finally arrived, he did nothing. For a week it remained unopened. Derek was sure that its contents had been meticulously examined before it left the barracks. His son's belongings aired and scrubbed before his commanding officer would sanction their removal. No signs of dust or blood allowed to sully the memory of his grieving parents. No hint of his last moments before his incineration in a flash of fire and metal.*

*Sapper Jason Hicks. Royal Irish. First tour of duty. He never knew what hit him. Season's greetings from Helmand.*

*

*Derek heard his daughter setting the table downstairs. He closed the bedroom door, then reached under the bed. He pulled open the straps securing the kitbag.*

*One ... two ... three. Next the zips. Working from the top, he removed Jason's beret, cap badge and identity tag. Then, he lifted out his well pressed dress uniform. Last, the boots. The leather was still stiff and unblemished. Obviously his spares.*

*'Dad, are you coming down?'*

*Derek was startled when he heard his daughter's voice. Since news of his son's death, he had become accustomed to the unspoken despair that consumed the household. Two officers stepping out of an unmarked saloon and a gentle rap on the door. Neither Derek or his wife had to be told why they were calling. They knew the protocol. Bad news given by senior staff – always in person. Invariably, a male and a female officer. Predictably courteous, if overly solemn. The details of Sapper Hicks' last hours, necessarily sparing. 'The medics made every effort to save him. He didn't suffer'. Heartfelt condolences from Jason's commanding officer. Unbridled messages of support from the lads in the platoon. And then they were gone.*

*Derek's wife hadn't spoken since. He could almost taste Irene's anguish, poorly camouflaged beneath a haze of diazepam.*

*Derek turned back to the empty kitbag. There must be something more. He ran his fingers along the side pockets. Empty. He pulled every toggle, clip and buckle. Nothing. A neat line of extra stitching, barely visible, caught his attention. That's my Jason, he thought, still an open book.*

*'Dad, your tea's getting cold.'*

*Ignoring his daughter's remonstration, Derek reached for his son's old army knife, lying on the sideboard. He carefully drew the blade along the stitches. Slowly, he pulled a crumpled envelope from its mooring. Typically, Jason was going to have the last word.*

Dear Dad,

If you're reading this then you've probably had a good nosey through my kitbag. I never could keep a secret. Remember the hash you found under the floorboards? Ma going ape and you with that silly grin?

What can I say about Helmand? Well, it's as different from Belfast as the frigging moon. Dusty, rocky, and brown. Hardly a blade of grass, but enough soil to feed the poppies!

Since March we've been billeted in a forward operating base north of Sangin. Can't say much more, official secrets and all that. The weather is pretty grim. In full kit it's like an oven during the day and a bloody fridge after dark. Lots of contact with dear old Talib. They keep us on our toes. You should see some of the kit they have. Sniper rifles, heavy machine guns and mortars. Mostly Chinese, but some of the stuff homemade. They work the farms most of the time, so you can never really tell who the enemy is. We lifted one of them yesterday. He claimed he knew nothing about the IED stashed behind the schoolhouse. We found detonators and fuse wires under his wife's burka, so well deserved extra rations for the sniffer dog!

We lost two of the lads in a firefight last week. If I'm honest, the Taliban are going to be a hard nut to crack. I don't hold with this shite about them being a bunch of ignorant ragheads. They're in for the long haul and will be around long after we're gone.

*'Ungrateful scum,' Salim al-Rashid muttered as he worked on the last of the graffiti decorating the shop front. Pakis Go Home, daubed, with patriotic fervour, in red, white and blue. To the ill-concealed delight of the smirking youths, watching him from across the street, their artistry had, once again, reduced his wife to tears and deepened her depression.*

*The cornershop had long suffered the twin perils of idle youngsters seeking cheap entertainment and a burgeoning out of town Tesco. Reaching his fiftieth year, it had all become an uphill struggle. Declining customers and falling profits. Perhaps, he thought, it was time to leave. Quite simply, Salim al-Rashid – grocer, tobacconist and amateur wine merchant – had lost his spark.*

*Ambitious plans to bring his son, Abu, into the family business had long been discarded. Solitary and self-absorbed, Abu had confined himself to his studies. Chemistry and applied mathematics had defiantly usurped his father's efforts to persuade him to join his sister behind the counter. As Abu embarked on his final year at school and, to his mother's delight, talked of a career in medicine, Salim concluded that the days of the cornershop were numbered. But while he had little appreciation of Abu's scientific endeavours, he admired his son's effort and stamina. It reminded him of the long hours he had invested in building up the business. As his most regular customer, Derek Hicks, had once remarked: 'Your Abu – a real chip off the old block.'*

*'Just think,' his wife squealed, 'a doctor in the family ... perhaps a suitable match for Eisha. Salim, we must have the Hamzas over soon!'*

*'Let's get Abu's exams out of the way first,' Salim had replied, in a tender rebuke that flew right over her head.*

*

*As summer approached, Mrs al-Rashid's maternal ambitions spiralled. Salim eventually conceded defeat and began to re-direct his energies towards his daughter, Jasmine, who, to his surprise, took to managing the shop like a fish to water.*

*At first, Abu's change of direction went unnoticed. More frequent visits to the mosque were judged a welcome sign of the young man's piety. His furious diatribes against Jasmine, for her immodesty, as she paraded her new outfits, drew only a gentle reprimand from her father. Then a new set of friends – bearded and zealous. Salim began to worry.*

*It was Abu's decision to abandon his studies altogether that proved the final body blow. For his mother, it spoke a wholesale rejection of all her aspirations. To Salim, Abu's detachment from the cornershop now seemed irreversible. The loss complete.*

*

*Giving up on the graffiti, Salim left his brushes to soak. He went into the living room at the rear of the shop. Four envelopes, three of which lay open and empty, sat on the sideboard. They bore different postmarks from Karachi, Beirut and Amsterdam, signifying a meandering trail. Like Russian dolls, they refused to yield their treasure until the last. Salim hesitated before opening the envelope. He glanced at the postmark. It was dated June 5th and had been posted in Kandahar.*

Dear Father,

I hope this letter reaches you safely. I pray that you and Mother are in good health and I apologise for my delay in writing. For security reasons, the Imam has warned us against direct communication with our families. God willing, I trust that my cousins have ensured the letter's safe delivery.

Since my departure you have never been far from my thoughts, I know that my unexplained absence must have caused great pain to Mother. Abandoning you and the shop, with only Jasmine to help, must have felt like a slap in the face. Please, believe me, I did not take the decision lightly.

The Imam reminds us that we carry a heavy burden. The path of righteousness is seldom followed without sacrifice. As your only son I may seem a disappointment. To throw away an education denied to you and my cousins must appear as ungracious as it seems dishonourable. But what greater honour than to lay down your life for your faith. To drive the crusader from the lands of the Prophet. Only jihad can make the infidel feel the pain of our brothers in Palestine and Bosnia.

Father, I hear you say that I am lost to my family. But here, in the camp, I have found a new family. Pashtuns, Kashmiris and Chechens. True brothers in arms. In their company, I no longer feel the outsider.

*'Dad, are you coming down or not?'*

*Holding his son's letter, Derek glanced towards a framed photograph of a young man, smiling and wearing the uniform of the Royal Irish Regiment. For a moment, he thought he could detect the sounds of the regimental parade ground – men marching and officers barking commands. Turning towards the wall, he stared at a framed and signed photograph of George Best, bedecked with a flag bearing the Red Hand of Ulster and a Rangers scarf. He looked back at the letter.*

To be honest I sometimes wonder why we are here at all. The Afghans keep banging on about new schools and hospitals, but there's no security to build them. The Royal Irish are doing their best to train up the Afghan army. Lousy shots, but always up for a scrap and they usually hold their ground when there's incoming. They're the first to return fire and the last to head for the bunker. The police are hopeless. Easily bought and untrustworthy. Best not to turn your back on them at the checkpoints. As for the women, don't ask!

The lads are looking forward to the Twelfth. Some of us got into the officers' mess and found a King Billy outfit. Pipes and drums too. We were up for a replay of the Battle of the Boyne until the CO got wind of it and that was that.

Just two contacts with Talib this morning and then hot grub brought in by chopper. Not a patch on Ma's cooking of course. We could all murder an Ulster Fry!

You know, it's not all doom and gloom out here. The lads are great. Nearest thing to family. It's a bit like home, they never miss a chance to wind you up, but always there when you need them. The biggest curse out here are the IED's. Your body armour has no chance. We took delivery of new Mastiffs and Ridgebacks last month. These monsters can take a direct hit from an RPG and you don't even spill your tea. According to the CO we're shaken not stirred.

I miss the craic at the Supporters Club. You remember that time I brought Abu down? Half a Smithwicks and clear off his head! His Ma none too pleased. What's he up to these days?

Being out here has given me time to think. I reckon I made the right choice with the Royal Irish. I know you always wanted me to follow you into the Paras, but this outfit has given me a chance to learn a trade. I've picked up more here than two years in that bloody call centre. Next year some of the lads are taking early discharge and plan to start up a garage in Dungannon. They say that there's a mechanic's job with my number on it. So maybe a fresh start next year.

My mate Paul says it's unlucky to send letters home before your last patrol. So being the superstitious type, I've sealed this one up in the old kitbag. You'll know where to look. You always did.

So, if you're reading this, Paul was right all along. Look after Ma and keep a good eye on Julie. And don't overfeed the fish!

Still smiling,

Jason

*'Salim, why didn't you tell me that Abu had written?'*

*Salim's attention was focused on his son's letter. For a moment, Rania sat in silence, watching her husband absorb the contents. In the well furnished room, framed photographs of the al-Rashid extended family populated the walls. A large black and white photograph of Muhammad Ali Jinnah sat on an ornate sideboard.*

*'Why did you read the letter, Rania?'*

*'Why not? ... I am just as entitled to know what is happening to Abu. I'm his mother. Salim, did you*

*know about Abu's plans. Why didn't you stop him?'*

*'Rania, I think we both saw this coming. You remember when Abu started to miss his classes? Then the visits to the mosque. It didn't seem so bad then. Better than chasing women.'*

*'Oh yes, a sign of your son's piety I think you said. Behaving as if his studies didn't matter as long as he took on the business. As if a career in medicine counts for nothing.'*

*'That's not true, Rania. Perhaps I should have seen what was happening, but you know I was always so busy. I couldn't leave everything to Jasmine.'*

*'Salim, you know how much I wanted a doctor in the family, a son to be proud of.'*

*'Listen, Abu said nothing about his plans – his beliefs. Anyway, I never heard you complain. You said yourself, his new friends may be a little zealous, but they were always polite. An example to Jasmine. Remember how they told us that she should show more respect and perhaps a little more modesty? I never heard you object.'*

*'Oh yes Salim, a fine example to Jasmine. Telling her she looks like a slut.'*

*'Rania, you see the way she dresses – showing everyone what should be reserved for a husband. What would your father have said? I think they had a point.'*

*'No, Salim, they did not have a point. They were just full of their own self-righteousness. Looking down on us ... condemning you, Salim al-Rashid,*

*the first Asian shopkeeper in East Belfast. Telling you not to stock alcohol. That you're forbidden to sell bacon to our loyal customers ... having you run the shop like some market stall in Karachi.'*

*'That's enough, Rania. I need to finish reading Abu's letter. Go out to Jasmine. See if she's cleared that muck off the wall. I will be with you in a minute.'*

Of course conditions here are harsh. The heat and dust is oppressive. I even miss the rain in Belfast! Remember our trip to Giant's Causeway? The rain never stopping. Curried chips in Portrush and poor Jasmine feeling sick all the way home. Out here, the food is plain and often in short supply. Where are Mother's spices now? She would be horrified at how much weight I have lost. But for all the hardship, there is room for laughter and always time for prayers.

Father, you know that I was never truly accepted at home. A different colour of skin and the wrong religion. You remember Mother trying to persuade my school friends to come to the house. Both of us waiting for them to arrive. Then phone calls from their parents with their weak excuses: Johnny is down with a tummy upset, Ian has pulled a muscle at football, and Mother telling me maybe tomorrow. Jason Hicks, the only boy to visit, though I think Jasmine was his main attraction.

Tomorrow we begin operations against the Americans and British. With all their firepower they have no stomach for a long struggle. Victory belongs to the pure in heart. I have no fear of death.

Tell Mother I am well and in good spirits. I miss Jasmine's mischief and laughter.
Pray for me,
Abu

*'Mrs Robinson rang this morning when you were asleep. Paid her respects. Says she'll call around later.'*

*Sitting motionless on a small sofa at the far end of the kitchen, Irene stayed silent. Her hands remained tightly clasped.*

*'There'll be some clearing up to do tomorrow. I hear the bin men are asking for double time. Some chance, eh?'*

*Julie ignored her father as he entered the kitchen and drew a chair up to the table. 'Bacon nice and crisp, eggs sunny side up, just as you like 'em, Ma.'*

*Derek looked towards his wife for a moment and drew a deep breath. 'Did you take your tablets this morning? Doctor Leary says they need to be taken with food. Now, where did you leave them? Shall I check the bathroom?'*

*Derek assaulted the fry with exaggerated relish. 'Irene, try to eat something. Do you want Julie to heat it up? It won't take a minute.'*

*'For God's sake, Ma',' Julie broke in, 'you can't go on like this.'*

*'Leave it. Irene, maybe you should go back to bed.*

*Remember what the doctor said about getting plenty of rest.'*

*Rising slowly from the table, Derek lifted his jacket from the back of the chair. He pulled a cigarette packet from his pocket. Two remaining. He moved towards Julie. 'Back in five.'*

*

*Standing in the drizzle, amongst the detritus of the marching season, with wilting loyalist flags and bunting looking down on discarded bottles, Derek watched Salim, down on his knees, tackling the remnants of the graffiti. The shopkeeper's head bobbed up and down next to a discoloured sheet peeling from a news-stand. Its headline announced: Another British Soldier Killed in Helmand.*

*'You'd do better with white spirit,' he said softly.*

*For a moment, Salim appeared unsure how to greet his favoured customer. His momentary look of embarrassment was overtaken by a warm smile.*

*'Ah, Mr Hicks, I was wondering when you would come to see us. Please, come in.'*

*Derek paused to observe Salim's daughter reach up to the top shelf to replenish the cornershop's apologetic display of men's magazines. She pulled her T-shirt down over her smooth midriff, then looked sympathetically towards him.*

*Salim placed his hand gently on Derek's shoulder. 'I am sorry for your loss. I had meant to pass our condolences in person, but, you know, the shop … never a spare moment.'*

*Derek placed one hand firmly on the counter. With the other, he drew some loose change from his pocket. 'Just a packet of the usual. Oh, and some digestives for Irene – it's all she can hold down since … well, you know.'*

*Gesturing towards Jasmine to leave the room, Salim looked directly at Derek.*

*'The loss of a son is a bitter blow for all the family, but is always worse for the mother.'*

*'It was all so sudden, Salim, I can't believe he's still not here.'*

*'How is Irene holding up?' Salim asked.*

*'She's saying nothing. She won't even talk to Julie.'*

*Salim lowered his eyes. 'We didn't even get much from the news – they say so little – an explosion and the name of the regiment.'*

*'It was his last patrol,' Derek murmured. 'They say he didn't spot the tripwire – never knew what hit him.'*

*'A mercy perhaps.'*

*'I got a call from his commanding officer in Helmand,' Derek continued. 'He told me that the medics did their best – that Jason didn't suffer. Oh, and the usual stuff about him being the brightest in the platoon – bravest of the brave and all that. Just words.'*

*'Words are never enough.'*

*'You know Salim, all this has me well beat. But it's hit Irene hardest. It's like she's been bloody crucified … sorry I didn't mean to … '*

*'A little blasphemy between friends is easily forgiven.'*

*'If only I could get her to talk. I think she blames me for Jason joining the army – not that he needed much persuading.'*

*'Just following the family tradition,' Salim replied.*

*'In a way, it was the making of him. He never settled in any other job. Always needed structure. To know where he was heading.'*

*'But not the life Irene wanted for him.'*

*'I know ... she never let me forget it. I think it was all the moving around after I joined the Paras. Never seeing her folks ... one lousy accommodation after another. Oh, and she never did get on with the officers' wives – a little too la de da.'*

*'No place to start a family then.'*

*'She always wanted security. To be like you and Rania, with the kids close by.'*

*'Is that why you came back?'*

*'Yes, that and missing her family. It became impossible.'*

*Salim threw up his hands. 'It is never easy. You know how I tried to get Abu to take over the shop, but Rania would hear none of it. She didn't want our son to get his hands dirty, then this talk of Abu going into medicine.'*

*Derek forced a smile. 'Can you blame her? You know yourself, the days of the cornershop are over – especially after the new Tesco.'*

*'You're probably right, but what a waste. After all*

*the years building up the business.'*

*'Have you thought about Jasmine taking over?'*

*Salim raised his eyebrows. 'Ah, that's the problem with tradition. I don't think I'm quite ready for women to run the show, whatever Jasmine thinks.'*

*'Times are changing old man,' Derek said. 'These young 'uns, especially the women – too bloody confident. They want it all now. Can't be bothered to wait. I don't suppose Jasmine is any different.'*

*'But that's just it. Because she has done a course in accounts, she thinks she can run a business. Jasmine doesn't understand it's about more than making a profit. It's about people – getting to know the customers – people like you. It takes time.'*

*'Time, that's the killer, isn't it? Jason was too bloody impatient too, not that it matters now.'*

*Salim held Derek's arm. 'Please, don't upset yourself.'*

*'Salim, do you remember them as kids? Jason coming over to the shop – the only white kid that bothered.'*

*'It was a long time ago.'*

*'You know, it wasn't just to see Abu.'*

*'You mean Jasmine?' Salim replied, grinning. 'I wasn't blind.'*

*'No, Salim, nor was I. The two of them, inseparable. What Jason and Jasmine had to talk about is beyond me. Poor Abu, he didn't get a look in. Has she said anything about Jason since ... ?'*

*'No, not to me. Perhaps to Rania.'*

*'I sometimes wonder if they would have made a good match,' Derek continued, 'though I'm not sure how that would have gone down at the Supporters Club.'*

*'Maybe a blow to local tradition,' Salim answered.*

*Derek smiled. 'We never let politics get between us, did we?'*

*'No, I think we had an instant meeting of minds. You, my first customer. I still remember the day you came in for cigarettes. Jason hanging onto your arm, begging for sherbet lemons.'*

*'You have a good memory, Salim.'*

*'And I remember you telling me who to watch out for the local kids. A little light fingered.'*

*'That was most of the bloody street in those days – Jason too, if he'd got half the chance.'*

*'Oh, don't worry, Jasmine kept a good eye on him.'*

*'It was a bit more than thieving then, Salim. Do you remember the workers' strike? The road blocks ... guns too. And your cornershop stuck in the middle of it.'*

*'It wasn't so bad for business,' Salim replied. 'The men in balaclavas never gave us any trouble – they were more interested in a steady supply of tea and biscuits. And they always paid on time.'*

*'Well, that was a break from tradition. You know, Salim, I'm glad I came out to see you. Being cooped up in the house. Then there's Irene ... I know I should be with her, but it's the bloody silence that's getting to me.'*

*Salim shook his head. 'We need to look after our friends in difficult times. You were there to help me when things got rough. Do you remember the time they left the bomb at the end of the street? You were the first to get Rania and little Jasmine out of the shop.'*

*'If I recall right, it was you that was the hardest to budge – lifting every penny from the till as if your life depended on it.'*

*'Tradition, tradition,' Salim replied, smiling.*

*'Look, Salim, I need you to do me a favour.'*

*'Anything.'*

*'Would you ask Rania to come over to see Irene – spend some time with her – get her to open up a bit, you know, talk.'*

*'I can try, but I can't promise anything. Rania ... she's not herself these days.'*

*'Sorry, Salim. Is there something wrong? If it's the graffiti that's annoying her, I can get some of the lads from the Supporters Club to clean it up.'*

*'No, it's a bit more complicated than that.'*

*'Look, if you want me to have a quiet word in the right ears – teach the little shites a lesson?'*

*'No, please, I don't want any trouble. I'll talk to Rania. It's just a bit difficult now. I need to find the right time.'*

*

*Standing alongside the shopkeeper in the yard, Derek pulled up the collar of his jacket and breathed in the dank summer air. He drew heavily on his cigarette, then turned towards Salim. 'Anyway, enough about me, how's Abu? I haven't seen him for weeks.'*

Chandler glanced nervously at Jabril – unsure whether his gentle nodding signified approval.

'Well, you *have* turned a corner,' announced Jabril.

'How do you mean?'

'You've finally taken the imaginative leap I've been waiting for.'

'I thought *all* my stories were imaginative.'

'In a *Western* sense, perhaps.'

Chandler cocked his head.

'Mr Chandler, your tales follow, how should I call it, a *classical* approach. Your protagonist faces a predicament. He knows he has a choice to make. Inevitably, he follows the correct path. But the strength of *this* story is that you leave the two fathers suspended in uncertainty. Will Salim tell his friend that his own son may bear some responsibility for Jason's death? How will Jason's father respond? It's anyone's guess.'

'The others – are you saying they're predictable?'

'Of course. Take Camilla, your young artist. You tell us that her father is caught in a predicament. Does he impose his authority or give the girl her freedom? Cliffhangers at every turn. But, inevitably, he allows her to follow her own path.'

Chandler pushed himself against the granite backrest. 'It's the way I've been taught. Sharkey always telling me to provide *resolution*.'

'Yes, but for *Arab* storytellers, ideas come in flashes – there is no striving for a final outcome.'

Chandler hung his chin disconsolately on his knees.

'Think of *A Thousand and One Nights*,' Jabril continued, 'no right or wrong path is set out. The hero's success is due more to providence than design.'

'Jabril, I don't peddle foregone conclusions. Look at Ahmed. He has to decide whether to rebuild his garage or join the rocket brigades. I leave the outcome entirely open.'

'That's true, but from an *Arab* perspective—'

'Okay, from an *Arab* perspective?'

'Well, the story makes no sense.'

'*I can't win*.'

Jabril threw Chandler a cigarette. 'Listen, even my uneducated neighbours will tell you that Ahmed can only follow the path that's written for him, it's foolish for us to try to control it. In Syria, we have a proverb: *The provision of tomorrow belongs to* tomorrow.'

Chandler sighed heavily. 'With all that's happened this week, I don't believe you really buy into this stuff. The only reason we're sitting in this temple is because we've both made difficult choices. Taken decisions that make a difference.'

Jabril glanced towards the road leading to the visitor's centre – alert to any sign of the car promised for their final leg to Beirut.

'Remember, the sheikh gave up three of his sons to get us here,' Chandler went on. 'General Abrash, even old Sharkey, personally intervened to save our skins. Providence had nothing to do with it.'

'Let's get back to your story,' Jabril said sharply. 'It speaks differently.'

'How?' asked Chandler.

'Well, like your other tales, you follow well-trodden themes – friendship, loss and so on. What intrigues me about *this* one is your sympathy with Abu.'

'So, for once, I'm not barking up the wrong tree?'

'No, not at all. Abu's break with his family is something I can identify with.'

'I never thought empathy was your strong point,' Chandler muttered.

'Which shows how little you know me.'

Chandler paused. 'I know you put family first.'

Jabril hesitated. 'Perhaps – but it comes at a cost.'

'You mean, losing your job over Zafirah?'

'I mean, selling my soul to Youssef.'

'It put bread on the table, didn't it?'

'It also taught me to spy on my neighbours.'

Chandler wiped the sweat from the back of his neck as the circle of shade narrowed in the afternoon sunshine. 'You blame your family for that?'

Jabril thought for a moment. 'It's ... *complicated.*' He looked back to the road. 'I'm not sure we've time to—'

'C'mon Jabril, it's the first time in a week that we haven't been in a rush to leave.'

Jabril blew out his cheeks. 'Okay, as soon as I was old enough to talk, my parents recognised that I possessed, what you call, *promise*. A never-ending supply of books, tutors, even private schools. No expense was spared.'

'It set you up as Top Gun in the university library, didn't it?'

'*Chief Librarian*, Mr Chandler. And no, there was no prospect of that then.'

'Why?'

'You must understand, in Syria, a professional position isn't easy to come by. Either you belong to the right family or you have connections. Like poor Habib, I had neither.'

'So, it must have been *providence*,' Chandler declared, with a broad grin.

Jabril motioned for a cigarette, ignoring the barb. 'On my last day at school, the Principal called me in. He told me that there was a scholarship from Moscow University on offer, but only for the most outstanding student in the district.'

'Meaning you, I guess.'

Jabril held up his hands. 'Well , I *had* achieved the best grade in the baccalaureate'.

'Why doesn't that surprise me,' groaned Chandler. 'I suppose everything was plain sailing after that.'

'No, quite the opposite.'

'I don't understand.'

'Think about it, Mr Chandler. Expectations were high. My parents ... the teachers, I couldn't afford to put a foot wrong – to let them down. While the other students drank and partied, I was, as you say, confined to barracks – usually the library or my room.'

'*The invisible student*,' Chandler mused.

'You know, the hardest part was returning home. My neighbours never trusted me. They had lots of questions about my time in Moscow, of course. But they always looked for signs that I had abandoned my Arab values.'

'Had you?'

'No, but I knew things had changed. Youssef was the first to point it out.'

'Go on.'

'Oh, he chose his moment carefully. At a family gathering to celebrate the end of Ramadan, he made a joke about a man who has a foot in both camps, but whose heart is in neither.'

'A bit of a comedian – how did that go down?'

Jabril bit his lip. 'Nothing was said, but I think everyone thought he had a point. I even began to believe it myself.'

'You sound like the fisherman in *Arabian Nights* – remember, the one who releases the jinni and—'

'I'm perfectly familiar with the story,' Jabril answered, curtly.

Chandler paused to think. 'I imagine your faith took a bit of a knock too.'

Jabril's face hardened. 'Whatever makes you think that?'

Chandler hesitated. 'Well, it's not rocket science. Three years abroad ... a different culture, enough to turn any young man's head.'

'Mr Chandler, I think you're mistaking idealism for atheism.'

'But *some* of it must have rubbed off. You had no problem keeping me supplied with Arak. And I also recall the way you talked about Miss Tuma in Krak des Chevaliers.'

'You'd do better to remember what I told you in Aleppo,' Jabril snapped.

'You said *a lot* of things in Aleppo.'

'*Think*. Outside the citadel, while we watched the pilgrims.'

Chandler scratched his chin. 'I seem to recall you telling me that I lived in a moral vacuum.'

Jabril slapped his thigh. 'There, you see? You have an excellent memory for insults. Perhaps the makings of a fine Bedouin.'

'I doubt whether they would take on an English unbeliever.'

'Or such a lousy marksman,' Jabril muttered.

Chandler gathered up his papers, then slid them back into the polypocket. 'I think we're getting off the point – you still haven't explained why you identify with Abu.'

Jabril leaned forward. 'I identify with his *frustration*.'

'How?'

'It's at the heart of your story,' Jabril snorted, 'do I really need to spell it out?'

'Indulge me,' Chandler sighed.

'Well, consider the position Abu finds himself in. His family invest in his education, but it's not enough. He craves acceptance from his neighbours – it's denied.'

'Is that enough reason to cut and run?'

'Why not,' Jabril shot back, 'neither of us are any different.'

'Yes, but with good reason,' Chandler said, forcefully.

'Listen,' Jabril went on, 'you have been the first to insist that we need to be given space. Abu is no different – he's simply chosen a new life, where he can remain true to his faith.'

'Find martyrdom, you mean?'

'No, Mr Chandler, find *purpose*. Isn't that what *we've* been doing for the last week?'

'I'm surprised to hear you say that – in Palmyra you called me a publicity-seeker.'

Jabril smiled. 'And in *Hama*, you proved me wrong.'

'Jumping ship, I'm not sure—'

'No, Mr Chandler, you turned down the offer of a scoop – your free pass out of the city. For once, you put self-interest aside.'

'In Hama, I think we *both* let our consciences get the better of us.'

Chandler eased himself out of his granite seat, before slinging his rucksack over his shoulder. 'Well, Jabril, do you *now* accept that we've made a free choice – that fate plays no bloody role in our decisions?'

Jabril closed his eyes. 'On this occasion, perhaps.'

✧

Chandler scanned the ruins while Jabril brushed the dust from his jacket.

'Are you going to return to Latakia?' asked Chandler.

'No, that's impossible – for the moment anyway.'

'What about Nadia?'

'She will remain with Qasim until he passes on.'

'And Zafirah?'

'I still haven't heard from her. But it's not safe for her in Damascus.'

'Is *anywhere* safe?'

'She talked to Nadia about moving to Australia with Theo. Maybe now's the time.'

They made their way slowly towards the visitors' centre. The Hezbollah flag hung limply in the dead air.

'You know, Jabril, you won't be able to stay in Beirut forever.'

'You're right. But for the time being, I'm content to remain the outsider.'

'Funny, that's how I used to see myself,' Chandler said.

'And how about now? Have you finally become, what did you call it, a *participant*?'

Chandler paused. 'No, but maybe I have *a foot in both camps*.'

Jabril grinned. 'I'm not sure about that – let's just say you have dipped your toe in the water.'

Chandler checked the road.

'Don't worry, they'll be here soon,' Jabril said. 'By the way, you never told me about *your* plans.'

'Pick up where I left off, I suppose. Attempt some sort of rapprochement with the ex.'

'Good luck with *that*,' said Jabril doubtfully.

'Well, at least get to know my nephew ... maybe we can take another crack at that climbing wall in Milton Keynes. '

'Ever the adventurer,' Jabril muttered.

'You never know, Jabril, I might even tackle a Munro or two ... you know, the ones you told me about before our trek over, sorry *through*, the mountains.'

Jabril chuckled. 'The success of *that* project may come down more to providence than design. You must keep a copy of *A Thousand and One Nights* with you at all times for inspiration!'

'I'll remember that.'

# Chapter Thirty-Eight

*All farewells should be sudden.*
Byron

Chandler woke to the strong whiff of cologne. Stretching his limbs under the linen sheets, he watched Jabril bear down on him.

Finally, Sleeping Beauty awakes.'

'Sorry, how long have I been asleep?'

'Twenty-four hours – I've never known a man sleep so long.'

Chandler propped himself up on the pillows. He looked around the hotel room. Expensive soft furnishings, abstract paintings and an enormous plasma flat screen adorned the suite.

'How are you feeling?' Jabril asked.

Chandler threw his legs over the duvet and took his first baby steps across the carpet. Shooting pains rose from blisters on his feet. His joints ached. Chandler thought back to the last mile of their trek across the Lebanese border, his infantile demands: *Are we nearly there yet?* Then the welcoming flash of headlights on the road.

'I'm not sure I can afford this luxury,' Chandler muttered.

'Don't worry, the cost of the room has been covered – an unknown benefactor, I'm informed.'

'*An Evil Cradling*, have you come across it?' Chandler asked.

'No, I don't believe so.'

'*Finally*, a book you *haven't* read.'

'And your *point*?'

'There's a passage that's stayed with me. It describes the author's release from captivity in Beirut into the hands of the Syrian security services. It's funny, leaving Syria, returning to Beirut – I'm getting the same feeling.'

'Except in reverse,' Jabril chuckled.

'Perverse, isn't it? The first time I've felt genuinely secure.'

'And so you *should*,' Jabril declared. 'Now, your flight to London has been booked. You need to be at the airport by eight. That gives you the rest of the day to get cleaned up and find something to eat.'

'What about you? How long will you stay in Beirut?'

Jabril shifted uncomfortably on his feet. 'I can't leave until I hear Zafirah has been given the go ahead to leave Damascus.'

'You need to ring her – check she's okay. Do it now.'

'I can't, all her calls will be monitored. I won't place her at risk again.'

'What about the baby?'

'The *baby*? You saw what Youssef did to him.'

'You could ring Dr Sadek.'

'Do you think I haven't tried? Nadia too. Neither of them are answering.'

Chandler stepped awkwardly across the room. He lifted a freshly laundered pair of slacks from the trouser press, then pulled his mobile phone from under the bed covers. He scrolled down for messages. The first, from an unknown number. He read the contents slowly and shook his head. The next, from Sharkey. *I did what I could old boy – the rest is up to you.*

'You should get some fresh air, Mr Chandler. It will be your last chance to see the city.'

'What about you?'

'Don't worry. I have plenty to get on with. But before you go, I have a small favour to ask.'

'Okay, as long as it doesn't involve *money* or *guns*.'

Jabril grinned. He reached into his jacket and lifted the Webley. Chandler stared at the weapon. He thought back to Jabril's advice in the mountains – *save the last bullet for yourself.*

'No, Mr Chandler, nothing like that. Your copy of *A Thousand and One Nights* – can I borrow it?'

'Of course, why?'

'It will help to get me started,' Jabril replied. 'I'd like to try my hand at fiction – something that I'll be able to read to Sami.'

'And written in the Western tradition, no doubt.'

'We'll see,' said Jabril, acidly.

'Children's tales are the biggest headache for an author,'

Chandler said. 'It's so bloody hard to get into their minds. I tried it with my nephew. Damn near impossible.'

'You're right, but I think it's time I should give it a go. Sami's too obsessed with his tanks and soldiers. He needs to broaden his imagination.'

'What do you plan to write?'

'Nothing too serious, a short story ... maybe something about a dog.'

Chandler paused. 'So you *did* have a soft spot for him after all.'

'Who?'

'The German Shepherd.'

'Surprisingly, yes, Mr Chandler.'

'You know, even if he had survived, we could never have brought him here.'

'So what better way to bring him back to life than through a story for Sami. Perhaps it will be included in a new edition of the *Nights*?'

'What are you going to call it?' asked Chandler.

'The dog?'

'No, the *story*.'

'I'm not sure, but I'll give it some thought while you're out.'

✧

Stepping into the afternoon sunshine, Chandler dodged the heavy traffic running down Rue Jeanne d'Arc. He stopped to check his street map. He was eager to spend an hour on the Corniche and planned to expose his sore feet to the sea air. Approaching the seafront, exhaust fumes gave way to the salty fragrance of the Mediterranean. Under a broad tarpaulin, stretched above a café, Chandler sat down and ordered coffee. He lifted a cigarette. From the promenade, he watched men and teenage boys cast their lines from huge fishing rods. Wives and grandparents sat on the rocks, laying out tubs of chopped cucumber, tomatoes and chickpeas. Small children scampered through puddles. They ignored the shouts of the men, celebrating their first catch of the day.

Leaving the café, Chandler made his way through the rear entrance of the American University of Beirut. He strolled past manicured lawns and smart low-rise office buildings. Fresh faced students, clutching files and laptops, hurried past. Reaching a three story block, housing the Faculty of Economics, Chandler stopped to check his watch. It was getting late, he thought.

Standing in the shade, he watched a slow convoy of black Chevrolets draw up. The doors of the vehicles opened simultaneously. Three men, wearing Lebanese army uniforms, disembarked, then gestured to their passengers to follow suit. The first man to step out was barely five foot. Chandler watched him arch his back. Squirrel-like, sucking on a sweet, his cheeks ballooned and deflated with a steady rhythm. The next to push himself into the warm air, had a solemn demeanour and wore a freshly trimmed beard. It did little to conceal the angry birthmark running down the length of his face. The last passenger took longer to exit. Older than his companions, he carried a heavy paunch and appeared breathless. Chandler noted his expensive shoes, before spotting his bushy moustache and black eye patch.

Oakshott was the first to spot Chandler, waiting in the shadows. Ignoring warning shouts from his security detail, he walked briskly over.

'You got my text message then? I trust you're happy with your accommodation.'

'Perfectly adequate,' Chandler replied.

'I remember our *last* encounter,' Oakshott went on, 'you seemed to be in a bit of a rush.'

'I had other priorities.'

'What a pity, Commander Said felt rather put out.'

'I can imagine.'

Oakshott reached into his pocket to lift another sweet. 'I would gladly have put a bullet in your skull myself when you failed to keep our appointment with the journalists. You left us all rather red-faced.'

'A shame you didn't have your gun to hand.' Chandler said.

'The Webley? Yes, losing that was *inconvenient*. Did you know it belonged to my father? The gun last saw action in El Alamein.'

Chandler glanced back to the cortege. He watched Commander Said and General Abrash talking in whispers. They leaned over a large map of Syria, spread over the bonnet of the sedan. Said lifted a green marker pen, then dissected the page into quadrants.

'I suppose you're wondering what's brought us together.'

'I'm getting used to surprises,' Chandler said, 'though I never expected to see *you three amigos* cosying up in Beirut.'

'Robert, they say a week is a long time in politics, but here, things move more swiftly. The situation in Syria is, how can I put it, *fluid*.'

'And deadly,' Chandler shot back.

Oakshott frowned. 'I told you in Hama, this is a dirty business. But it *will* reach a satisfactory conclusion – provided we can help the interested parties reach agreement.'

'I still don't understand how *I* come into this?'

Oakshott hesitated. 'Listen, Robert, people say the President's days are numbered. His wife knows that – she's looking for a way out. Strangely, she suggested *you* as a bargaining counter.'

'*Me*?'

'Yes, she was willing to trade *your* safety for guarantees for herself, though you never heard me say that.'

Chandler watched Oakshott stare at a group of female students, exchanging jokes and cigarettes on the lawn. 'Still playing a double game?'

'Of course, the Foreign Secretary was none too impressed when he heard about your recording,' Oakhurst continued. 'A fly in the ointment, I think he said. After that, your safety wasn't on the top of his agenda.'

'So the rescue was down to Abrash then?'

'Yes, but it wasn't for *your* benefit, Robert. The general's loyalties lie exclusively with Jabril and his father. *You* never featured in his calculations.'

'But I wouldn't be standing here without Abrash's help.'

'I agree, but you must understand, the general's interests, and those of *our* government, overlap, for the moment at least. As soon as we got the green light from Washington, and the nod from the President's wife, we gave General Abrash free rein to organise the rescue. You know, *he's* the real winner in all this.'

'How do you make that out?'

'Well, he's paid off his debt to Jabril's father and will, no doubt, escape a charge of war crimes. In the coming months, we'll have to rely on him and the old guard to prevent the army fracturing – we can't afford another Iraq.'

'And then you'll drop him?'

Oakshott cracked on his lozenge. 'That's a decision somewhat above my pay grade. What I can tell you is that the future belongs to men like Commander Said. He has the respect of the younger fighters on the ground.'

'But he's a fanatic – I thought the government wants no truck with fundamentalists?'

Oakshott shook his head. 'On the contrary, we regard him as something of a moderate. The real fanatics are waiting in the wings, so no time to waste.'

'What are you saying? Britain and America stands back and lets the like of Said take over? Bring in Sharia law, relegate women to the kitchen?'

'*Realpolitik*,' Oakshott replied. 'It's the only way to get the big boys in the region to play ball.'

'You mean the Saudis?'

'I mean the *Sunnis* – they're the majority in Syria after all. In any case, we can't risk Iran getting a foothold.'

'Or upset Israel.'

'As I said, Robert, it's *realpolitik*.'

'Sounds like you have everything sewn up.'

'Not yet, there's a lot more work to be done – the Russians and Chinese, their blasted vetoes in the Security Council – diplomacy never ends.'

Chandler lit a cigarette. The students giggled on the grass

behind him. He checked his watch. Jabril will be worried, he thought.

'What are you doing about Jabril's daughter? She needs to get out of Damascus – that was part of the deal.'

Oakshott sucked in his cheeks. 'Zafirah? Her safety isn't in my gift.'

'I *still* have the recording.'

Oakshott winced. 'It's difficult, we're still working on a *local* solution. At the moment, *you* remain my top priority – so you would be well advised to catch that flight to London.'

'You're all heart.'

Oakshott placed his hand gently on Chandler's shoulder. 'Believe it or not, Robert, my chief concern has always been your personal safety. After all, we can't let a good writer go to waste.'

Chandler watched Abrash and Said exchange cigarettes, then turned back to Oakshott. 'Isn't it time to rejoin your amigos? Looks like they've finished mapping out the future.'

Oakshott smiled. 'Sealing some deal, no doubt – I'd better check to see if they're planning to spring any surprises.'

Chandler raised his hand. He mustered a half-hearted wave.

'Well Robert – until the next time?'

'Adios,' Chandler muttered.

✧

Leaving the front entrance of the university, Chandler made his way along Rue Bliss, then cut through a series of side streets until he reached Hamra. Pausing next to Byblos Bank, he spotted the Palestinian boy selling plastic carnations. The tobacco tin lay empty at his feet and he wore the same mud-spattered trousers. Nothing had changed.

Ignoring the pains in his feet, Chandler stopped outside the Mayflower. Barely a week since he had encountered Jabril in the hotel breakfast room. His sore feet told him it had been a lifetime. The hum of traffic began to recede. For a moment, he stood opposite the hotel's unassuming entrance and watched the journalists scurry out of the lobby. None of the hacks appeared to notice him. Still the *invisible man*, he thought, and walked on.

Sidestepping the porters, lifting suitcases from the marble steps of the Crowne Plaza, Chandler tried to catch the eye of the smartly uniformed receptionist. Perched on a high stool, behind a forest of glass and steel, her head was bowed, engrossed in a novel. Chandler moved from the reception towards the dining room. Then he checked the bar. No sign of Jabril. He returned to the main desk.

'I'm sorry, are there any messages from Mr Mansour?'

The receptionist looked up wearily. Chandler noted a fine silver mesh, failing to halt the sideways march of her crooked teeth. Too little, too late, he mused.

'No, nothing from Mr Mansour, but I think he has a visitor.'

'Who?' Chandler exclaimed.

'I'm not sure, he said he is a relative – that he has to deliver some important news.'

'When did he get here?'

The receptionist glanced towards the clock. 'About an hour ago.'

Chandler banged his fist on the desk and raced towards the lift. He slammed the ascend button. Nothing moved. He took to the stairs, leaping three steps at a time. With his feet stinging, he stumbled breathlessly across the threshold of room 301.

✧

Resembling something between a game of noughts and crosses and a map of the Central Line, Jabril's body lay face up. His chest criss-crossed with tracks of scarlet, punctuated by deep gouges between his nipples. With his back turned, Youssef straddled Jabril's slim torso on the bed. Chandler heard Youssef muttering in Arabic. It sounded like a blessing. He saw Youssef's hunting knife lying beside the pillow. On the floor, papers lay scattered. Chandler's eyes were drawn to a sheet of paper bearing a rough sketch of a dog. Human-like, the animal stood on its hind legs, paws outstretched. Above the cartoon, two words. *Animal Magic*.

Youssef spun on his haunches. 'You should never have come here.'

Chandler's gaze was drawn to Jabril's feet. The soles, smooth and unblemished. They lacked history. Chandler could detect no physical signs of his trek across the mountains.

'I am sure that you must be blaming yourself,' Youssef said.

Chandler felt the roof of his mouth dry up.

'Why didn't you listen to my advice in the mountains, Mr Chandler? I told you, my argument has never been with you. My quarrel with Jabril is *private* – you were unwise to interfere.'

Chandler turned his head towards the open cabinet at the far side of the bed. His copy of *A Thousand and One Nights* lay on its side. Behind the book, almost hidden from view, the Bakelite handle of the Webley.

'You know, my cousin always looked down on me,' Youssef continued. 'He never missed an opportunity to remind me about his qualifications.'

Chandler edged towards the body. He brushed his fingers gently across Jabril's eyes.

'I suppose Jabril told you how I was jealous of his fine education. Nothing is further from the truth. How can I envy a man who has lost his soul?'

Chandler kept his eyes fixed firmly on the Webley.

'It's not just the way *he* betrayed me. I could have forgiven him that. What I cannot understand is why he let Zafirah turn away from me – to run off with that Armenian pig.'

Chandler stepped hesitantly around the bed. Youssef maintained his gaze on Jabril's body. Chandler reached into the cabinet.

'Taking a *position* – that was my cousin's big mistake. I told him not to listen to Abrash. The general has no future in Syria. The President will deal with him when the time is right.'

Chandler gripped the revolver. His hand began to shake.

'Aren't you forgetting our little skirmish in the mountains?' Youssef said. 'I remember how you hid behind the rock like a frightened rabbit. *Courage*, Mr Chandler. Didn't you learn anything from the Bedouin?'

Chandler eased the pillow from Jabril's head. Still, Youssef failed to respond. He held it firmly against the mouth of the barrel. Youssef smiled, then dropped his legs nimbly from the bed. He lifted a corner of the bed sheet and began to wipe blood from his hands.

'*Go home*, Mr Chandler – leave it to my countrymen to write the next chapter.'

Chandler watched Youssef pick up the knife. He jammed it into the inside pocket of his jacket. Moving towards the door, he cast him a backwards glance.

'Mr Chandler, you don't have the *balls*.'

# Epilogue

*We walk alone in the world.*
*Friends such as we desire are dreams and fables.*
Ralph Waldo Emerson

In a high speed dive reaching two hundred miles per hour, the peregrine falcon was about to break her personal best. A hundred feet above Regents Park Mosque, she snatched her prey. Clamped firmly between her talons, she began her ascent. Even in its death throes, the plump woodpigeon managed a brief struggle, obliging its captor to drop gear. For a few seconds, she searched for a suitable runway, then decided to land in the grounds of the Italianate Gardens.

Lying in a reed bed, close to the water's edge, the boy was almost hidden from view. His eyes trained skywards – a sole witness to the magical spectacle. Chandler edged towards him, intent not to break the spell. The air was still. Nothing moved.

Chandler turned towards a procession of school children leaving the Boat House. They set up camp on the perimeter of the lake. He switched his gaze to a young woman with olive skin. Clutching a buggy, she stood near the water. Chandler heard her call over to a man sitting astride a yellow pedal boat. He had a neatly trimmed beard and wore long shorts and a black T-shirt. Hearing her shouts, he moved his muscular quadriceps in a steady rhythm – propelling the craft swiftly towards her.

'He seems to be in his element,' Chandler said.

'Theo?'

'No, *Sami*. He hasn't moved for nearly an hour.'

Zafirah crouched down to lift the baby's dummy from the grass. Wiping the teat on her sleeve, she dropped it into her handbag. 'He gets his patience from his grandfather. All his stories about the fighting on the Golan Heights. Qasim telling him how he always made his gunners hold back until the enemy was in range, then making every shot count.'

They looked down at the sleeping infant. Cocooned in a navy Babygro, his feet were twitching.

'He must be dreaming,' Chandler said.

Zafirah smiled. 'I think he's destined to play for Armenia, but Theo says we should aim higher.'

Chandler spotted a crusty ridge running down one side of the child's neck, the skin around the scar still inflamed. Then, for a moment, he turned back to the boy hidden among the reeds.

'Zafirah, I lifted a sketch your father drew in the hotel in Beirut – a mountain dog. I think he was hoping Sami might take more interest in wildlife.'

'Robert, if Qasim heard that, he would be sorely disappointed.'

'Probably,' Chandler muttered.

'He doesn't say much these days, but he always had other ambitions for his little soldier.'

'Odd, isn't it?'

'What is?'

'*You* calling me *Robert.* Jabril never called me by my first name, it was always *Mr Chandler.*'

'That doesn't surprise me. After all, you were a paying customer.'

Chandler shook his head. 'I think we both know that I was ... *became*, a little more than that.'

Zafirah glanced back to the lake. She watched Theo step out of the boat, then call over to Sami, before lifting him onto his broad shoulders. The boy kicked his heels against Theo's chest. Rider and mount began a steady canter towards the Boat House.

'Have you heard from your mother?' Chandler asked.

'A short telephone call – she is barely speaking to me.'

'Because of what happened to your father?'

'No, because of Theo. She's furious about his plans to take us to Melbourne. I told her, it's his best hope of finding work. His cousins have offered to train him up as a silversmith. He would be crazy to turn them down.'

'What about Sami?'

'He's coming with us. There's no future for him in Syria – it's why my mother arranged for Sami to join us in London.'

'So that leaves Nadia on her own then,' Chandler said.

'Not quite, she still has Qasim to look after, though he hasn't got long.'

'Perhaps she will join you later.'

'Perhaps.'

'Zafirah, you know she can't stay in Latakia. Your father left too many enemies. They'll take their revenge any way they can.'

Zafirah screwed up her eyes. For a moment, Chandler feared the serenity of this little corner of the park was about to shatter.

'Robert, did you know I spoke to my father on the phone before Youssef got to him?'

'No.'

'He told me about your conversations – the stories. He said you never stopped telling him that he was free to make choices, even in the most difficult circumstances. In the end, I think he understood what you meant. He even joked about his conversion on the road to Damascus.'

Chandler smiled. 'When we first met, I was full of my own self-importance.'

'Yes, he told me *that* too.'

'Then the tables were turned. I had a difficult choice to make.'

'It seems strange,' Zafirah went on, 'everyone is talking about taking difficult decisions ... you, my mother, Theo – all convinced that they've made the right choice. Now it's *my turn*, and I can't decide what's best for us.'

Chandler watched Theo and Sami gallop across the grass. Theo was breathless. Giggling, Sami dismounted and landed at his sister's feet. Chandler knelt down. He gripped Sami firmly by the shoulders, then whispered into his ear. He reached into his pocket and held the Roman silver coin between his thumb and forefinger. Sami looked at it intently.

'What is it?' Zafirah asked.

Chandler pushed the coin into Sami's hand.

'A gift for the boy.'

# References

Chapter Eleven. 'Blind Faith', by Anthony Viney, first published in the *Impartial Reporter*, 2010.

Chapter Eighteen. 'The Orentes', in *Syria: Through Writers' Eyes* (2006) by Marius Kociejowski.

# Acknowledgements

Leigh Braiden and Helen Hunt, for their patience in preparing the manuscript.

Brian Langan and Paul Corcoran for their editing skills.

Inklings Writers Group, for their ideas and encouragement.

The staff of the Annebrook Hotel, for their hospitality.

Peter Byrne, Ian Butler, Dianne Ashcroft, Lisa Kenny and David McKeegan for their creative input.

My colleagues, in the Fermanagh Community Mental Health Team, for putting up with my Syrian chatter.

Dr Stephen Moore, for his advice on emergency procedures.

The late Robert Fisk, for his constructive criticism.

My daughters, Connie, Ruth and Faith. Also, my grandchildren, Cian, Lucy, Éire, Lenny and Fae. All acting as reminders of what is important in life.

My wife, Kathy, for her company and counsel on the road travelled.

Barney, for his canine patience and happy company.

Averill Buchanan, whose technical wizardry ensured the birth of this novel.

Finally, the people I encountered during my travels in Syria. In particular, Radwan, my driver and 'minder'. Their generosity, stories and humour remain with me. May peace be upon you.

# About the Author

*Anthony Viney (right) with war correspondent, Robert Fisk, in Beirut (published in the* Impartial Reporter, *November 2013)*

Anthony Viney lives in Mullingar, in the Republic of Ireland, with his wife, Kathy. After stints in the defence industry, the BBC, teaching, and working with the Traveller community in London, he settled on a career in social work in Northern Ireland in the early 1990s. He has published a number of academic papers and texts and is a regular contributor to his local newspaper. In retirement, he remains an avid swimmer and kayaker. He also spends his spare time being taken for walks by his American Akita. His debut novel, *On the Road to Damascus*, is inspired by his love of thrillers as well as his real-life journey through Syria as an independent traveller in 2011.

Twitter: @AnthonyViney5
Email: tonyvineyis@gmail.com

Printed in Great Britain
by Amazon

19027550R00181